The Bowman Legacy

NOT FOR SALE

The Bowman Legacy

NOT FOR SALE

A Novel

F. Haywood Glenn

Ambiance Publishing Company
Philadelphia, Pennsylvania
USA

Cover Art by LaReine M. Nixon
Author Photo by D. Scott

ISBN: 978-0-9820101-6-7

ACKNOWLEDGEMENTS

I serve an awesome God and give praise to him for all blessings now and forever. In Him I trust.

Once again I must acknowledge the work of my editor, Alicia (Adlals) James, for her exceptional attention to detail. Thank you Alicia.

Special thanks to my cousin LaReine for allowing me to use her artwork for my cover. Besides being an awesome artist, she has also been a constant source of encouragement.

DEDICATION

To my weird, quirky, creative, and sometimes loud family. I love you all. You may not understand this obsession I have for creating stories but you love me just the same. Thank you.

Forever rejoicing in the memory of my mother
Jessie Marie Witherspoon Haywood

The Bowman Legacy

NOT FOR SALE

Prologue
September 1842 – A New Life

". . . old things are passed away;
behold, all things have become new." II Corinthians 5:17

From the moment they left the ferry, Lillian felt as if they had entered a new world. This feeling of newness was as peculiar as it was over-whelming. The sky seemed brighter, clearer, even bluer. It was a warm day but a cool, misty breeze blew across the river. The sweet smell of honeysuckle and wet earth hung faintly in the air. Lillian took a deep breath, inhaling the earthy aroma.

As Louis assisted her climbing into the waiting wagon, she looked at the faces of the others and wondered why they were not filled with the same joyful anticipation that she felt. Louis and Jacob were quiet and appeared completely unmoved, while the women all looked so sad.

Althea looked ill. Lillian hadn't realized that Althea was nauseous from the short ferry ride. She was also having trouble breathing and her face was flushed and dotted with beads of perspiration. She held a small handkerchief, which she often used to mop the sweat from her brow.

Nan and Denny didn't look sick but they didn't look happy either. Lillian just couldn't understand why they were all so sullen. She hoped that they could each find some happiness in the new lives that lay ahead of them in the small village of Timbuctoo.

The wagon moved slowly over the narrow dirt road. They passed fields of corn and the occasional farmhouse with cows in the pasture. Lillian rode in silence for a while. She was trying to, not only understand her own feelings about this move, but looking for the cause of the gloominess that seemed to effect the other women. She reached over and linked her arm with Louis. He put his hand over hers and smiled down at her.

It was at that moment that Lillian realized that her happiness did not only come from the move to Timbuctoo, or the promise of reuniting with her daughter; it was love. It was a love that was returned in equal measure. She was in love and it was like nothing she had ever felt. She realized now that the feeling she had for David for all those years, was not love at all. She had been David's slave and his lover. It was the only kindness ever offered to her and she took hold of it with both hands. It sustained her through the worst of times, but it was hardly true love. David set her free when he learned that their coupling was incest. He took the easy way out by taking his own life and left her, although free, she would have to live with the stigma that she foolishly thought was love. Whether it was love or something else entirely, she refused to be burdened with its vile mark of shame any longer. What she felt now was a new love. Right or wrong, what she felt for David could not compare to what she felt now for this wonderful, beautiful man. She had no doubt that Louis was the reason for her happiness.

He was not only strong and handsome; he was a genuinely kind person with a big heart. Even though the Vance family was unknown to him before meeting James, he took care of this new brother as if they had shared the nursery. The blood ties bound them until James' death. He saw to all of James' affairs and settled his estate before coming back to Philadelphia.

Louis refused to own slaves. He freed most of them but some of Gloria's field hands were sold after Louis found a planter he was certain would treat the slaves of the Gloria Plantation humanely. Some of the slaves that had been the most loyal to him during his time on Gloria were freed and they were now riding in this very wagon, on the way to new lives in Timbuctoo; Jacob as a free man and Nan and Denny as free women. Yes, Lillian loved everything about Louis Bissett. She glanced up at him again, "I love you, Louis," she whispered.

He leaned down and kissed her. "And I love you, Mrs. Bissett."

"Aren't you all excited to see Timbuctoo," Lillian said.

"Not especially," Denny sulked.

"We don't even know where we're going," Althea complained.

"Sure, we do," Lillian answered. "We're going to Timbuctoo Village. Rebecca writes that we will all be able to build new lives in this village. I'm excited to see our new homes and learn where our new lives will take us."

Her excitement had no affect on the other women. Lillian was quiet for a few minutes but the more she thought of it, the more she understood their sullenness. "Nan," she said. "You and Jacob are free now. You don't have a Massa. No one to tell you where to go or what to do. That alone should make you both happy. This is what freedom feels like. I don't understand why you aren't as excited as I am about this move. You too, Denny."

"Well," Nan said thoughtfully. "I guess I ain't excited cause I got no idea what freedom is supposed to feel like."

Denny rolled her eyes toward the sky. "We ain't never heard of no Timbuctoo," she said with a smirk.

The wagon shook and bounced over the badly rutted road. Both Louis and Jacob exchanged knowing glances but said nothing. "There's a lot of things you ain't never heard of, Denny," Lillian said in a low voice. She wished she could make them all see the beauty and joy of being able to begin again. Lillian was happier than she could remember and she vowed not to let their skepticism bring her down. "You know, it really doesn't matter that you've never heard of this village. Rebecca writes that it is a small town and the people are close, like a really big family. Most everything in the town is owned by black folk."

"No white folks?" Jacob asked.

"Well, there are some. Rebecca writes that some white folks helped to settle the town years ago. Most are of the Quaker religion and they don't believe in slavery. The important thing is that you will not have a Massa. You will be your own man. Life is gonna be different for all of us. You'll see."

"So, how we gone live without a Massa?" Jacob wanted to know.

"You're going to work, Jacob. We all must work. You have to work and make money to care for yourself. That's what it means to live free. It says so in the Bible. But you won't have a Massa and Althea, you'll be able to own your house again."

Lillian looked back at Althea expecting to see her broad smile but Althea was just staring straight ahead. Several minutes passed before she spoke. Her voice was as soft as a whisper and Lillian could barely hear her speak. "I guess you forgot, Lil. I ain't got a penny to my name. I ain't likely to be able to buy a house with no money." The look on Althea's sullen face said more to Lillian than the few words she spoke. It was obvious that her friend was still battling the depression that had stolen her joy after the loss of her houses and the death of her husband. Lillian wished that she could make Althea see that life would be different now. She wished that she could remove all of Althea's pain but all she could do was smile and place a reassuring hand over her friend's hand. Lillian looked back at Althea and saw eyes that were filled with unshed tears. She was somber and heart-broken and Lillian's heart ached for her friend.

The church was the first structure seen from the road. It's steeple bright and white, stretching tall and erect against a clear blue sky. It seemed to float above a sea of high lush green grass. As the wagon plodded forward, more of the village of Timbuctoo came into view. They passed small farms and houses sporadically spaced on both sides of the road. Soon the town's main street came into view. The first sign, about a mile outside of town read, "Welcome to The Village of Timbuctoo."

Another crude wooden sign nailed to a post with the words, "Freedom Road," carved into the wood and painted in bold white letters marked the village's main street. It was a wide road with business establishments on each side and a wide wood-planked walkway. First was the wagon and wheel maker's shop, which was right next to the farriers. There was a general store with fabrics shown in the window. The sign hung on the outside of the establishment said they sold pots, pans, and brooms. Next was the bakery and you could smell the freshly baked bread and pastries for miles. Fresh fruits and vegetables were sold from crates that lined both sides of the street. The largest building was the hotel which was the last building on the left side of the street. The people were mostly black folk. Very few white people were seen around town on that day.

"We're here!" Lillian said excitedly. "This is it." Right across from the hotel was a very wide three-story building. It looked to be about three lots put together. There was a cloth awning that stretched over the wood-planked walkway. The front of the building had a large plate glass window. The gold and black letters arched across the window read, Bowman Catering Company. The two stories above the catering company was where the family resided with entry doors on the side of the building and also in the rear.

As soon as Jacob helped her down from the wagon, Lillian ran up the walkway toward the side door. Rebecca must have been watching from the window because before Lillian could cross the few yards to the door, it swung open and Rebecca came running. Her movement was labored. "You're here!" she screamed and mother and daughter embraced.

"Oh, my," Lillian said as she noticed Rebecca's protruding belly. "You didn't write that you were expecting. You look like you're ready to have that child at any moment."

"Soon Momma, very soon." As she spoke, she noticed the others. Rebecca released her mother and threw her arms around Althea's neck. "Miss Althea!" she said through tears. "I'm so happy to see you. Momma wrote to me about your troubles and I am so sorry."

Althea was so surprised that she could hardly speak. She and Rebecca had never had a warm relationship and Rebecca's obvious concern was curious, to say the least. Her embrace was so strong that she nearly knocked Althea off of her feet. 'Oh my,' Althea thought. 'Apparently, the spoiled, self-absorbed teen had grown into a caring and thoughtful young woman.' Althea returned Rebecca's embrace and smiled warmly for the first time in many months. "It is good to see you, Rebecca," she whispered.

Nan, Jacob, and Denny stood apart, watching the small family reunion. "I'm so happy that you decided to come with my mother to our little village. You will be happy here, Miss Althea. I'm sure." Rebecca said as she seemed to notice the others. She stepped away from Althea, recognition slowly creeping into her face. "I remember you," she said to Denny. "We played together under the steps in the big house on Gloria Plantation."

Denny smiled. "Sure did. Whenever I could get away. That was so long ago."

Lillian came forward to introduce the others. "You were very young Becca. You may not remember Nan and Jacob."

Rebecca was thoughtful for a moment. She stared at them all, trying to match the faces and names in her vague memory. "You worked in the kitchen house with Bell," she said to Nan. "I remember that you often gave me an extra biscuit or cookie."

"Yes, that's right," Nan said. "And this is my husband Jacob."

The look on Rebecca's face said that she didn't remember Jacob but she smiled at him anyway, taking his hand and shaking it vigorously. "Welcome Jacob," she said.

Finally, she turned her attention to Louis. "Well, well, Mr. Bissett. I hardly expected to see you here."

Lillian came and stood beside her husband, taking him by the hand. "Louis and I are married, Rebecca. I didn't have time to write about the wedding."

Rebecca looked shocked at first. She could hardly believe what she was hearing but when she turned her attention to her mother, all she could see was joy. Lillian was happy and you could see the joy in her face. Rebecca didn't remember ever seeing her mother so happy. She smiled broadly as she came forward to embrace Louis. "Welcome," she said. "You are welcome to my home and to our family."

"Well, how far along are you?" Althea asked.

"Where is my grandson David? I can't wait to see him." Lillian said.

"Davey is taking his afternoon nap and Miss Cathy is at the Methodist Church. She volunteers there a couple of days a week, and I'm near about six months. Miss Cathy says it's a girl because of the way my bundle is so high and I'm always craving sweets."

Rebecca led them through a side door and up a narrow staircase to the family's living quarters above the Catering Business. The door at the top of the steps opened into a large, modestly furnished dining room with a heavy wooden table and chairs. A buffet sat against the wall. To the left was a small but cozy sitting room with two comfortable stuffed chairs and a small sofa. Heavy curtains hung at the windows but the walls were bare. Rebecca explained that the kitchen was on the other side of the dining room and three bedrooms were on the upper floor. Soon they were all seated around the table. Rebecca made a pot of tea and brought in a freshly baked apple pie.

Supper that evening was a feast. The food was as delicious as the company and everyone laughed and talked until late in the evening. "Where is Benjamin?" Lillian asked.

"Oh, he's down in the big kitchen working. He has some big order for this evening. He likely won't be back until very late."

After Rebecca and Lillian made room for everyone to sleep, Lillian and Louis decided to wait up with Rebecca until Benjamin came home. Lillian and Louis were dozing on the sofa while Rebecca sat knitting in an armchair by the window. It was well after midnight when they were aroused by Benjamin's heavy footsteps on the stairs. Rebecca dropped her knitting and ran to the door. "They're here," she whispered as she opened the door.

Benjamin embraced his mother-in-law first and shook hands with Louis. "I'm so glad you came," he said. They spent a few minutes catching Benjamin up before they all went to bed.

The Bowman house was quite crowded over the next few weeks but they all found joy in acquainting themselves with one another. All the women helped with the cooking and cleaning and Lillian was most happy to spend the evening hours playing with her grandson. Davey was a beautiful little boy with pale skin and the same striking green eyes of the Vance family. He smiled easily, enjoying the attention, and quickly became attached to his doting grandmother. Little David looked like a white child and favored the grandfather for whom he was named. The green eyes and thick curly black hair were Vance traits. Lillian silently prayed that Rebecca's experience with racism would make her determined to teach her children to be proud of their blackness.

The next day Miss Cathy happily gave the women a tour of the Village. Nan and Denny were awestruck as they had never seen free blacks who owned their own shops and houses. Most everything in the small town was owned and managed by black people. Some were freed slaves, some were fugitives, but many were born free. The few white people who lived in Timbuctoo were from the Quaker church. Miss Cathy explained that they were strict abolitionists and were responsible for helping settle the town.

After Benjamin gave Louis a brief tour of his catering business, Louis and Jacob spent the next several days searching for available properties. Within a couple of weeks, Louis had purchased a large three-story house right in the middle of town. It had four bedrooms on each of the upper floors and a modestly modern water closet on each floor. There was a large kitchen with two ovens, and a spacious dining area. There was also a small parlor in the front of the house. It was fully furnished with large, heavy pieces and besides the layers of dust, it looked as if it had been recently occupied by a large family. However, Louis learned that it was a boarding house owned by a Quaker couple. The wife died and her husband wanted to sell the property as soon as possible and move back to his family in Pennsylvania. He gave Louis a good price and Louis did not hesitate to make payment and take possession of the keys.

Days later Louis also bought a small, 170-acre farm just outside of town. The property included a sizable Victorian house. It was a family home with two floors and an attic. There were four large bedrooms. The entire house was stone with a large flat wood porch in front. The only exception was the kitchen which was red brick and apparently added onto the original construction. Louis was told by the property owner, that the house was built by a prominent Pennsylvanian, related to William Penn. Apparently, Mr. Penn's relative later sold the house to the Quakers. Louis was ready to buy the farmhouse even without the history lesson.

That evening Louis was fidgety as he tried to hold onto his good news until what he thought might be a perfect time. Lillian noticed his agitation right away. She and Rebecca were preparing dinner while the rest of the family helped to set the table and bring in the food from the kitchen. Denny was playing a game on the floor with little Davey and didn't notice anything out of the ordinary. Lillian came into the dining room carrying a basket full of fresh-baked biscuits. She sat the basket down gingerly as she watched her husband pace the length of the room. "Louis," she finally whispered. "Is there anything wrong? Why are you so jumpy?"

Louis turned with a jerk as if he had been caught at something secret. A smile slowly spread across his handsome face and he went to Lillian. He wrapped his arms around her and kissed her soundly, vanquishing any misgivings she may have felt. "Everything is wonderful," he whispered in her ear as he held her tightly and Lillian melted into his embrace. She snuggled closer, leaning her head on his shoulder. She was lost in the intimacy of the moment until she felt a tug at her skirt and glanced down to see Davey with both arms stretched upward. It was a silent plea for Grandma's attention and Lillian's heart easily warmed to this new love. Both Lillian and Louis smiled as she lifted her grandson into her arms and nestled her nose into his soft puffy cheeks.

Dinner was a pleasant affair as usual. Nan and Jacob talked about how amazed they were to see so many free blacks walking the streets of their small village. Everyone seemed genuinely happy except Althea. Her broken heart and spirit were evidenced in the new lines etched into her sad face.

When she and Lillian had met in Philadelphia, Lillian thought Althea was the happiest woman she had ever encountered. That was when she was free, owned two houses, and a vegetable garden that awarded her a comfortable, if not substantial, living. When her husband was away, which was most of the time, Althea was free in every sense of the word. She was an independent black woman, a rare existence anywhere. Now Althea was nothing like the woman Lillian met in Philadelphia. She owned nothing and was completely dependent on the kindness of others to sustain her living. 'What a difficult thing for a woman as proud as Althea to bear,' Lillian thought as she looked across the table at her only friend. Her heart ached for Althea.

When the meal was over, Louis could contain himself no longer. He tapped his glass with his fork to get everyone's attention. "Rebecca and Benjamin," he began. "We are all so grateful for your hospitality and I take this opportunity to thank you both, from all of us. Rebecca, I feel as if you are my real daughter and I am so happy that you chose

Benjamin for your husband. He is a good man and I am confident that he will continue to take great care of you and keep you happy. I have no doubt that he will also be a great father for little David."

Rebecca blushed. "Thank you," Benjamin said. "You all know how much I love Rebecca. She and Davey are my life now."

Rebecca echoed Benjamin's thank you. "You sound as if you're going somewhere, Louis," she said. Lillian was staring up at him, silently holding her breath because she knew that there was more to come.

"You're right, Rebecca. I am leaving." Everyone gasped. "We are all leaving but we won't be going too far. We're a family now, and I don't expect any of us will venture too far away from each other." One by one, they each breathed a sigh of relief. Then Louis produced a set of keys that he held out to Lillian. "I have just purchased a small farm and house just outside of town for Lillian and myself." Lillian stood and beaming with happiness and gratitude, she took the keys from Louis before she threw her arms around his neck and kissed him. "The house is large and we will certainly have to hire farmhands to help work the land and a housekeeper to help Lillian with the house." Louis paused as he watched their faces intently. "Nan, Jacob, and Denny, you are all welcome to come to live with us, if you choose. Keep in mind, it is a farm. There will be work for all of us and we will all reap the benefits of whatever profit the farm produces. They all sat wide-eyed but said nothing for a few moments. Louis could easily read their faces. "You are not slaves. Remember, you are free people who will now be paid for your labor. You don't have to work on my farm but if you do so, I will pay you handsomely and I will also share the profits with you."

Jacob was the first to speak up. "I'm most grateful Massa, I mean Mr. Louis."

"Just Louis, just Louis, Jacob. I don't want to be anybody's Massa."

He hadn't mentioned Althea and her heart seemed to visibly sink. Lillian glanced from Althea to Louis. She knew that Louis would not leave Althea out but still, she was bewildered. Althea pushed her chair back, ready to leave the table.

"Hold on, Althea," Louis said. "I didn't forget you. I just saved you for last because you are so very special to my wife and me and I hope that this will finally make you happy again. I've come to miss that broad smile and hearty laugh as much as Lillian. Your happiness is very important to both of us." He produced another set of keys and held them out to Althea who didn't readily accept the keys. "You are now the proud owner of, 'Althea's Place.' These are the keys to Althea Brown's Boarding House."

Althea finally lifted her head and looked at Louis. Her eyes filled with tears and her hands began to tremble slightly as she reached for the keys. "Thank you," she whispered. Lillian came to her and the two women embraced. "You and Lillian are the best friends anyone could ever have and I love you both. God, bless you."

The entire family began to applaud Lillian and Louis.

The family had gathered for a modest dinner that ended as a wonderful celebration.

❦

Rebecca gave birth to twin girls on December 17, 1843. They were named for both grandmothers, Catherine and Lillian. Cathy and Lilly were welcomed by big brother David.

Lillian was right about everything. This move began a new life for each of them. Denny accepted employment and room and board from Althea at the boarding house. Althea had lost her houses in Philadelphia, but she was now the proud owner of a boarding house. Louis dubbed the house, "Althea's Place," as soon as he saw it and before Althea had laid eyes on the property.

Nan and Jacob lived and worked on the farm. However, Nan and Althea became good friends and whenever Nan wasn't working, she could be found in Althea's kitchen, helping wherever she could.

The town was a marvel to them all. Timbuctoo was a friendly town and so small that it was easy to know most everyone. To take a stroll down Main Street, one would be blessed with friendly greetings from everyone to cross their path. Most businesses were owned and operated by black families. Some were born free in Pennsylvania, Delaware, or New York. Many were runaway slaves from southern or midwestern states. It was easy to settle into such a welcoming town.

Lillian couldn't wait to share what a wonderful town they found in Timbuctoo. She decided to write to Beth as soon as she could.

April 4, 1843

My Dear Friend Elizabeth,

I sincerely hope that this letter finds you and Jefferson well. Louis and I are happy and doing very well. I can't tell you what a joy it was to finally be with Rebecca and Benjamin again.

Their family has grown since we last communicated. Besides little David, who is adorable, Rebecca and Benjamin had twin girls shortly after our arrival.
This town is a wonder. The people seem to move slower than people in Philadelphia. No one is in a hurry and everyone is polite. None of us have ever seen anything like this town. Most everything is owned and run by Negros. There are a few whites, mostly Quakers. I am told that Quakers were instrumental in settling the town.

Louis bought a small farm just outside of town and I quickly fell in love with our quaint little farmhouse. He also bought a boarding house for Althea. Can you imagine? She is finally able to break free from the depression that took away her joy when she lost her houses. Now, she is slowly coming back to herself.

Moving to this small town was the best thing that could have happened for our family. I miss you dearly and hope that you will be able to visit soon. Until then, I remain,

Yours Affectionately,
Lillian

That was the first of many letters between the two unlikely friends. Their bond may be hard to understand by those who did not know their history, but it was no less powerful. They kept each other abreast of their families, the current state of affairs in Philadelphia, as well as New Jersey, and the politics that seemed to be altering all of their lives.

After Lillian and her family had lived in Timbuctoo for more than a year, she learned that the town was a haven for runaway slaves. It was one Sunday, after service ended and when many parishioners would linger in the sanctuary conversing with one another, Lillian heard Benjamin refer to Reverend Evans as a conductor. She and Rebecca took turns serving Sunday dinner and on this particular evening, she and Louis were to host the family dinner.

Separate conversations were buzzing around the table and Lillian used that time as an opportunity to ask Benjamin about Reverend Evans. "Does Reverend Evans have some work on the trains?"

Benjamin looked puzzled. "No," he said in a questioning voice.

"You called him a Conductor this morning."

"Ah," he understood her confusion. "Reverend Evans is a Conductor on the Underground Railroad."

Lillian squinted her eyes as she looked at her son-in-law. Now she was really confused. Others around the table stopped talking and began to pay attention to their conversation. "I don't understand, Benjamin."

"You see," Benjamin lowered his voice. "There is a sophisticated network of people, who are both white and black, dedicated to helping runaway slaves find freedom in northern free states in America and Canada. Some people provide refuge to hide slaves away in barns, underground rooms, even caves. They may help by transporting them from one place to another or providing new identities and other paperwork to aid in their escape. This network is called the Underground Railroad and the people who help these runaways are called conductors. Reverend Evans is not the only Conductor. I am also a Conductor, as is Constable Willis. Eventually, I'm sure Louis will join us."

Louis smiled. "Lillian, remember you wanted to know why I've been digging in the barn so much?"

"Yes," she said slowly.

"I've been hollowing out a room under the barn for just that purpose."

Lillian put one hand to her heart and the other over her mouth. She was suddenly awash with emotion. She was impressed and happy that her family was engaged in something so courageous and meaningful while at the same time, she was afraid of what could happen if they were ever discovered. "I am so proud of you both," she said. "I don't mind saying that I am also a little afraid for you."

Benjamin came and put an arm around her shoulders. "Don't be afraid, Mom. I feel as if God has called me to do this work for our people and He is with us always." The others began to applaud Benjamin's words.

Chapter One
Maryland/New Jersey

Spring 1857 - Escape

The sound of his own frantically beating heart was all that Josiah heard as he crawled his way up the river bank. The two others who had embarked on this dangerous journey to freedom, were lost in the murky depths of the Delaware River. Josiah met them both just days before the tragedy. The three had been introduced to one another at the home of Miss. Carrie Markel, an abolitionist known for helping runaway slaves seeking freedom in the North.

For five days, the three young men were sheltered in an underground room beneath Miss Carrie's home. Life went on as usual in the rooms above them and they could hear the comings, goings, and voices of Miss Carrie's family, friends, and neighbors. The underground room was devoid of light, except the little shown through the worn floorboards during daylight hours. Once the sun went down, they were submerged in complete darkness.

The two others were brothers but neither talked much. The older of the two was likely near Josiah's age. The younger brother was just a boy, maybe in his early teens. His brother called him, Choppy. Josiah assumed it was a nickname of sorts but so far, he had no reason to call him anything. At night, the brothers whispered to each other which reminded Josiah of his own brother and the events that led him to this dark room that smelled of wet earth.

A couple of weeks ago, running away never crossed Josiah's mind. He and William worked together on the Atkins plantation. Massa Atkins had been fairly good to them since he bought them from the Georgia plantation where they were born. Josiah was eleven and William was nine when they came to the Atkins plantation in Maryland. Both boys were large in stature. Josiah had all the physical characteristics of a warrior but the gentle soul of an angel. He had grown to over six feet tall with bulging muscles and the strength of a bear. He learned quickly and was quiet by nature.

However, William was also tall, but lean, and strong with a more playful nature. William was also likely to be disobedient sometimes. With no mother or father to guide them, Josiah and William learned to lean on each other and they were both fiercely protective of one another. That kind of devotion between slaves was never looked upon favorably by planters and Massa Atkins was no exception.

Josiah had become quite a skilled carpenter and furniture maker. William was allowed to stay with Josiah as a helper and apprentice. The two young men had become so skilled that Massa Atkins began hiring them out to perform certain home repair jobs in town. When on the plantation, Joe and Will created wonderful pieces of furniture which Massa Atkins then sold in town for a hefty profit. William had no passion for carpentry but he loved going away from the plantation with Josiah to perform small carpentry jobs in town.

A warm day in the spring of 1857, Josiah and William were summoned to the big house. They entered Massa Atkins' study with heads bowed. "You wants to see us, Massa Atkins," Josiah softly asked.

Mr. Atkin's head was down as he scrutinized one of the many documents that covered his desk. He didn't look up or answer right away. The brothers waited patiently. Finally, he said, "Yes. I got a complaint about your work." He leaned back and folded his arms across his chest. "Mrs. Shrewsbury sent me a note early this morning. It seems William, you sold her a table with uneven legs."

William snickered behind his hat and Josiah nudged him into silence. He had no idea what Massa Atkins was talking about but he knew by William's snicker that his brother knew and likely expected the complaint.

"Is there something funny about Mrs. Shrewsbury's complaint, William?" Atkins asked.

"No sir, but the legs on that table are perfectly fine."

"Then why is she saying that they are uneven. The table is wobbling, for God's sake. I went to see it with my own eyes."

"It ain't the table that's uneven, Massa Atkins. It's the floorboards in that rickety old house," William said through more snickers. "I tried to tell Mrs. Shrewsbury that the house needed new floorboards but she hushed me." He smiled broadly as if it were all a big joke.

"And that, somehow tickles you, eh boy."

Josiah nudged his brother again, hoping to hush his snickers, but he said nothing.

"No Massa."

"Ah, Massa," Josiah intervened. "You know Will. He just puts a smile on everything. He don't mean no harm."

"Yes, I do know your brother Josiah, but I've had just about enough of William's playful ways. I've no doubt that twenty lashes will wipe that simple smile from your face William."

With their heads hung low, the brothers left the house. Josiah had a bad feeling twisting in the pit of his stomach. He put an arm across William's shoulders as he whispered in his ear. "You got to stop that laughing at everything, Will."

William didn't answer. All he could think about was the whipping he would soon endure. What he found funny was the old lady's continued attempts to get him into trouble. She knew that her floor boards were uneven. He had even moved the table to a different spot to prove that it was not the table that was uneven. He even believed that Massa Atkins would see exactly what he saw, the table was fine. He was shocked to hear Massa order twenty lashes.

"I'm sorry Joe. I just never thought I would get whipped for laughing."

Atkins watched as William's shirt was torn from his body and he was strapped to a tree, planted in the front yard for just this purpose. The Overseer, Mr. Gale, would carry out the master's orders. Soon after the first couple of lashes sliced through the flesh on William's back, Atkins turned and walked away. He didn't wait to see his orders carried out but the rest of the slaves soon gathered and watched in mutual pain. They all winced with each lash.

Josiah counted the lashes and when the twentieth lash ripped through William's skin, Josiah stepped forward. "That be twenty, Mr. Gale," he whispered. Mr. Gale paid no attention to Josiah. Most of the slaves could not count and those who could, would not readily let it be known, but someone yelled from the back of the crowd.

"Twenty! Massa said twenty lashes, Mr. Gale." But Mr. Gale did not stop. Blood leaked from every lash on William's back.

"I said, that be twenty," Josiah said as he stepped closer to Mr. Gale intent on snatching the whip from Mr. Gale's hands

"Boy! I swear, if you don't step back, I'm gonna take this whip to you too." He stiff-armed Josiah with his free hand, pushing hard at Josiah's chest, causing him to fall backward.

With tears in his eyes and both hands balled into fist, Josiah got quickly to his feet and did step back. He counted twenty more lashes.

"He's gonna kill that boy," someone in the crowd yelled.

At first, William screamed out in pain with every lash but now his screams were barely a whisper. Then, he suddenly stopped crying. With the next lash, William's head swung to one side before falling forward into the tree to which he had been tied. Josiah watched the blood pool at his brother's feet and he knew that Mr. Gale was killing William. No one could live after losing that much blood.

Mr. Gale had beat his brother to death. Grief and rage filled Josiah and took over his senses. He suddenly lunged forward, snatching the whip from Mr. Gale's hand and throwing it to the ground. Gale tried to throw a punch to defend himself, but Josiah grabbed him by the throat with one powerful hand. Mr. Gale fought with everything in him but he was no match for the strength and grief-filled rage that had taken hold of Josiah. He could hear the roar of the other slaves as they shouted at him, "No, Josiah! Don't kill him! Stop!"

But Josiah could not stop. He lifted Mr. Gale by his throat, squeezing the life out of him with one mighty hand. "You killed him. You killed my brother for laughing," he said through his sobbing. After what seemed like only a few minutes, Mr. Gales' body went limp in Josiah's hand and he released him, letting his dead body fall to the ground, in a pool of William's blood.

Other slaves had already taken William down from the tree and as Josiah already knew, his brother was dead. He sat down on the ground with his back against the tree and took William into his arms. He rocked him back and forth as if he were a small child, tears streaming down his face. "I told you to stop all that laughing," he said through sobs. "Now they done killed you. They killed you for laughing."

"Run," somebody said. "Run, Josiah," he heard again. Josiah was suddenly aware of the situation. He had killed a white man with his bare hands. If he didn't run, he would soon be as dead as William. He moved William's bloodied corpse from his lap and slowly stood, looking down at his brother. He began to back away. "Run Josiah. Run," he heard again. This time he recognized the voice of his dead mother, so he ran. He ran as fast and as hard as he could. He had no idea where he was going. He only knew that he needed to getaway. He ran through the deep foliage of the wooded area behind the plantation. He ran through streams and over rocky hills. On the other side of one of those hills, the earth sloped down suddenly, and he found himself sliding uncontrollably. Sharp rocks and twigs tore at his thin shirt and into his flesh until finally, he plunged into the river. Once he was able to swim to the nearest bank, he began to run again. He ran until sheer exhaustion dropped him to his knees. He was too tired to run anymore. He took time to catch his breath and gather himself, then looked for a safe place to hide.

He stayed off the main roads, hiding wherever he could find the slightest bit of shelter, covering himself with dirt and leaves to blend into his surroundings. He hid in the daylight hours and moved north once the sun went down. After three days, he was both hungry and tired but knew that there was no turning back now. He prayed day and night and did his best not to lose hope. He was bone-weary when he discovered a large dead tree in the forest whose trunk had a deep hollow at its base, probably from some small animal. Josiah dragged bushes and branches toward the tree before he climbed inside and covered the opening. He was so tired that he fell asleep at once.

He didn't know how long he'd been inside the tree but he thought he might be dreaming when he felt himself being poked with a stick. He realized that he was no longer covered by leaves and thought he may have thrown them off during the night. He was poked again and knew that he wasn't dreaming. He quickly scrambled out of the tree, looking around as he got to his feet. An old black man with white hair on his head and face, stood there with a stick. A a nag and a wagon stood nearby. The man stood a few feet away watching Josiah intently.

"Hey Boy! You runnin?"

Josiah nodded.

"You ain't got no idea where you goin, does ya?" the man asked.

Josiah nodded again.

"If you that boy from the Atkins place, the whole county is out looking for you. If they catch you, you as good as dead. They say you killed that mean old son-of-a-bitch Gale with your bare hands."

Josiah didn't answer.

"Seems to me, you did a service to a whole lot of black folks. You ain't the first to want to kill that man."

They were both quiet for a time and Josiah sat down on the ground and dropped his head into his hands as he realized just how desperate his situation had become, and he knew that he needed to keep moving. There was no time to feel sorry for himself or even grieve for the loss of his brother.

"You ever heard of Miss. Markel?" the old man asked.

Josiah shook his head again, wishing the old man would just take his nag and move on. Couldn't he see that Josiah just wanted to be alone?

"Folks say she's one of them abolitionist," the old man said. Josiah gave no indication that he knew or had ever heard of an abolitionist. "That means she don't believe that slavery is right in the eyes of God. She's been known to help run-away slaves get north to the free states. She's a good white woman. She is what folks call a conductor."

Now the old man had Josiah's attention. "A conductor? This woman got a train?"

"Well," the old man took off his hat and scratched at his head. "There is a train, of sorts, but you can't see it and it don't belong to her."

"Ah, old man you talkin crazy."

"Look boy, you need to listen more and talk less. Just know that Miss. Carrie Markel can help you. That's what she does. She helps run-aways on their way to freedom."

"How do I find her?" he whispered.

"Well, thank God. I was beginning to think you were daft, boy," the old man said as he flashed a toothless smile. "I'm gonna take you some of the way. I can get you pretty close."

"Thank you," Josiah said. He eyed the old man with suspicion. "You slave or free?" he asked.

"I'm a slave, just like you were."

"How is it that you just walking along with a nag and this here wagon?" Josiah walked close to the wagon to see what he carried.

"My Massa trust me. He sends me all over the county running errands."

"Then why ain't you run away to this Miss. Markel yourself?"

"I'm too old and I got too many folks here that I don't want to leave behind. Like I said, my Massa trust me and I can move around as I please." He walked toward the back of the wagon. "Enough talk, boy. You best get into this here wagon. Scoot down behind these grain sacks and pull some of those empty sacks over you. I'll get you as close as I can to Miss. Markel's before dark."

Josiah did as he was told. "Thank you, sir."

"No thanks needed. Just be still and quiet. If we run into patrollers, I don't know you and I got no idea how or when you got into my Massa's wagon. Understand?"

"Yes, sir."

"Now drop down and cover-up. We best be movin along."

Josiah soon felt the wagon lurch forward and realized that he was on the way. With his body still slightly trembling from fatigue and his heart heavy with guilt and grief, Josiah hunkered down and began to silently pray.

Sleep was impossible on the ride to Miss. Markel's house so when the wagon finally came to a stop, Josiah kept still and held his breath. "Come on, boy. Time to be on your way."

Josiah came from under his covering and jumped down to the ground. They were in the thick of a wooded area off the main road. The sun was just beginning to set and the meadow that stretched westward before him was cast in an orange glow. "See those trees on the other side of this flat land?" The old man didn't wait for an answer. "That's where you'll find Miss. Markel's place. You can count, can't you?"

"Yes, sir."

"Go to the side door and knock three times. Count to ten and knock twice more. Do you understand?"

"I understand, but how will I make it across this here flat land without being seen? It's wide open."

"Look boy, I ain't got all the answers. You just do it." The old man had climbed back into the wagon and snapped the reins, moving the nag back to the main road. "Now go. God be with you."

"Hey, what's your name?" Josiah called but the man did not answer.

Josiah waited until it was completely dark before he sprinted across the meadow to the side door of Miss. Markel's house. He was immediately admitted with no questions asked. Miss Carrie, as he was told to call her, had dark hair and eyes, rosy cheeks and a warm smile. She embraced Josiah as if he were her child. "You must be tired and hungry. I will have food brought to you very soon. Follow me," she whispered as she quickly led him to a trap door at the back of the house which led to an underground room where the two other run-away slaves waited.

After five days underground, Miss Carrie graciously provided the three run-away slaves with a rowboat. It was late April and Miss Carrie assured the young men that the river would be so busy that three young men would hardly be noticed among the fisherman, large passenger steamboats carrying people from Delaware to New York, and barges for carrying cargo to almost every city on the East coast.

However, Miss Carrie's well-meaning intentions could not have anticipated the storm that was moving steadily north along the East coast with a deluge of wind and water. They were well on their way when the first few drops of the spring rain fell. Less than an hour into their voyage, the wind began to pick-up. Josiah noticed that the larger steamboats had moved so far ahead that they could hardly be seen and the smaller rowboats of fisherman had disappeared from the river altogether. It seemed that they were all alone on the water.

The plan was to dock in Philadelphia. However, the storm made this an impossible task. At first, the wind blew softly, but suddenly it began to whip in strong gust. It rained harder and harder and soon the rain was pounding and the wind began to swirl. The tiny rowboat was no match for the fierce storm as it dipped and climbed the swells of the river. The oars were useless and all the men could do was hold fast to the sides of the boat and pray. Then a wave, larger than any had ever seen on a river, came crashing down onto the rowboat, submerging it under water. All three men were tossed from their seats toward the sky before falling into the furious current of the Delaware River.

"Swim Josiah, Swim," Josiah heard his mother's voice in his head again. His head bobbed above the water for only a second before the river pulled him down toward the bottom. He felt the weight of the water pulling him down below the turbulence of a raging river and suddenly it was peaceful and he was content. He was subconsciously letting the current carry him to a final resting place at the bottom of the Delaware River. "Swim Josiah," he heard again and he opened his eyes. "Josiah, swim and live!" It was as if his mother was right there with him in the river. "Josiah," she called him a third time. "Live boy! Swim Josiah and live." In that instant, he began to fight his way to the surface which seemed completely out of his reach. Finally, he reached the surface and he could lift his head above the water. He took a few deep gulps of air before going below the surface again. Under the water, he swam as hard as he could, finally reaching the river bank on the New Jersey side of the river, just as the storm seemed to pass over and away.

Exhausted from both fear and exertion, Josiah lay on the muddy riverbank thanking God for his survival and trying to steady his rapidly beating heart. Then he heard the sound of trotting horses and whispered voices. All his senses became alert and he quickly got to his feet. Josiah knew that he was a fugitive and there would be slave catchers searching for him.

Dense foliage lay just a few feet away and Josiah used all the strength he had to push himself forward. He moved quickly to hide in the cover of the forest, behind a large tree whose roots were partially hidden in a thick ground cover. The mud and grass stains from the river bank helped to camouflage his body. His nostrils filled with the smells of the forest and the river and Josiah had to cover his mouth and nose to stifle a sneeze. While holding his breath, he folded his large frame into an awkward position and hid in the small space behind the tree. He did not know how long he could hold such an uncomfortable position but he knew that he could not reveal himself to these men, who were likely slave catchers.

"It's a good thing we docked as early as we did," one of the men said. "An hour later and we would have been on the river when the storm hit." Josiah couldn't see his face but his voice was a little squeaky and not one that he recognized.

"I think we picked the wrong side of the river," another said. "That nigger is probably moving northwest through Pennsylvania."

"Well," said a third voice, "if we don't find him soon, we will have to cross the river back into Pennsylvania and continue to search."

Josiah's spine stiffened as he recognized the voice of Arthur Gale, eldest son of the Overseer George Gale who had beat William to death and who Josiah had killed. How could he be here, Josiah wondered? Arthur Gale had left the Atkins plantation years ago with his mother. Was he searching for Josiah because he killed his father or, was he just a slave catcher who had not yet heard of the tragedy in Maryland?

After a time, the horses moved on and the voices began to fade into the distance. Only after he was sure that the men had moved on did Josiah scrambled to his feet. He tried to wipe the river mud from his face and hair as best he could, but he knew that nothing would get rid of the smell except a bath.

Just as he had done back in Maryland, Josiah thought it best to travel at night under the cover of the dense forest. He stayed away from the main roads. The afternoons were warm but April evenings were cool and sometimes cold. What little belongings he had been given by Miss. Markel were at the bottom of the Delaware River. Josiah had nothing to keep him warm during those nights. He had been walking for two days, trying to use the night stars for direction. One morning, after a particularly cool and damp night, Josiah awoke in a dew-covered brush to a large white man standing over him. He wore a big hat and had a couple of rabbits strung together by the feet and hanging over his shoulder. He nudged Josiah with the barrel of his shotgun.

"Come on out of there, boy," the man said. Josiah didn't move. With a kind face but sharp words, he said again, "Come on. Ain't no harm to you, boy. Just come on out." Josiah slowly got to his feet. "You ain't from around here, are you boy?"

"No sir," Josiah whispered.

The man looked Josiah up and down. "A run-away, I'm guessing?"

"Yes, sir," Josiah said.

"Relax. I mean you no harm. You ain't the first and ain't likely to be the last run-away to pass this way."

Josiah breathed a sigh of relief.

"Well, my God, you're soaking wet. Follow me," the man said as he turned and began to walk away. "The house is less than a mile away. My wife and I will get you warmed up and fed, then you can be on your way." Josiah followed quietly for a few minutes. Then he was suddenly suspicious of the old man and stopped walking.

"Why?" Josiah asked.

The man stopped and turned to look at Josiah. "As I said, we have seen many run-aways, but you the first to question our help." The man took off his hat and scratched at his thinning hair. With his hands resting on his hips he looked into Josiah's eyes. "It ain't a mystery, son. My religion tells me that all men are created equal in the eyes of God.

We don't believe that any man should own another." He squinted his eyes against the sun as he spoke and his casual smile put Josiah at ease. Josiah smiled back as fear fell away from him and they began walking again, together.

"May I ask what is your name, and what religion are you, sir?"

He kept walking as he spoke. "I am George Housman, from Pennsylvania and I am a Christian sir, of the Quaker Church and a farmer here in New Jersey."

"I am happy to meet you, Mr. Housman."

Housman didn't seem to be worried about being seen with a fugitive slave. He just walked on like it was the most natural thing in the world. "My wife and I came here from Pennsylvania about ten years ago. We like it here. Nice people, a nice church and we like the idea of helping our fellow man." They came to a clearing and Josiah could see a small farmhouse and a field with a few cows.

Mrs. Housman was as nice as her husband. Their house was cozy and comfortable and they insisted that Josiah stay the night. After a meal of rabbit stew and fresh bread, sleep came easy. He was completely exhausted. Almost as soon as he settled himself on the sofa offered him for the night, he slept long and hard. He awoke to an empty house. It was probably late in the afternoon as the front of the house was flooded with the yellow light of a fading sun. Apparently, the Housemans went about their normal duties of running the farm. He sat up and stretched. Mrs. Housman came in carrying an empty bucket in each hand.

"Well, now. You've slept the whole day away."

"Yes, Ma'am. I was pretty tired and I am so grateful to you and your husband. I can't thank you enough."

She smiled. "I found some clothes for you. They may not fit as they should but they will do." She put down the buckets and pointed to the clothes folded neatly over a chair. "You can wash up in the shed. Hot water and everything you need is there in the back."

Josiah nodded his thanks and went to clean himself up and change into clean clothes. Both the Housman's were in the kitchen when he came out. She handed him a bundle of sliced ham, fresh-baked bread and a canteen of tea. To his surprise, Mrs. Housman opened her arms, as an invitation for a hug. Josiah leaned close and Mrs. Housman threw her arms around his neck and hugged him briefly. Josiah returned her embrace. "Take care of yourself, Josiah. We'll be praying for you."

Mr. Housman came forward and shook Josiah's hand. "The sun will be going down soon. I don't know where you're going, but I'm praying that you get to freedom safely. May God be with you."

"I don't know how to thank you both. I know that I will never forget your kindness."

Mr. Housman pointed Josiah north. "Good luck to you Josiah." They shook hands again and Josiah took to the forest again. He moved quickly through the dense brush, hoping to get as far as he could before daybreak.

He heard no one and saw no one as he moved north. The sounds of the forest at night were sometimes eerie. The squeaking and barking of squirrels, the high pitch squeal of raccoons, and the howl of dogs in the distance could be frightening, but Josiah just kept moving. When the hooting of owls was replaced by the sweet songs of birds high up in the trees, he knew that the sun would soon rise and he looked for a place to hunker down and hide. It wasn't long before he came across a large tree, partially obscured by a boulder. Tired and hungry, Josiah made himself comfortable behind the boulder with his back against the tree trunk and opened the bundle Mrs. Housman so graciously packed for him. He mumbled a short prayer before he began to munch on honey baked ham and bread, licking the sweet juices from his fingers.

He took a long swig from the canteen and that's when he saw her. She was partially hidden in the trees but the first thing he saw was big gray eyes that looked very sad. She didn't move, she just watched. They stared at each other for some time before she scrambled from her hiding place and walked right up to Josiah. She made some sort of sign with her hands and motioned for him to follow her. Josiah glanced around, wondering why this young girl was all alone in the forest. Where were her parents? Was there anyone with this child? Seeing no one, he followed her silently.

She walked deep into the woods and Josiah followed. Every couple of minutes, she would turn to see if he still followed. Finally, they came to a well-hidden cave. Inside, it was easy to see that the child had been living alone in this hovel. A pallet for sleeping was made of straw and old clothes. There were cups, likely stolen, for drinking and rusty cans that she probably ate from.

"What's your name?" Josiah asked. But the girl just shook her head no. "Can you speak?" she shook her head no again but took a stick and drew a big *"S"* in the dirt. Though Josiah never learned to read and write, he had been able to pick up some words and letters over the years and he recognized the *"S"* from the word sale, on the furniture tags Massa Atkins sold. "Susan," Josiah asked.

She shook her head again and pointed to a pile of straw. Josiah figured she wanted him to lay down. He bowed deeply from his waist, grateful to the girl for a place to lay his head and made a pallet of straw a few feet away from the pallet she used. He tried to guess her name again, going through a list of female names beginning with the sound of "S," and she continued to shake her head no. Eventually, she stopped answering him and curled up on her own pallet to sleep. The night air was cool but the girl didn't seem to be bothered by the cool air. She was asleep in just a few minutes.

❦

The girl had watched Josiah from the trees for some time just as she watched the three very large white men that were tracking him. At first, she was just watching the black man, wondering who he was and where he had come from. He only moved at night and hid when the sun came up. She was sure that he was a run-away. She decided that she would offer him a safe place to sleep for the night but before she came close enough for him to see her, the air was suddenly filled with the stench of old tobacco and whiskey. She scurried up the nearest tree to see who approached.

They hadn't seen her hiding in the trees but she saw them and knew that they followed the runaway. The tallest of the men was probably the leader. He was very fair with bright blue eyes and white hair. At first, she followed them hoping that they might make camp, giving her the opportunity to pilfer some food or water from their rations. She soon realized that they had no intention of making camp and would make it back to town before nightfall.

"He's one big buck," she heard the leader say. "I'm surprised that he survived the storm on the river, but it's only a matter of time before we catch that nigger." The other two just nodded their heads in agreement.

"They say he strangled Gale to death with one hand," one of them said.

"No matter," another said. "It won't be long before he's back in chains."

"It's for sure, he's in these woods somewhere."

"We'll find that nigger," the third man said. "It just a matter of time."

"Yeah. He didn't just kill a white man. He killed my Daddy and I'll track this son-of-a-bitch to the ends of the earth if that's what it takes. I won't rest until I witness him take his last breath."

"Amen to that!"

"He can't get very far," another said.

"Yep. Maybe we'll have better luck tomorrow," the white-haired man said.

The girl stayed hidden in the trees until she knew that the men had moved far enough away not to hear her. Then she began to search for the man they hunted. It wasn't long before she came upon Josiah hiding between a large tree trunk and a boulder. She watched him for a while before she made her presence known. He was really tall and broad but he had a kind face and he trembled some. The girl could tell that he was afraid but he smiled when he saw her and she knew that she had no reason to fear him. She gave a motion for him to follow and he did so without question. She didn't know why but she wanted to help him, so she took him to her cave so that he could rest for the night but as the sun rose, she wondered what else she could do to help him on his way. She didn't know but she was sure that the Bowmans would know what to do. She just had to make them understand her.

Chapter Two
The Innocent
1857
Timbuctoo, New Jersey

She made no sound as she moved into the Bowman yard. This wasn't her first time. She came often but silently. Sometimes she watched Rebecca from the other side of the road. Many evenings, after the sun had gone down and nothing stirred outside the Bowman house, the girl would be daring enough to walk right up to the house and peer through the window.

David is now sixteen, and the twins, Lilly and Cathy are fourteen years old. The family has made a practice of reading to each other every night after supper. The father often reads from the Bible and the girls read from their storybooks. David rarely reads but he enjoys listening to the Bible stories and the stories read by his sisters. The girl watched from the window and was filled with envy. She sometimes imagined that this was her family, her parents, and her brother and sisters. She had never known her father and it had been so long since she saw her mother that she couldn't remember what she looked like. She wished that she could stay there and watch this family forever, but often the pangs of envy and loss were so great that she had to turn away. After wiping her tear-stained cheeks with a dirty hand, she would scurry back into the cover of the woods, behind the Bowman house.

Today was different, though. She wanted to tell the Bowmans about the man in the woods. She wanted to tell them how she had watched him being tracked by three white men on large horses. She was afraid that the man might be caught and she wanted to help him in some way.

It was a cool April morning but the sun was warm and welcoming. Rebecca didn't see or even hear the girl coming. It seemed as if she just appeared. Rebecca hung one sheet on the line and bent over her basket to gather another. That's when she saw the girl standing just inside the fence. She couldn't have been more than ten or eleven years old, Rebecca thought. They stared at each other, both taking in the essence of the other. Rebecca saw a dirty, shabby white child with sad gray eyes. The girl saw the mother she had dreamed of since she was a small child.

"Hello," Rebecca softly said. There was no answer. The girl just continued to stare as if she was expecting something. Rebecca dropped the sheet back into her basket and took a step closer, but the girl backed away. "Can I help you with something?" Rebecca asked.

Vacant eyes stared back at her and then the girl lifted her right arm and pointed to the back of the house, but she said nothing.

"The house?" Rebecca tried to understand. "You want something from my house?"

She shook her head, "No."

"You want to go into my house?" Rebecca asked. "No? What are you doing here? Where is your Mother?"

"Mama," it was David coming through the back door as he spoke. "She can't speak, Mama."

Rebecca turned to look at her son. At sixteen, David was nearly as tall as Benjamin. "How do you know that, David? Who is she? Where is this child's family?"

"I don't know all that, Mama. I'm not sure she has a family," he said with a shrug of his shoulders. "I ain't never seen nobody but her. She's been hanging around our house for a couple of months now. That's how I know that she can't speak. I don't think she has a home either. I think she sleeps in the woods."

"Oh, my God," Rebecca whispered.

"I've been giving her food whenever I see her hanging around the yard. I guess that's why she keeps coming back. She goes away but she always comes back." David nonchalantly shrugged his shoulders again and Rebecca could hardly believe what her son was saying. "She's real nice Mama until I start asking questions. Then she just runs off."

Rebecca stood for a moment, taking it all in and wondering what she could do to help this child. "Oh my God," she whispered again more to herself than either the girl or David. This child is mute and homeless, she thought. Pushing her apprehension aside, Rebecca waved the girl forward.

"Come," she said, and the girl slowly came forward. Rebecca intended to take her hand but after seeing the dirt crusted between her fingers and under her broken nails, she quickly changed her mind. As the child came closer, the acrid smell of excrement and urine was so overwhelming that Rebecca had to cover her mouth and nose with the hem of her apron and turn away from the sickening smell. "Take her inside, David, and get her something to eat. Then boil some water for the tub. This child needs a bath." Rebecca eyed the girl again. "I'll be back as soon as I can, hopefully with some answers."

David was wary but he did as he was told. Ignoring the stench, he reached a hand out to the girl. She gave no protest but took his hand and let him gently guide her into the house. He motioned for her to sit at the table. Then he filled a plate with cold baked chicken, biscuits, and some warm grits leftover from breakfast. She scarcely let the plate touch the table before she began to stuff her mouth with both hands. "Hey," he said with some alarm. "You're going to choke if you don't slow down." He watched the girl eat in awe and sadness. He was saddened at the child's great hunger and angry that whoever was responsible for the girl had allowed her to be in such a state. He left her eating a second plate of food while he went to gather wood for the stove and water for her bath.

⁂

Unsure of what she should do about the child, Rebecca headed straight for the Constable's office. A portly, middle aged, black man who had been living in this town his entire life, Constable Willis was the law in Timbuctoo. Her thoughts raced ahead of her quickening footsteps. She thought, 'keeping a white child in my house could bring all kinds of trouble. Benjamin will not be happy about this,' she thought. By the time Rebecca reached the Constable's office she was anxious and out of breath. "Mr. Willis," she called as she opened the office door. Constable Willis looked up in surprise and Rebecca didn't wait a second before a torrid of unintelligible words spilled from her mouth. She spoke too quickly and too loudly and the Constable could barely understand a word.

He held up his hand to stop her in mid-sentence. "Mrs. Bowman! Take a breath." He came from behind the desk and led Rebecca to a chair. "Have a seat." He calmly sat across from her and his composure seemed to have a calming effect on Rebecca. She took several deep breaths in an effort to settle herself.

"Now tell me what happened?" he said in a low voice.

Rebecca relayed the events of the morning. She told the Constable everything, just as it happened. She even told him that David had seen the girl many times before today. She had apparently been hanging around their property for some time. Constable Willis was thoughtful for a moment. "Mrs. Bowman, if you're worried about the child, maybe you and your family might be kind enough to take her in for a while. Once the child is comfortable, maybe she will tell you about herself and her family. Just give it some time."

"But, Constable Willis, she's mute and she's white."

"Mute?"

"Yes, so I don't think she will be telling us much of anything."

"Oh my," Constable Willis said with a sigh. "Well, that could be a bit of a problem but it should also make finding her family a little easier. A mute child? Someone must be missing her," he said. "I'll do my best to find out where she came from and get back to you when I know something." He stood as he spoke and with a hand placed at Rebecca's elbow, he gently steered her toward the door. Once outside he released her. "In the meantime, just take care of the girl. You may be able to get some information from her in one way or another."

"Thank you," Rebecca stammered.

"Good day to you, Mrs. Bowman," he said.

"Good day, sir," Rebecca said but did not immediately walk away. There was a strange look on the Constable's face. He stared off in the distance and Rebecca couldn't help but follow his gaze across the street to where two strangers were just dismounting their horses in front of the town hotel. Timbuctoo was such a small town that it was nearly impossible not to notice a stranger.

"Is there something wrong?" Rebecca whispered.

"Not yet," Constable Willis whispered. "But there could be trouble brewing." He turned his head and looked in the other direction, not wanting to gain the attention of the two strangers. "Those two men presented themselves to me earlier as bounty hunters on the lookout for fugitives but I've seen their kind before, many times. They say they look for criminals and I don't doubt that they are looking for fugitive slaves, but the truth is, they are also looking for bodies, black bodies that they can sell back into slavery. Slave catchers, if I had to guess. I can't say more at the moment but tell your husband and keep your son and the rest of the family close until the danger passes. I will be in touch as soon as I am able. I promise."

The Constable's warning of slave catchers in town unnerved Rebecca. She knew she had to alert her husband and Louis as soon as possible. She also wanted to get back to her home as soon as she could. She had a bad feeling about the girl she'd left at the house with David. The fastest way to notify Lillian and Louis, Rebecca thought, would be to send a messenger to their farm. She was sure that Althea would be able to send a message, so she stopped by the boarding house on her way home.

Rebecca entered through the back door. Denny and Nan sat at the table snapping a basket of string beans. "Morning, Becca," Denny said. Nan nodded her head to echo Denny's greeting.

"Good morning," Rebecca said.

"You look upset. Is there something wrong?"

"Not yet, Nan, but the Constable thinks that there could be trouble."

"Trouble?" Althea yelled from the pantry as she came down the small ladder set to help her retrieve items from the top shelves. "Good morning Rebecca, now what's this you saying about trouble?"

"Well," Rebecca washed her hands before taking a seat at the table. She began to help Nan and Denny snap string beans as she spoke. She relayed everything from the arrival of the young girl at her back door to the brief conversation she had with the Constable, who told her of the strangers in town. "Constable Willis says they claim to be bounty hunters but he knows a slave catcher when he sees one." Rebecca barely paused. She didn't notice that the women had stopped snapping the vegetables and stared at her wide-eyed with mouths agape. "I came by to ask if someone would go out to my Mother's place and let her and Louis know about the slave catchers." Rebecca looked up to see all three women's eyes on her and she realized that they were afraid.

"Denny," Althea called. "Go next door and get Esau. It wouldn't be safe for any of us to be on the street."

"Who is Esau?" Rebecca wanted to know.

"Esau Ayers is the son of the Quaker family that lives next door. It will be safer for him to go tell Lillian and Louis about the slave catchers. Besides, his parents would want to know this too. They often take in runaways."

Denny hurried out of the back door while Althea and Nan went about locking doors and windows. "I better get back home," Rebecca said. "There is still a mute white girl at my place and I'm not sure what I'm supposed to do with her."

"Do?" Althea questioned. "Clean her up, feed her and take care of her till someone tells you differently. You know that's what Lillian would say. Now go. Get home and tell Benjamin and David to stay off of the street."

"You're right, Althea." Rebecca gave Althea a hug and left by the back door.

Church bells rang, signaling the noon hour just as Rebecca entered Bowman Catering by the front door. Benjamin was busy explaining the details of an upcoming event to a group of employees when he noticed Rebecca quietly enter. She eased the door shut, then turned to peep at the street through the dark linen curtains. Rebecca never came down to the company dining room and seeing her immediately alarmed Benjamin. He excused himself and made his way quickly through the maze of tables to Rebecca's side. "What is it? What's happened?" he asked as he enveloped his wife in his arms. Rebecca leaned into his embrace. He only held her for a moment but that was enough for Rebecca to exhale, releasing much of the anxiety that she felt from the moment she saw the girl. He led her to a table and Rebecca told her husband everything as he gently stroked the back of her hand.

"Get Grandma from the church," he calmly instructed. "The two of you go home and tend to this homeless child. I'll get our girls from the schoolhouse and be home as soon as I can." He embraced her again and led her to the back door. "Hurry Becca, and keep David indoors."

Rebecca explained everything to Mom Cathy on the walk from the church. She didn't say much but her eyes squinted, making a crease in her forehead between her eyes. This was the only indication of her dismay. "We will take care of this child. That is the only Christian thing to do and you know that your mother would agree."

"Yes, Ma'am. Althea said as much, too."

They found David sitting on the back steps. "Where is she?" Rebecca asked.

"I left her in the room behind the kitchen with a tub full of hot soapy water. I pointed to the water but she didn't understand, so I just left her there."

"You did good, David. Thank you." He shrugged his shoulders. "Look, honey, the constable says that there may be slave catchers in town. You are going to have to stay close to home until the danger passes. It isn't even safe for you to sit out here."

A sad expression crossed David's face but he did not protest. He dutifully went indoors with his mother and great-grandmother.

Rebecca tapped on the door before entering the room they used for washing. The water was still hot and a cloud of steam rose from the wooden tub in the center of the room. The girl stood in the corner of the room examining the ceramic bowl under the potty chair. Though this must have been new to her, its use was apparent as she motioned with her hands and arms that she wanted to use it. "Yes, yes. You may sit." Rebecca said.

The girl stripped off her tattered clothing quickly and plopped down onto the potty chair. Rebecca gathered the soiled clothing into a bundle and set it outside the door as she called for Mom Cathy. When the child had finished with the potty chair, Rebecca showed her how to clean herself before taking her by the hand to the tub. She pulled away as if to say she had no intention of getting into the tub of hot water.

Rebecca swished her hand in the water to show her that it was no longer as hot as she thought. With some coaxing, Rebecca was able to get the girl into the tub. She scrubbed her clean. She washed away all the mud and removed the dried leaves and twigs tangled in her hair. She cleaned the dirt that was caked under her fingernails and toenails and cut them short. She also had to cut some of her hair, as much of it was just too matted and tangled to comb. Mom Cathy brought one of Lilly's old dresses and a petticoat that fit their new house guest perfectly. Rebecca rubbed oil on the girl's arms, legs, and face. The transformation was remarkable. The dirty matted hair that looked almost black, was now cleaned to a light Carmel colored brown.

When she was finished grooming the child, she took her to her own bedroom, where she could look at herself in the full-length dressing mirror. She took one look at herself and threw her arms around Rebecca's neck and Rebecca returned her affection.

Mom Cathy was in the kitchen preparing the evening meal. By this time, the entire family was home. When Rebecca and the child walked into the dining room, all eyes turned in their direction. "Hello," the girls said in unison. David just stared with his mouth open. He couldn't believe that this was the same girl. The girl only smiled her greeting.

As plates were heaped with food and dishes passed back and forth around the table, the child never took her eyes away from Rebecca. A plate was prepared for her and sat in front of her and she immediately went to grab a handful of greens, but when she saw that Rebecca shook her head, "No," she stopped immediately and put her hands in her lap. "What is your name?" Little Cathy wanted to know. The girl made a sign with her hand but no one knew what she was saying.

Benjamin blessed the table and everyone said, "Amen." Only then did they take up their forks and begin to eat. The girl watched and did the same.

"I think she is speaking sign language," Lilly said. "Our teacher told us that is how the mute speak."

"If that were true Lilly, that would mean someone had to teach her this sign language. The girl has been living in the woods, for God's sake. No one has taught her anything." David said.

"You don't know when she became homeless," his sister shot back.

"If she could tell me her name, she would have," David argued.

Suddenly, the girl stopped eating. She stood and slammed her fist on the table so hard that dishes, flatware, and the Bowman family jumped at the sound. All eyes turned to the young white girl. "Saaaamtha!" she stammered. It sounded more like a grunt than a word or a name. The family just continued to stare at her. She tried again. "Saaama tha . . ." More grunting.

Rebecca stood from her chair and went to put her arms around the girl. "You are all talking about her like she can't hear. She hears and understands you all," Rebecca said. "Is that your name, Sweetie? Samtha?" She shook her head no. "Samantha?" The girl smiled, relaxed and sat down again. "Her name is Samantha!" Rebecca was happy to finally know the girl's name. "I would like you all to meet Samantha," Rebecca turned back to the girl and said. "I am very glad to meet you, Samantha. Where is your family, Samantha?"

Samantha pointed to the window then made a sign with her hands like sleeping.

"Sleeping in the woods?" Lilly asked.

"No!" She shook her head and then began to eat.

"Do you have a Mama?" young Cathy wanted to know.

"No!" She shook her head again.

All through supper, Samantha made signs with her arms and hands and the Bowman girls tried to guess what she was saying. It became a sort of game. The Bowman girls were fascinated with Samantha and they wanted to learn all they could about her life. Over the next couple of days, they learned that Samantha's mother may have died in a fire and she had been alone and living in the woods for a very long time. She wasn't as young as she looked. She lost track of the time in the woods but she guessed that she was about fourteen or fifteen, close to the twin's age. She remembered that before the fire, her mother had schooled her in their home. She also remembered that before the fire her father had left and never came back. The more they learned the more Rebecca's heart ached for the girl. After Supper, Samantha was put to bed with the twins wearing one of their nightgowns.

Once Rebecca learned that Samantha had some schooling, she decided to buy her a small chalkboard. Rebecca couldn't wait to present the small gift to Samantha. Though Samantha could not spell very well, she could write the way words sounded to her. Once she got the chalkboard, she was better able to communicate with the family.

꩜

After the Constable told Rebecca about the slave catchers in town, she kept the children and especially David, close to home. David usually spent time helping his Grandfather Louis out at the farm, but for now, his parents agreed that it was just too dangerous. Benjamin made sure that the twins and his grandmother got back and forth to the church where Mom Cathy volunteered and the twins went to school nearby.

There had been no word from Constable Willis about Samantha's family and, considering the things Samantha was able to tell them, Rebecca and Benjamin didn't expect the Constable to have anything of importance to add. Nevertheless, Samantha seemed to be adjusting well to living with the Bowmans. She got along well with the twins and was eager to help with the housework when asked. It was obvious to any who cared to notice, she had a special affection for David.

The Bowmans were very comfortable with Samantha and she seemed comfortable with the family. But on her third day with the Bowmans, Samantha rose early and packed a bag full of left-over food and left the house before anyone was awake.

That morning, Mom Cathy called for the girls to come down for breakfast. Lilly and Cathy bounced into the dining room with their usual exuberance. "Where's Sam?" Mom Cathy wanted to know.

"Don't know," Lilly offered with a shrug of her shoulders.

"She's gone," Cathy said.

Rebecca dropped the sock she was darning back into her sewing basket and slowly walked into the dining room. "What do you mean, she's gone?" Miss Cathy asked.

"Where could she have gone?" Rebecca said.

"I don't know Mama," Lilly said. "She left her bed before the sun came up. She had some food tied up in a rag. I thought she must still be hungry."

"She's always hiding food," Cathy offered.

"That child was hungry for a very long time. I am not surprised that she's hiding food," Mom Cathy said as she moved around the table filling the bowls with oatmeal.

David came in from the back staircase. "Morning," he said as he found his seat at the table. One look at his mother and grandmother and David knew that something was wrong. "What's wrong? Why are you looking so sad, Mama?"

"Samantha's gone," Rebecca explained.

"Gone? Gone Where?"

"We don't know. She left early this morning."

"She'll be back, Mama. I think she was really happy here."

"I think so, too," Mom Cathy offered.

"I hope so."

The girls and David went back to eating their breakfast, Mom Cathy went to the kitchen and Rebecca went back to her basket of socks to continue her darning while saying a silent prayer for Samantha's return.

❧

Josiah didn't know how long he slept but when he woke up the girl was gone. He knew it was late afternoon because the sun was high in the sky with its rays shining through the canopy of the trees. He wondered when or if the girl would come back. He also wondered if he should stay in the cave or strike out on his own again. The girl had been a blessing and he was grateful to her for giving him a place to sleep. However, living in a cave with a homeless white girl might be asking for trouble that he really didn't need. Rested but confused and with his mind made up, Josiah decided that the best thing for him to do would be to move on, but he had no idea where to go. As soon as he started out, he noticed the tiny footprints of his homeless host and decided to follow them to see if they would lead him to wherever the girl had gone.

He followed for quite some distance until the footprints disappeared into a fragrant leafy ground cover. The growth that covered the ground went as far as the eye could see and the forest seemed to go on forever. If there was a road, Josiah could not see it and had no idea in which direction he should travel.

He moved steadily and quietly through the foliage. A dog barked in the distance and Josiah couldn't help thinking of the hounds used to hunt runaway slaves in the South. Then he heard the muffled voices of men who could not be far away. He became anxious. Could those voices belong to the men who were hunting him? Did the dogs bark because they had picked up his scent? He didn't know the answers to those questions but he knew that he must move away from the danger as quickly as he could. He turned and began to move as fast as he could in the opposite direction but not having any idea where he was going. The trees of the forest were so dense that the sun was almost completely blocked out. The sounds of the forest seemed to grow louder. Birds chirped, frogs croaked, and insects buzzed. Josiah could hear running water of a nearby river. Then he was suddenly over-whelmed again and began to fear that he could be running into danger.

He decided that it might be best to find his way back to the cave, at least for now. This decision proved to be more difficult than he had anticipated and he was soon lost and wandered aimlessly through the forest for hours. As afternoon became evening, the wind picked up, blowing cool, damp air. The evening also made the sounds of the forest come alive again, but the late hours brought different sounds. Crickets chirped in loud unison. Birds sang their evening songs calling to distant mates. As darkness encroached, Josiah became even more anxious. Finally, tired and hungry, he breathed a sigh of relief when the surroundings became more familiar and he knew that he was close to the cave.

He crawled back into the cave and pulled some fallen shrubbery and tree limbs in front of the cave's opening just as he had seen the girl do two nights before. He was cold and hungry but he felt safe and he settled in for the night. He could hear the wind gently rustling through the trees. Sometimes the gusts were strong and threatening and he could hear tree limbs being torn and flung several feet away from the tree that grew them. Josiah curled his body, bringing his knees to his chest and wrapping his arms around himself for warmth.

As he lay there, trying to fall asleep, his mind went back to the plantation. Visions that he would prefer to forget suddenly became very vivid. William was strapped to the tree, the flesh on his back torn away and blood pooling at his feet. Mr. Gale stood there with a familiar scowl on his sunburned face. Josiah heard his own voice tell Mr. Gale, "no more." He shook his head from side to side as if that would somehow erase that awful memory. He blinked back tears and tried again to fall asleep. His mind lingered somewhere between sleep and awake. He knew he wasn't asleep because he could still hear the wind blowing, but he wasn't awake either. "I am with you, always," he heard. This time, it was not his mother's voice and it was not his own voice. It was a very serene voice, a whisper. "I will always be with you, Josiah," he heard. The soft voice was like a gentle breeze. It just brushed across his face and all anxiety seemed to fall away and he slept.

Hours later he thought he smelled warm bread and bacon. He must be dreaming. Slowly unfolding his large body, he realized that he was no longer cold. He stretched and yawned, willing his body from the stillness of slumber. One more sniff and, Josiah knew that he wasn't dreaming. As he opened his eyes, his stomach churned reminding him that he hadn't eaten in days. He pushed himself upright and there she was, sitting cross-legged across from him. At first, he thought it was someone else because she looked so different. Her face and clothes were clean and her hair was pulled back and tied with ribbon. It was only after she smiled that he could see that it was the same girl.

A small fire burned and he could see that she had heated some food in a tin plate. She smiled broadly as she handed him the warm plate heaped with biscuits, bacon, and grits. He smiled back. "Thank you," he whispered as he began to eat hungrily.

The girl didn't eat. She just watched Josiah. There were so many questions he wanted to ask her, but he just smiled at her between bites. Where had she gone? Where did she get this food? Could she tell him which way was north?

After Josiah had eaten, he reclined against the wall of the cave and watched as the girl seemed to be cleaning the cave. She kicked dirt on the fire to smother the flame. She stacked her tin cups, cans and plates on a nearby bolder against a wall and then turned to face Josiah. She took a branch and wrote the word "come," in the dirt.

"Come? You want me to come with you?"

Samantha shook her head, yes and Josiah followed her from the cave and through the forest. They moved quickly. Samantha took so many twists and turns that Josiah knew that he would never be able to find his way back to the cave now. Finally, after almost an hour of walking over well-worn paths and often taking a turn off the path and into dense woods, they came to the edge of the forest and Samantha stopped. A lush green meadow stretched before them for a few miles. Josiah could tell that they were behind the main street of the town. They were facing the back of several businesses. Behind one of those buildings was a home with a large fenced in yard. Clothes hung from a line and Samantha put her hand up, signaling that Josiah should wait there for her.

"Wait? You want me to wait here?"

"Yes," she confirmed with a shake of her head. She smiled before she ran across the meadow to the back yard.

Suddenly a woman came running from the back door. They embraced briefly before the woman took her hand and led her into the house. Josiah made himself comfortable against a tree to wait.

Samantha was gone all that day. Rebecca's anxiety grew with each passing hour. The sun had just begun to go down when Rebecca gazed out of the back window to see Samantha coming through the gate. She dropped everything and ran across the yard to meet her. Rebecca was so happy to see Samantha that, for a moment she didn't even care where the girl had gone.

After their embrace, Rebecca couldn't help noticing that Samantha seemed tense. "What is it, Samantha? Has something happened?" Rebecca questioned. Samantha shook her head, "no," but took Rebecca by the hand and tried to pull her toward the house. At first, Rebecca pulled back, not wanting to go inside. "No, Samantha."

Samantha stood for a moment, apparently baffled by Rebecca's refusal to go inside the house. She smiled, hoping to reassure her that nothing was amiss, then she darted across the yard and into the house. Mom Cathy was preparing the evening meal while David helped the twins with their school lessons. Samantha nodded a silent greeting to each of them before she retrieved her chalkboard from a shelf in the dining room. By that time, Rebecca had come inside the house.

Samantha wrote, "Run-away man," on her chalkboard and held it up for Rebecca to see. Rebecca just stood looking from Samantha to the chalkboard. She was stunned and didn't know what to say. Samantha banged the palm of her hand against the board with a loud smack. "Runaway," she tried to say with grunting.

"Where is this man?" Rebecca asked.

Now, Samantha had the attention of everyone in the house. Mom Cathy came from the kitchen, wiping her hands on her apron. Samantha was pointing out the window. "Is he out there?" Rebecca asked. "He's out there, now?"

Samantha shook her head, "Yes."

"David, go and get your father. Take the stairs. Do not go outside."

"Yes, Ma'am."

Minutes later, Mom Cathy, Rebecca, and Samantha stood huddled at the window watching Benjamin as he crossed the open field toward the trees marking the edge of the forest. Benjamin glanced around as he approached the trees then he disappeared into the forest.

The forest was dark and Benjamin walked slowly and carefully, looking behind him often. He walked no more than a few minutes before he saw the young man sitting with his back against a tree. At first, Benjamin thought he was hurt. He carefully approached but his footsteps crunching on dry leaves and twigs alerted the young man to his presence and he looked up with a jerk. He stood quickly and his full height loomed over Benjamin. "Hey," Benjamin said. "Did Samantha bring you here?"

The man just stared for a moment. Benjamin could tell that he was afraid. "It's all right. You're safe here."

"Is she, all right?" He whispered.

"Sam is fine. She's worried about you." That seemed to ease his mind and an awkward smiled flashed for only a moment. "I'm afraid you're gonna have to stay here in these woods well into the night. It just isn't safe for me to take you into our house right now."

"I understand."

"Here," Benjamin said as he handed him a small bundle. "What is your name?"

"Josiah Gilbert."

"Well, now, I'm happy to meet you, Josiah." Benjamin extended his hand and Josiah gave him a hearty handshake. "I am Benjamin Bowman. I certainly wish we were meeting under different circumstances." Benjamin smiled hoping to put Josiah at ease. "I brought you some food to eat and a blanket." Josiah took the bundle from Benjamin who couldn't help but notice the look of anxiety that crossed his face. "Stay out of sight and I swear, I'll be back as soon as I can."

"Thank you," he whispered.

Back at the house, the family was full of questions that Benjamin just couldn't answer. He only spoke to Samantha. "He's fine Sam. Don't worry. I'll help him as much as I can, I promise."

Benjamin left the catering company as early as he could and went to the Bissett farm. He found Lillian and Louis just finishing their supper. "Hey Mom," he said to Lillian. He hugged her briefly and gave her a kiss on the cheek.

"Hello Benjamin," she said. "You hungry?"

"No thanks. This isn't a social call."

That got the attention of both Lillian and Louis, neither did they miss the anxiety in his voice.

"What is it?" Lillian wanted to know. "What's happened? Are the children all right?"

"Everyone is fine," Benjamin said. He took a deep breath and sat down at the table. He took his time and explained everything. He told them about Samantha and Josiah.

"Wait until almost dawn before you bring him here. I'll be waiting and don't worry. This isn't the first time we've had a freedom seeker." He patted Benjamin on the shoulder in an effort to reassure him. "Everything is going to be fine. Remember, I'll be waiting."

Benjamin wanted to move Josiah as soon as possible, but to do so now would be to put both their lives in jeopardy. It would be a long and apprehensive evening for the entire family. Samantha stationed herself at the kitchen window, where she had a clear view of the Bowman land right up to the edge of the forest. Mom Cathy took the twins with her to church for Bible study. David stayed with his mother and Samantha. Rebecca was busy knitting socks while keeping a watchful eye on Samantha. Benjamin tried to carry on his business as if nothing were amiss, but the fluttering in the pit of his stomach made that nearly impossible. He found himself peeping through the curtains at the back door more than usual. He worried about the young man he left hidden in the trees and whispered a prayer that he would not be found before he had a chance to move him. The work day seemed to drag and he checked his pocket watch often. Finally he called an early day and sent his workers home. As soon as everyone had gone, he locked up the business and went to join his family upstairs. Samantha met him at the top of the steps, her eyes were bright with anticipation. She made a sign with her hands, and even though he did not speak with signs, he knew she asked about Josiah. David came to her side, eager to act as her translator. "She wants to know if the man is still in the forest. She's afraid for his safety."

"He's fine, Samantha. He is right where you left him." That was all Benjamin could offer but it wasn't the answer Samantha wanted to hear. She began to grunt and throw her hands in the air, her anxiety rising as she tried to sign faster than her hands would move.

"She wants to know why he is still hiding in the forest," David said.

Benjamin put a hand on Samantha's shoulder, in an effort the calm her down but she threw his arm away and turned to run into Rebecca's waiting arms.

Rebecca held Samantha closed as she assured her that Benjamin would do all he could to save Josiah. Benjamin turned to go back down the steps but David stayed close, concern etched into his young face.

"Josiah must stay hidden until Benjamin feels that it is safe to move him," Rebecca tried to assure Samantha. "This is a very dangerous situation and Benjamin is trying to be cautious. If Josiah is a

F. Haywood Glenn

fugitive and he is captured, he could be sent to prison, executed or even sold into slavery. Do you understand what I'm saying, Sam? We must be very careful."

Samantha made a sound that wasn't her usual grunt. It sounded like she said, "Yes." That single word stopped everything. Benjamin stopped in the middle of the stairs and turned to face Samantha. Rebecca took a step back from Samantha and David just stared in disbelief. Samantha knew immediately that she had made a grave mistake.

She had been staying with the Bowmans for almost a week and hadn't uttered a single word. David was the one who thought she was mute because she hadn't spoken a word during the months he had encountered her outside their home. The sign language and the chalkboard was all a hoax. Why, was the question on everyone's mind. Rebecca took Samantha by the shoulders and held her away from her so that she could look into the girl's eyes. "You can speak?" she softly accused.

Samantha shook her head no as she made a sound close to her usual grunt.

"You can speak," Rebecca accused again. "I heard you say, 'yes."

"I heard you too," David said. "What kind of game are you playing with us?"

Samantha shook her head vigorously, all the while grunting, making incoherent sounds, and attempting to sign her protest. Tears filled her eyes and she soon began to cry. For reasons that the family could not understand, Samantha seemed content to go on pretending to be unable to speak, no matter the consequences. Rebecca looked at her husband. Benjamin was still in the middle of the staircase and he looked up at his wife. Neither spoke but Benjamin shook his head slightly and Rebecca understood. The look said that this was not the time to confront Samantha.

David didn't know what to make of Sam's deception. He felt betrayed because he trusted her and felt sorry for her. Now, he wasn't sure how he felt about her. He only knew that she lied and she was continuing to lie.

To David's surprise, his parents were willing to go along with the charade. "It's all right, Sam. Maybe we both heard wrong. It isn't worth getting yourself so upset. I'm sorry if we upset you." Rebecca said to the girl and she could plainly see that Samantha was relieved.

David just stood there, his eyes wide with disbelief, but he went along with his mother. "I'm sorry too, Sam," he whispered.

As Samantha descended the steps, she touched Benjamin's hand, as a way to express her apologies. He embraced her briefly to signify his acceptance of that apology.

Later that day David came upon his mother as she pulled weeds from her vegetable garden on the side of the house. Sam could not possibly see them from her perch in front of the back window. "She's lying, Mama," David said. "You know she is lying."

Rebecca stood and removed her gardening gloves. "Yes, David. I know."

"Then why are you going along with her lies."

"Because there must be a reason for her lies. She hung around our house for months, according to you. She has been living with us for close to a week. She came to us because she wanted us to know about the young man hiding in the woods. She saved his life and she appears to be genuinely concerned for his well-being. I'm not sure why, but she is obviously hiding more than her voice. What would prompt a young white girl to do such things?"

"I don't know but whenever one of the twins or me tell a lie, we're scolded. She is using us, Mama." David said.

"Maybe. Or maybe she just needs us."

David really didn't understand and Rebecca wasn't sure she understood any better. She wanted desperately to speak with Benjamin about this but she also knew that now was not the time. She would wait until things settled down a bit. She also vowed to visit the Constable's office again as soon as possible.

Dinner that evening was as hectic as it ever could be with the twins and David yelling back and forth while Rebecca and Mom Cathy tried to restore order and serve the plates. Benjamin tried to hide his growing anxiety, but as the evening wore on, he kept an eye on the mantle clock. The family went to bed as usual but Benjamin lay awake, staring at the ceiling until he thought it was safe enough to move Josiah. In less than an hour, the sun would rise and he needed to be at the Bissett farm before sunrise. He took the only unmarked wagon of the two owned by his catering company.

Josiah dozed as he sat with his back against the tree and waited. Shortly after the sun went down it began to drizzle. The cool air was pregnant with moisture and a heavy fog hung low over the forest. Josiah unrolled the blanket that Benjamin had given him earlier in the afternoon and was grateful for the little warmth it provided. It was near dawn when the sound of wagon wheels awoke Josiah and he sat bolt upright in alarm. He got to his feet quickly and gathered his meager belongings, rolling them in the damp blanket. He secured the bundle with a vine and slung it onto his back. Cautiously, he moved further into the woods, hiding behind a large bush where he could see who approached.

"Josiah," Benjamin whispered, surprised that the young man was not exactly where he'd left him earlier that afternoon. He moved closer to the tree. "Josiah, it is Mr. Benjamin." A strong wind blew through the trees, releasing some of the water that had gathered on the leaves. A nearby bush shook as Josiah stepped from behind its cover and Benjamin let out a long sigh of relief. "Come," he whispered before leading the way to the wagon.

Josiah was surprised to see that a space in the bottom of the wagon had been hollowed out. It was such a small space that Josiah wondered if his large body would fit into that space. Benjamin apparently read his thought. "Get in. You'll fit. Larger men than you have fit into this space. Just bring your knees to your chest and duck your head. It won't be a very long ride. You'll be fine."

Josiah did as he was told and Benjamin covered the space with sacks of grain, rice, and flour. He then covered the entire shipment with a tarp. The street was virtually empty but Benjamin chose to use the back roads and keep close to the edge of the forest. He arrived at the Bissett farm in no time, pulling the wagon behind the shed. He tapped lightly on the back door before letting himself inside the dark kitchen.

"Louis," Benjamin softly called as he made his way through the dark house, toward the bottom of the steps. He could hear the sounds of movement as Louis and Lillian were roused from their bed. Lillian appeared at the top of the steps, wrapping a shawl around her shoulders, a single candle in her hand. Benjamin met her at the bottom of the steps and they embraced briefly. "Mom, you should keep that door locked. Especially since we now know that there are slave catchers in town?"

"I'm aware, Benjamin," she said.

"He's right, Lil. We have to be very vigilant now," Louis said as he descended the steps.

"The news about the slave catchers is all over town." Benjamin took a deep breath trying to calm himself. He didn't know why he was so nervous. They had hidden many run-aways in the years since they came to Timbuctoo. "That young man hiding in the back of my wagon right now is the reason those men are here. We know he is a run-away, but he could very well be a fugitive too."

"Oh my," Lillian said. "It has been a while since we've had such a guest."

"I haven't had the time to really talk with him yet but right now, it's important that we hide him and do what we can to keep him safe."

"Pull the wagon into the barn and I will meet you there in a few minutes," Louis said.

Benjamin nodded and gave his mother-in-law and sweet peck on the cheek before leaving by the back door just as he had come.

Once the wagon was inside the barn, Louis dropped slats of wood into metal slots that had been bolted on the inside of the doors. Benjamin began to move the heavy bags of grain so that Josiah could climb out of the small space. He jumped down and stretched, thankful to be able to stand to his full height. Then, he took one look at Louis and froze, his eyes were wide with fear. He took several steps backward.

At first, Benjamin and Louis were both baffled at Josiah's sudden fear. It was Benjamin who realized that the young run-away thought that Louis was a white man. "It's all right," he said as he took a few steps closer to the young man. This is my father-in-law, Louis. He ain't white. He's just light-skinned because he's half white." Josiah was still skeptical but he nodded his head as if he understood and came forward.

Louis smiled in an effort to reassure the frightened young man and Josiah seemed relieved. He came forward and said, "I'm Josiah Gilbert." He extended his hand toward Louis who readily took it for a manly handshake and a fatherly pat on the back.

"Good to meet you, Josiah," Louis said. "Maybe one day we will have time to get to know one another better but right now, we've got to get you to safety before the sun comes up." All three shook their heads in agreement.

Louis led Josiah and Benjamin through a trapped door in the ground, hidden inside one of the horse stalls and beneath a mountain of hay. They proceeded through a narrow passageway into a larger room beneath the house. Louis lit a single candle so that Josiah could see where he must stay for the foreseeable future. A makeshift bed and some blankets stood against a dirt wall and there was a barrel filled with water. Louis let a few drops of wax from the candle fall into a tin cup before he pushed the candle into the center of the cup "This was only lit so that you might get an idea of where you are but once I leave, you must blow out the candle and don't light it again until morning. The barrel of water is for drinking and bathing and you can relieve yourself in the pan in the corner. My wife or I will bring you food and empty your waste when we are able. In the meantime, just get comfortable. You're safe here, for now."

"Thank you," Josiah said before he turned to Benjamin. "Thank you too, Mr. Benjamin." Benjamin just put a friendly hand on his shoulder and he and Louis turned to leave.

"Sir," Josiah said. "Please tell Sam thank you and let her know that I am all right." Benjamin nodded his head then they left Josiah alone.

Josiah made himself as comfortable as he could. Apparently, the hours of anxiously waiting and wondering what was going to happen next had taken a toll on his body. He was exhausted and fell asleep almost as soon as he stretched out on the make-shift bed. He slept hard and dreamless. There was no way to know exactly what time it was when he awoke. His underground refuge was as dark in the late morning as it had been in the middle of the night. He lit the single candle in the tin cup which provided just enough light to relieve himself and wash his face. Then there was nothing left to do but wait. Mr. Louis came almost every morning to empty the waste pan and Miss. Lillian came every morning and evening with a meal.

There was nothing to do and nothing to see. Hours turned into days and days into weeks. Josiah lost track of time and couldn't remember how long he waited in that dank hovel. He was alone with only his memories to keep him company. He thought a lot about his mother. He thought about William and the laughing that often caused him trouble. He thought of the girl Sally, who had taken a liking to him and followed him around the plantation. He also thought about Samantha and wondered why she chose to help him.

A familiar scripture came to mind. " . . . behold, I am with you always, to the end of the age," he whispered. This was a scripture that he had heard many times. It was often recited when slaves congregated together in the barn for church on Mr. Atkins' Maryland plantation.

Josiah also remembered his mother whispering that same scripture as she was tied and loaded onto a wagon to be sold away from her family and the only home she had ever known. "You boys don't worry about me. I be fine. God is with me and you. The Scripture says he be with us till the end of time so you boys don't be worried about me." Josiah could still hear her as they shackled her and loaded her onto the back of the wagon. He and William could only tearfully watch and whisper their goodbyes.

The room was damp and smelled of earth. Josiah went down on his knees on the dirt floor and recited that same scripture. Then bowing his head and putting his hands together, he prayed.

F. Haywood Glenn

Chapter Three
Pursuit

1857
Josiah Gilbert, Runaway Slave, over six feet tall and strong,
dark complexion, a skilled carpenter,
the property of Mr. Joseph Atkins, St. Mary, Maryland

There were three of them and they were hardly the kind of men to go unnoticed. They were big men, well over six feet tall. The tallest was clearly the leader. He wasn't just tall, he was broad, muscular, and lumbering. With fair skin, red hair and beard, he looked like a scary figure from a child's fairytale. Heads turned as the three strode down Main Street as if they owned Timbuctoo. Their clothes and speech gave away their origins. They were southerners and it was obvious to some that they were hunters of men, bounty hunters, slave catchers. The Fugitive Slave Law passed in 1850 made the pursuit and capture of run-away slaves a very lucrative business for those men who had the stomach for such an inhumane practice. These men were to be feared and avoided.

They took rooms at the hotel and spent a good bit of time just walking up and down the street. They asked a lot of questions, but mostly they just stood around town watching people. In the three weeks since their arrival, they were seen more than once moseying around some of the farms just outside of town.

It was not unusual for Louis to rise at dawn to begin his work for the day. He carried a pail of chicken feed as he left the house by the back door and moved quickly toward the chicken coup. The night sky was divided with hues of orange and yellow as the sun rose over the tall trees, revealing the bright blue sky of the new day. Louis shielded his eyes against the glare of the sun as he glanced toward the road. That's when he noticed the large white man on horseback at the edge of his property. The man just sat there watching. Louis put down the bucket of chicken feed and moved toward the road. He had seen this man in town a couple of days ago and he knew why he was there at his farm.

"Morning," he said as cheerfully as he could. There was no response. "Is there something I can do for you, sir?"

The man scratched at the whiskers on his chin, then slowly removed his hat. He ran a soiled hand through his wet hair. "Yep," he said slowly. "You may be able to help me. I'm looking for a fugitive. A big black nigger, goes by the name of Josiah. He's a really big fellow. That nigger killed a white man back in Maryland." He scratched at his whiskers again and spit a stream of brown tobacco juice through his rotting teeth. "Seen anyone like that around here?"

"No, sir," Louis said. An eerie feeling crept up his spine and the air suddenly became heavy, making it difficult to breathe. "No, I ain't seen nobody like that," he said. "This is a pretty small community. Strangers don't go unnoticed."

The man looked Louis in the eye and smiled. He adjusted his hat and nodded toward Louis. "The name is Roy Williams. I'm in town for the next week, just in case you run across this fugitive." He spat again and wiped the spittle from his chin with his sleeve. "Good day to you," he said as he made a clicking sound with his tongue and urged his horse forward. He slowly rode away. Louis nodded and watched the man as he moved down the road. It wasn't until he was completely out of sight that Louis felt he could continue with his work.

The three bounty hunters made their presence known all over town. Besides their frequent trips to Constable Willis office, they questioned as many people as they could with no results. At the end of June, when the summer was just beginning, the three bounty hunters left Timbuctoo but they didn't go alone.

♨

Mrs. Ida Simms owned the only bakery/haberdashery in town. She sold everything from books to bread, but it was the freshly baked bread that really kept the shop running. Miss Ida, as most folks called her, was born free in New York City. She moved to Timbuctoo with her new husband Isaac more than twenty years ago. Isaac died of pneumonia as a young man but not before fathering two healthy boys. Isaac, Jr. was now eighteen and his younger brother, Jesse was sixteen. They were good boys. Miss Ida taught them well and kept them grounded in the church.

Both boys helped with the business and were well known and liked around town. Isaac was a serious young man who had visions of a grander life away from Timbuctoo but Jesse was a happy and playful young man.

One hazy, hot day in June, Ida sent Jesse to the hotel, which also housed the only post office in town. Miss Ida was expecting a delivery of supplies. "Mama," Isaac said with a worried expression on his serious face. He untied his apron as he came from behind the counter. "I think I should go. It may be too much for Jesse to carry."

"Aww no, Isaac!" Jesse protested. "I'm sixteen now. I don't need you looking over me like I'm some little boy." Jesse lifted his shoulders and pushed his chest forward as he spoke.

"Yes, yes." His mother said. "You are old enough to run on down to the post and pick up a package for me. I wouldn't send you if I thought it would be too heavy. Now go." She shoved the postal notice into his palm and Jesse bolted for the door. Then she turned to Isaac. "Follow him, but don't let him see you. Make sure he gets there safe."

"Yes, Mama," Isaac said.

Isaac did follow his brother and Jesse went exactly where he was supposed to go. Isaac stood against the wall on the side of the hotel and waited for his brother to come out, but after almost eight minutes, Isaac began to worry. He went to the desk in the lobby where an older man sat. "Excuse me, sir." The man looked up, his eyes vacant as if he were going blind.

"Can I help you?"

"My brother came in to pick up a package from the post and . . . ,"

"The Post Office is in the back. Just walk straight back. You can't miss it."

Jesse was not in the post office. Isaac's heart began to race and his palms began to sweat. Sunlight streamed from the back indicating that there was a back door and Isaac began to run toward the light. He pushed it open and nearly stumbled over a package in the middle of the walkway, but Jesse was nowhere around. When Isaac picked up the package, he realized it was the package his mother had sent Jesse to get from the post. He ran from the building and began to stop people and ask if anyone had seen his brother. Most people just shook their heads and kept walking. Even as he asked, he somehow knew that the slave catchers who had been hanging around town had taken Jesse. Feeling defeated and filled with remorse, Isaac sat down on the walkway and dropped his head into his hands. How could he tell his mother that Jesse was missing and likely kidnapped by slave-catchers?

He had no idea how long he sat there on the walkway but when he got up, he headed for the Constable's office. The Constable was sitting on the walk, in front of the office. An abandoned checkerboard game sat on top of a barrel beside him. "Hello Isaac," he yelled cheerfully when he saw the young man approaching.

"Not well, sir," Isaac said with a disheartening expression. "I think those bounty hunters got my brother Jesse."

"What?" The Constable stood quickly, pushing his chair backward and toppling the checkerboard. "What makes you think such a thing? Did you see them?"

"No sir, but I found the package he was supposed to pick up from the post at the back of the hotel. Jesse wasn't there. It seemed like he just disappeared." Isaac said.

Constable Willis was quiet for a moment as he scratched at his balding head. "When did you last see your brother?" he asked as he made himself ready to ride. "Tell me everything."

"Mama sent Jesse on an errand to pick up a package from the post. She told me to follow, to watch so he wouldn't get into trouble. I didn't want Jesse to know that I was watching him, so I hung back a little. When he went into the hotel, I thought he would just be a minute or two. I waited for a while before I went into the hotel. Like I said, when

I got to the post office at the back of the hotel, there was no sign of Jesse. The package he was supposed to pick up was on the walk outside the back door."

"Maybe Jesse just went home. Did you check?"

"No, sir. There is just no way Jesse would go home without that package."

"Go home, Isaac. Let me handle this," Constable Willis said as he pulled his revolver from a drawer and pushed it into the holster at his hip. "I'm going to bring Jesse back. Just go home and be with your mother."

"What do I tell her, Constable? I can't tell her that Jesse is missing."

"Isaac, go and tell your mother that I'm going to find Jesse and bring him home." He put his hat on and walked to the door. "Now, go home Isaac. I'll be in touch soon."

"Yes, sir," Isaac said. With his hands thrust deep into his pants pockets and his head hanging in despair, Isaac slowly walked home. How could he tell his mother that Jesse was gone? What could he say? That short walk took longer than ever before and when he finally opened the door to the bakery, the sight of his mother brought tears to his eyes. Ida was busy with a customer. She handed her customer a bag of freshly baked dinner rolls and thanked her for her business before she turned to face her son. One look at Isaac's face and she somehow knew that something had happened to Jesse.

"No," Ida whispered. "No! No! No!" she began to shout, her voice getting louder with each word. "Not Jesse. Not my baby boy."

Isaac wrapped his arms around his mother and she sobbed against his chest. "Constable Willis is out looking for him, Ma. I think the slave catchers got him from the back of the hotel. If Constable Willis and the police can catch up to them before they get to the river, they can save him. Constable Willis has known Jesse all of his life and can vouch that he isn't the runaway slave that they're looking for. I'm sure of it. We just have to wait."

"I pray that you are right," Ida said. They closed the bakery early that day as Ida was too distraught to continue to work.

The news of Jesse's abduction spread through town like wildfire. People were afraid. Boys were kept close to home and everyone was more vigilant. Lillian was heartbroken when Louis told her about young Jesse. "How do you know?" she asked.

"I ran into Constable Willis. After he contacts the police in Burlington, he will be getting a search party together."

"Ida must be heartsick," Lillian said.

Louis didn't answer but his feelings for Ida and her family were written in the frown lines of his face. He took a leather saddlebag from the closet and began to pack provisions for the search. Lillian finally looked up from her needlework. "Oh no, Louis!" She dropped the fabric into her lap. "You are not thinking of joining that search party, are you?"

"That's exactly what I'm doing. I just can't sit here and do nothing, Lillian." He continued to prepare to leave. "We know that they snatched Jesse because they couldn't find Josiah."

"Yes, but we knew the risk."

He took Lillian by the shoulders and looked into her eyes as he spoke. "For us to take the risk to free our people is one thing, to risk the life of another young black boy is another."

"But . . ."

"No buts, Lillian. We need to bring Jesse home. Ben and I are going to meet Constable Willis at the Police Department in Burlington so we can help in the search. I'm sure we will be joined by some

members of the Abolition Society of Gloucester County. We're going
to meet at the Methodist Church."

He pulled Lillian toward him and kissed her soundly.

"Be careful, Louis," she said as she blinked back tears that stung
the back of her eyes. "I know you're right." Louis paused at the door
and looked back at his wife. "Go," Lillian said as she waved him on
and walked behind him toward the door.

⁊

Josiah continued to languish in a dirt room beneath the Bissett
barn. Well-fed and rested, his only complaint was boredom. He began
to look forward to seeing the Bissett's when they brought him food and
water. Mr. Louis would sometimes sit and talk a bit but Mrs. Bissett,
although kind, was much less talkative. She wore a pleasant smile and
always asked how he was feeling and if he needed anything. However,
on this day, her smile was missing.

Josiah heard the soft paddle of her feet as she moved down the
narrow stone steps at the back of the barn. When he knew that she was
close to the door, he stood up and brushed the dust from his clothing. It
was a useless act, but he wanted to look as good as he could. "Good
morning Miss Lillian," he said.

"Good morning, Josiah," she handed him a tin plate of grits, eggs,
and biscuits.

Josiah couldn't ignore the somber expression on her pretty face.
"Is something wrong Miss Lillian?"

She didn't answer but gave an exasperated sigh. "Well, everyone
else knows. I see no reason to keep it from you." Josiah just waited for
her to finish. She sighed again and cleared her throat. "Sit and eat your

breakfast." She pulled an empty pail toward the bed and settled herself there. "A sixteen-year-old boy was abducted this morning by three bounty-hunters. These bounty hunters/slave catchers have likely been hunting for you since your escape."

Josiah just stared, wide-eyed and saddened. "I'm sorry," he whispered.

"No need to be sorry. It isn't your fault. Let us just pray that my husband and the rest of the search party can get the boy back."

"Yes, Ma'am."

"Once those men have moved on, you will be able to join our small community here and leave this hovel."

"Yes Ma'am," Josiah said again. "But right now, I am so grateful for this space. I have never known people as kind as the people I've met since I climbed out of the river and I thank God every day for you all."

Lillian smiled at Josiah before she made her way back into the house and settled down to wait for news from the search party.

❧

The police department in Burlington would only send two police officers on the search, but more than twenty black men from Timbuctoo and surrounding towns joined the search party. Some were white Quakers from the Abolition Society, but many were just folks from Timbuctoo and other free black towns of Southern New Jersey.

They kept to the back roads on horseback until the sun began to set. The party camped in the forest a few miles from the Delaware River. According to Constable Willis, they needed to get to the bounty-hunters before they crossed over the river into Pennsylvania. The search would begin again at sunrise.

The canopy of leaves from the forest was so dense that only small slivers of orange and pink peeked through the trees signaling the sun's rise. Louis had not slept. He nudged Benjamin. "You awake?"

"Yes. I don't think I slept more than an hour or two. I'm eager to find Jesse and get back home."

They glanced around the camp and was surprised to see that most of the men were awake. Constable Willis got to his feet. "Let's get ready to move. We're close enough to the river to leave the horses here and move on foot. Maybe we will catch them by surprise. Let's go."

The men split up but Benjamin and Louis stayed together. Ears and eyes alert to any sound or movement in the forest as they moved forward toward the river. By now the sun had completely risen, giving some light to the forest. It was a very hot and humid day. The air was thick with hidden moisture that promised to spill at any moment. The trees were still and the forest seemed eerily quiet as the men trudged forward.

Suddenly, the sky darkened and trees began to sway ominously as a strong gust of wind moved through the trees. A gunshot sounded in the distance causing the men to stop in their tracks. "It came from that way," Benjamin said. Both men turned and headed in the direction of the gunfire. Three more shots rang out and Benjamin and Louis started to run toward the sound.

Others heard the gunshots and were all moving in the same direction. When Benjamin and Louis reached the road, they saw a wagon with three young black boys shackled by their hands and feet and tethered to the floorboards of the wagon. Jesse was among the boys. Louis signaled with his hand for the boys to get down and they did so quickly. The man left to guard the boys, heard the sound of the chains as the boys moved and he turned with a jerk. He pulled a pistol and began to shoot at Louis, who took cover behind a tree. Benjamin used the cover of the forest to move toward the front of the wagon. He threw a twig in the man's direction and when he turned toward the sound, Louis shot him.

Thunder began to clap in the distance making it difficult to tell the difference between the brewing storm and gunshots. Another man seemed to appear out of nowhere and Benjamin shot him. Louis told the boys to stay down and he and Benjamin began to move toward what was a gunfight near the banks of the river.

There were five men. The three who had been seen around town and two others who had searched nearby towns. As Benjamin and Louis moved toward a clearing, close to the road, it sounded like a fierce gun battle. Again, there was a sudden loud clap of thunder and the skies opened up. A blinding, torrential downpour made visibility difficult but they could see the bodies of the three slave catchers sprawled in the mud. They were all dead now.

The storm only lasted about fifteen minutes. When the rain slowed to a drizzle, Constable Willis ordered the men to dig the graves. Benjamin found the keys to the shackles and released the boys. He found a shovel in the wagon and he and Louis took turns digging. The five bounty hunters/slave catchers were buried in the woods, close to the bank of the Delaware River.

The men nodded their heads toward each other before they parted ways. This wasn't the first time this group had been called together to save a young black man from being sold back into slavery. In some cases, as was the case with Jesse, slave catchers would even sell free black men into slavery if they could. Timbuctoo wasn't the only free black community in South Jersey, but all of them were determined to stay free and to keeping their citizens free.

Chapter Four
The Sweet Taste of Freedom
1857

"Now the Lord is the Spirit, and where the Spirit of the Lord is,
there is freedom."II Corinthians 3:17

There was no way to tell the time of day from his small underground room. Days and nights seemed to blend, making it hard to keep track of time. It had been nearly five days since Josiah had seen the sunrise or feel a fresh breeze brush against his cheek. He used to be able to tell the difference between night and day by the amount of activity above his head. Now, there was very little movement on the floor above. His only light was the one candle that burned whenever he was awake. The smell of wet earth and old wood was so thick that Josiah sometimes felt as if he could taste the dirt.

Waiting was difficult. Although he was grateful to the Bissett's and Bowman's for sheltering him, he wanted desperately to leave his underground hovel. He longed to take a breath of fresh air. To make matters even worse, just knowing that a young man was abducted because the slave catchers couldn't find him, filled him with guilt. He didn't even know the young man, but he couldn't help feeling responsible.

After a time, the activity that he usually heard from the floor above suddenly stopped. There was complete silence. Josiah knew that something was happening but he could do nothing except say a prayer for this young man's safe return. That night he prayed for young Jesse. "Lord, lord, it's Josiah again." Once he started, he prayed until he was weary. With his worries and fears given over to God, Josiah was able to sleep soundly.

The next day, Josiah was anxious as he waited for word about Jesse but no one came. Mr. Louis brought him breakfast but said very little. "Did they find the boy yet?" he asked.

Louis didn't answer the question. He just patted Josiah on the shoulder and said, "Everything is going to be just fine. Don't worry." Before Josiah could ask anything more, Louis was gone.

As the day wore on, Josiah knew that something was happening because there seemed to be a lot of activity above his head. Footsteps marched back and forth. Some were heavy enough to cause dry dirt to fall between the wood planks of the floor above, while other footsteps were soft. No one came in the afternoon but by evening, Josiah could smell food cooking. He laid down on his makeshift bed and waited.

The next time he heard footsteps, they were heavy, sure steps. He expected to see Mr. Louis but it was Mr. Benjamin who appeared at the bottom of the steps. "Mr. Benjamin!" he said. "Did they find the boy?"

"Oh Yes, Jesse's fine," Benjamin said.

"What about those slave catchers?"

"They aren't doing so well," he said with a grin. "We don't have to worry about those slave catchers anymore. They're gone. Left Timbuctoo for good."

"They might send other men."

"They might, but we will worry about that when and if it happens. Now, it's time you came out of hiding. The family is having a little celebration for you and Jesse. Can't wait for you to meet everyone."

Josiah smiled, then he looked down at his wrinkled and dirty clothes and back at Benjamin. He brushed his right hand across his left shoulder and a cloud of dust took flight. Benjamin knew exactly what Josiah was thinking. "Oh, I get it. You would like to clean up before meeting anyone."

"Yes sir, Mr. Benjamin."

"No Mister. Just Benjamin."

"Yes, sir," Josiah said uncertainly.

"Just Benjamin," Benjamin said again as he threw his arm around Josiah's shoulders. "Its time you get out of this hovel. Let's go," he said as he guided Josiah toward the steps. Benjamin led him out of the barn and through the kitchen to the back stairs. The steps were narrow and steep and Benjamin urged Josiah up the steps. On the second floor of the house, they went down a narrow hallway toward the back of the house. At the back of the house, the last door opened into a beautiful room. A large wood bed sat in the middle of the room. It was covered with a brightly colored quilt. There was a washstand, a bedside table with a hurricane lamp, and a bench that enclosed a chamber pot. The ceiling was slanted on one side and a large round window at the very top of the wall that looked out on the land behind the house. Tall windows lined the outside east wall with sheer curtains that would catch the morning sun. There were clothes laid out on the bed. Josiah looked back at Benjamin who smiled. "This is your room, Josiah, courtesy of Louis and Lillian Bissett."

"Yeah? Mine and who else?"

"No one else. Just you."

A smile slowly spread across his handsome face as he glanced around the room. "I've never had a room of my own. This is a very fine room, Mr. Benjamin."

"The clothes are yours too. There is more in the closet and the drawers. As I said, we're having a little celebration. Water for your bath is on the way. You better get cleaned up fast. Everyone is excited to meet you."

"Yes, sir."

As soon as Benjamin left, Josiah took a walk around his new room. He could hardly believe his good fortune. He ran his fingers along the edge of the dresser, marveling at the craftsmanship. Furniture was something he knew and he knew that this room was furnished with quality furniture. He sat on the bed and bounced a little. The mattress must be feather filled, a welcomed change from the straw-filled mattress that he was used to on the plantation or the pallet on the underground dirt floor. The closet was filled with suits, the drawers of the chest were filled with underwear, socks, and nightshirts; everything a man could need.

He sat down on the bed and smiled to himself for a moment. He could hardly believe his great fortune. "Thank you, Lord," he whispered. There was a knock on the door before a young man came in carrying two buckets of hot water for the tub. Josiah took one of the buckets and poured the steamy water into the tub. Another bucket was handed to him before the young man came into the room. He handed Josiah a towel, washing cloth and a bar of soap.

"Hello," he said as he extended his hand. "I'm Isaac."

"Good to meet you, Isaac. I'm Josiah."

"I know. Better hurry it along. They're all waiting to meet you."

"Yeah, I'm a little nervous about meeting you all."

"Don't be. We're all family here. You'll see." Isaac went to the door. "I'll be waiting down in the kitchen. When you are finished with your bath, tap on the floor and I'll come to help empty the tub."

"Thank you," Josiah said.

♨

Josiah met Isaac down in the kitchen and Isaac could see that he was visibly shaking. He reached up to give Josiah a friendly pat on the shoulder. "Take it easy, man. This is a big day for you. Smile, this is your liberation day. You will wake up tomorrow morning a free man. Smile, brother!"

Josiah heard the voices of the people who waited to meet him. He couldn't even imagine how many people were crowded into that room. As Isaac led him down a short hallway between the kitchen and the dining room, the voices became louder. Isaac stepped in front of Josiah and pushed open the door. A much shorter version of Isaac stood on the other side of the door. A slight young man with a deep brown complexion and a cheerful smile. "This is my younger brother, Jesse," Isaac said.

Josiah reached out to shake young Jesse's hand but thought better of it and pulled the boy toward him in a crushing embrace. "I am so sorry for what happened to you," he whispered.

"I'm all right. It wasn't your fault. Mr. Benjamin said that if it wasn't me, they would have taken someone else."

"Mr. Benjamin is right," Isaac said.

"Well, I'm sorry you had to go through anything and I'm just happy that you are all right."

The next thing Josiah knew, Miss Lillian grabbed him by the arm and pulled him further into the room. "Here he is everyone," she shouted. "I would like you all to meet Josiah Gilbert," she said proudly.

It was a room full of people, both black and white. It was a scene that Josiah could have never imagined in his entire life. They were all smiling or laughing, enjoying each other's company. They all seemed very happy to meet him. Miss Lillian pulled him along and introduced him to everyone individually. The town constable was there and he was introduced to Miss Ida, Isaac and Jesse's mother, Althea, Nan, and Jacob. He met young David Bowman and the Bowman twin girls. He was surprised to see so many white faces in the crowd. Miss Lillian said that they were neighbors and members of the Quaker church. There was one face in all of those people that he recognized. She looked different from what he remembered. She had hair slightly darker than corn silk. Her skin wasn't dirty, but smooth and unblemished. It was her eyes that he remembered most. Large, gray eyes filled her small face but they no longer looked so sad. She smiled and her eyes twinkled brightly. Josiah embraced her and she returned his embrace. "Thank you, Samantha. You saved my life," he whispered. Samantha's face brightened as she smiled up at Josiah and nodded her head.

Rebecca came forward. "Hello, Josiah. I'm Benjamin's wife, Rebecca. It is so good to finally meet you."

He met so many people, he wasn't sure he could remember all of the names and faces. They all seemed happy to meet him. Next, they all sat down to a feast which he was told was prepared by all of the women. Miss Althea seemed to be the real cook among them. She shouted orders and passed plates from the kitchen to the sideboard. Fried chicken and catfish, cornbread, collards, baked sweet potatoes, rice, roasted pork, and bean soup, it was truly a feast. Josiah hadn't seen that much food in a very long time. The woman ushered him toward the table, patting his back and urging him to eat as much as he wanted. There was strawberry punch and Mr. Louis secretly spiked his glass with a dose of bourbon, which warmed his stomach and eased his frayed nerves. When the meal was over, Isaac brought out a harmonica and soon there was singing and dancing.

It had been a very exciting day and with the food and a couple of glasses of bourbon, Josiah was tired. He slumped into a chair close to the front window hoping to rest for a moment or two. He closed his eyes and leaned his head back but there would be no time to rest. "Let's talk on the porch," Louis whispered to Josiah and Benjamin, who stood close by nodding his head in agreement.

The three settled themselves in the three rocking chairs on the front porch and Louis began to stuff his pipe with tobacco. "Well, how does it feel?" Benjamin wanted to know. "You are a free man Josiah."

"I'm not really sure, sir." He cleared his throat and glanced from Louis to Benjamin. "I am happy now that I'm free but how do I know that Mr. Atkins won't send others looking to bring me back to Maryland? Will I ever really be free?"

"You are free. The men they sent didn't even know who you were," Louis said as he clenched his pipe between his teeth. He lit the pipe and the smell of tobacco filled the air as he took a long drag. "They knew of your crime but all they cared about was that you were a fugitive. They're gone now and you will become part of the Timbuctoo community."

"But what if others come looking?"

"Others will come looking, you can be sure," Benjamin said.

"Josiah, you are not the first run-away slave to take refuge in this small village. Yes, others will come and we will deal with them and protect those who seek freedom as we have always done," Louis said. "You can live here with me and Lillian as long as you like but you must work to be able to take care of yourself. Do you understand?"

"Yes, I understand. On the plantation, Massa Atkins hired me and my brother out."

"What work were you hired out to do?"

"I'm a carpenter, sir. I can do all most anything with wood. My brother and I made furniture."

"If you don't mind my asking," Benjamin said, "why didn't your brother run with you?" Josiah was quiet for a few moments. Both Louis and Benjamin could see sadness creep into his face. Josiah dropped his chin to his chest and sighed heavily. "If you would rather not speak of it, it's all right."

Josiah lifted his head and stared straight ahead; a blank expression came over his handsome face. "My younger brother William was a joker. He angered Massa Atkins one too many times and Massa ordered twenty lashes." Tears clouded his eyes as he spoke but Josiah continued to stare straight ahead. "The Overseer, Mr. Gayle, had a different idea. He would not stop after the twenty lashes. I begged him to stop but he just kept slashing that whip across William's back. There was so much blood at the bottom of the tree and he still would not stop. When I saw that much blood, I knew that William was dead." He blinked now as tears began to stream down his face. Louis handed him a handkerchief to wipe his face. "I told him to stop after I counted twenty lashes but he just kept on slashing that whip. I grabbed Mr. Gayle by the throat. I could hear everyone screaming for me to let him go, but I just couldn't let him go. He killed my brother. He killed him for laughing. When I realized that I had strangled Mr. Gayle to death, I dropped him in the dirt. I can't say if I felt anything but hate. I was so filled with the horror of seeing William beat to death, that I couldn't even think. I bent down pulled William to me. I held my brother's bloodied body in my arms. I could hear everyone around me telling me to run, but I kept thinking that I couldn't leave William. Then, I think I heard my mother's voice telling me to run. I moved William's body from my lap and I ran." Josiah told them the whole story of how he winded up in that cave with Samantha. When he had finished talking, Louis gave him a pat on the back while Benjamin sniffed back tears.

"It's over now Josiah. I am truly sorry about your brother. You have a chance to start a new life here and Benjamin and I will help you as much as we can. We'll be your new brothers. Of course, we can't replace William but you are part of our family now."

"Thank you," Josiah said. "I have never met people as kind as you people have been to me."

"I think we should rejoin the celebration before Lillian and Rebecca come looking for us," Louis said.

The cake was being served when they rejoined the party. In the kitchen, Rebecca and Constable Willis were having a serious private conversation. "I think our mysterious houseguest is not what she appears. I'm sure I heard her speak," Rebecca said.

"You don't say?" Constable Willis scratched at the whiskers on his chin. "I had the opportunity to inquire about her when I was with the Burlington Police a few days before Jesse went missing."

"What did you learn?"

The Constable looked around to make sure there was no one close enough to hear. "Officer Kent told me that she could be Samantha Hunter. Her father, Todd Hunter, ran off years ago and her mother, Caroline died in a fire at the home at least four years ago. The child, who couldn't have been more than ten or eleven, was never found."

"Really?" Rebecca was surprised. "Was the child mute?"

"No, but they say Caroline was unstable. Set her own house on fire. She likely wanted to kill herself and her daughter. If this is Samantha Hunter, she got out of that burning house and has been living on her own ever since. I think it is highly likely that suffering a thing like that could cause her to be mute, at least for a time. The girl is probably about fourteen or fifteen."

"I'm not sure I understand."

"The child has been living hand to mouth, in the woods, no less. She hasn't had anyone to talk to until you and your family took her in. If you heard her speak, I'm sure she is trying to find her voice."

"So, what are we to do?"

"I'm sure I don't have to tell you. Do exactly what you have been doing. Care for her and talk to her. She will eventually open up. It's the Christian thing to do."

"I know you're right, Constable, but there is something about that girl that gives me the willies. Thank you. I guess I just needed to hear someone say it to me."

Constable Willis walked away and Rebecca scanned the room until she found Samantha sitting in a chair near the mantle. Samantha's eyes darted around the room from face to face. She smiled slightly and nodded her head whenever anyone addressed her directly. Constable Willis's words had softened Rebecca's heart toward her young house guest. She now saw a young girl who had suffered a tremendous loss. Rebecca continued to watch as David offered Samantha a cup of punch. Her face brightened as she saw him approach. He handed her the cup and she happily accepted, smiling as David took a seat beside her. Guess I should have seen that coming, Rebecca thought.

Rebecca found Benjamin and pulled him aside. "What is it, Becca? You look like you're about ready to burst into flames." Benjamin chuckled.

"It isn't funny, Benjamin."

"What?"

Rebecca tilted her head toward David and Samantha. "Look! I think our son is sweet on Samantha."

Benjamin glanced at David, who was squatting beside Samantha and looking up at her with adoring eyes. "Ah, that's nothing. So, he's got a little crush. There is nothing to worry about." He bent down and kissed his wife on the cheek. "You worry too much, Sweetheart."

Rebecca frowned and walked away.

🙢

During Josiah's time in hiding, his beard and hair were able to grow wild. Louis thought Josiah's facial hair and the massive mound of untamed hair on his head changed his appearance. They both agreed that he looked older and such a change was probably a good idea. Louis decided that the hair could be tamed somewhat. So, with a good pair of shears and a sharp razor, he trimmed Josiah's facial hair and cut the hair on his head close until he looked like an older more sophisticated young man. When the transformation was finished, they went down to the kitchen. Lillian looked up with a gasp. "Josiah!" She said. I barely recognize you." Josiah couldn't help but smile. "So, you were hiding a very handsome face under all that hair?"

"Not Josiah, Lillian," Louis corrected. "May I present Mr. Joseph Bissett, my half-brother, all the way from Louisiana."

"Well, my, my," Lillian said. "I am happy to meet you, Joseph, my new brother-in-law." Lillian hugged Joseph and they all laughed.

Chapter Five
The Winds of War
1859

"Those who deny freedom to others,
deserve it not for themselves." Abraham Lincoln

On May 25, 1859, abolitionist John Brown lead a raid on the federal armory in Harpers Ferry, Virginia. Brown thought his raid would be the catalyst that would start a slave revolt. He was wrong. His raid was an utter failure. Besides losing his two sons, he was wounded, captured and tried by the state of Virginia. John Brown was hanged on December 2, 1859.

After John Brown was captured, things began to change in Virginia. More legislation was passed to place even more limits on the little freedom that slaves had enjoyed prior to the raid. Timbuctoo also began to change in ways no one could have predicted. You could almost feel the change in the air. The community was growing as more people poured into town. Some were former slaves who had been able to buy their freedom; others were ex-slaves, freed by dying planters;

and some were definitely runaways. Most were able to blend in with the citizens of Timbuctoo, while others just passed through on their way to other northern cities or Canada.

Some of the newcomers were definitely slave catchers. In September 1850, Congress passed The Fugitive Slave Act which stated that the government was responsible for finding and returning runaway slaves to their owners. This emboldened Slave Catchers and there was a constant flow of man hunters through town.

Louis and Benjamin attended more anti-slavery meetings than ever before and everyone seemed just a little more tense. There was a lot of talk about State's Rights. Although some states abolished slavery, the southern state's economy flourished under the free labor slavery provided and they were desperate to preserve their way of life. Many believed that their desperation would lead to war. Everyone knew that a war was coming, they just didn't know when.

&§

It had been two years since Josiah ran away from Massa Atkins' place in Maryland. Now, he was Joseph Bissett, a free man. He was certainly happy to be free but, Joseph knew that freedom was fragile. Staying free required vigilance. He learned to always be aware of his surroundings, to quickly notice a new face in town. Sometimes he was able to tell where the newcomers were likely to have come from by their speech, clothing and other tell-tale signs. Besides the constant watchfulness, Joseph found a good life in Timbuctoo.

The town enjoyed a period of relative peace for a few years. Life went on in the Bowman house. The twins would soon celebrate their sixteenth birthday. Lilly would be leaving the family in a few weeks to study education at the Institute for Colored Youth, in Cheney, Pennsylvania. She would return to Timbuctoo, after two years and she hoped to be able to teach the youth of Timbuctoo. The school was just outside of Philadelphia and she would be able to visit often.

Cathy had no such ambition. She shared her father's love of cooking and was delighted when he offered her a job in the kitchen of the Bowman Catering Company. To everyone's surprise, Cathy was a great cook and took to the business very well.

It was the middle of September and Rebecca planned an outdoor celebration for the twins birthday and Lilly's acceptance in the Institute for Colored Youth. The weather was perfect. The searing heat and humidity of August had died out, leaving a pleasantly warm day with a gentle breeze. The family gathered behind the Bowman house. Long tables were set up with yellow table cloths and folding chairs with yellow cushions. The tables were crammed with all of the twin's favorite foods and you could smell the honey-dipped fried chicken and buttermilk biscuits for miles. Those succulent aromas were carried on the wind, inviting others in the community to come and join in the celebration.

Within an hour of setting out the food, so many neighbors came to join the celebration that it seemed as if the entire town was at the Bowman place. There was a lot of laughing, singing, eating and just enjoying each other's company. Children of all ages ran over the grass kicking a large orange ball. Isaac was eager to speak with Joseph alone. They both brought their fishing poles and snuck away down to the creek at the first opportunity. Neither was aware that Samantha followed them to the creek. The young men perched themselves on a large boulder at the edge of the creek and threw their lines into the water.

Isaac was more interested in sharing stories of his most recent female infatuation, than any fish that might tug at his line. Isaac's attention to females was fleeting. Almost every week he had a new infatuation and could hardly wait to tell Joseph about the latest female to take his breath away. Joseph liked to hear about Isaac's fanciful ideas about love and women.

A few yards away Samantha climbed up into a tree where she could watch and listen to Joseph and Isaac.   They were all close enough to hear the laughter and excited shrieks coming from the birthday party.

A soft rustling in the bushes caught Isaac's attention. "Shush," he whispered. "Did you hear that?"

"No, I didn't hear anything. Maybe you heard a squirrel or some other small animal."

"Sure," Isaac said but he wasn't convinced. Moments later there was another rustle in the bushes and Isaac was sure someone was hiding in the thicket. "I'm not crazy," he said to Joseph. "Someone is out there."

"Yeah, you're right," Joseph whispered as he pulled his line from the river and dropped it on the bank. Isaac did the same. "Someone is out there, all right." Isaac and Joseph slowly moved into the thicket, looking for whatever or whoever was there.

Samantha heard it too and her eyes quickly scanned the area. She saw an older black man and a young woman with a small child tied to her back. They were dressed in rags and their feet were bare and bloodied. Samantha watched as they crouched behind an area of dense shrubbery. 'Runaways,' she thought as she climbed further up into the tree to look out over the forest. Not more than a mile away she could see men with rifles moving fast on foot. By this time, Isaac and Joseph had come upon the group of runaways.

"Hey," Isaac whispered as he took in the tattered clothes, matted hair, and bare feet. "You're not from around here, are you?"

Joseph gave him a sidelong glance for the stupid question. "You could tell that with just a glance, huh?"

"No," the man said. "We run all the way from Virginia."

Samantha could see that the men with the rifles were getting closer. She immediately started to climb down, intent on warning all of them of the danger.

"I think we can help you if you come with us," Joseph said.

Just as the man stood and came out from his hiding place, Samantha saw one of the white men lift his rifle and aim."NO!" she screamed. They all turned to look up at the tree and Samantha scampered down as fast as she could. Once she was on the ground, both Joseph and Isaac were staring at her in disbelief.

"You spoke," Joseph whispered. In the two years, Joseph had known Samantha, this was the first time he had ever heard her speak. "You spoke," he said again.

"Yes, Joseph, but there is no time to explain now. I promise I will explain."

For the moment, time seemed to stop. Joseph trusted Samantha from the moment they met and he trusted her now. Although hearing her speak was a great shock. She was right, there was no time to explain now.

"This way," she said, pointing further into the forest. No one moved for a few seconds. "Come on," Samantha whispered as she turned and began to run through the trees. Joseph shook off the shock of hearing Samantha speak and began to follow her. The others were soon close behind. Although Isaac was a bit skeptical, Joseph knew that Samantha knew these woods better than anyone and he trusted her to lead them away from danger.

Eventually they came to a cave that was well hidden behind dense shrubbery and a couple of trees felled by recent storms. Joseph couldn't tell if this was the same cave she had led him to three years ago. Samantha walked them deep into the cave. The further they walked; the more Joseph realized that it couldn't be the same cave. Once they came to a clearing inside the cave, it was obvious to Joseph that Samantha must have lived in this cave at one time.

"You will all have to stay here until I can bring help," she said. "Joseph, you and Isaac will have to stay too. It isn't safe for you either."

Joseph grabbed Samantha by the hand and pulled her away from the others. "How is it that you spoke," he said? "I thought you couldn't speak."

"I couldn't."

"You just all of a sudden can speak? How is that, Sam?" he sounded angry? His face was a mixture of fear and confusion.

"I'm sorry, Joseph. When I found you in the woods, I couldn't speak. Until the Bowmans took me in, there was no one to speak to and no reason to speak. My speech has been coming back slowly. I can't explain it. I don't understand myself. I didn't even know I could scream until I actually screamed. When I heard my own voice, I was as shocked as you are, but I was happy because my voice had come back to me at that moment. I was able to save all of you by warning you of the danger. Please don't be angry with me."

"I'm not angry, Sam." He pulled her to him and they embraced. "You know that I can't stay angry with you. You saved me, just like you are saving this family now." She smiled up at him and he hugged her again. "Go. Get help and come back as soon as you can."

"I will. I promise."

Samantha hid just inside the opening of the cave until there was no sound or movement in the forest. She moved quickly and quietly, careful not to step on a twig or have her feet crunch on the hard ground. After moving a few feet, she climbed up into a tree, where she could look out over the forest for miles. She saw that a wagon was very close to where Isaac and Joseph had been fishing. Horses were tethered close to the road, but the three men that she had seen earlier were gone. Where could they have gone, she wondered as she climbed down from the tree? Still being as careful as she could, she made her way back to the Bowman house.

By the time Samantha made it back to the Bowman house, the celebration had ended. Most of their neighbors had already gone home. Mom Cathy and Rebecca were busy packing up to take everything back into the house. Lillian was talking with the twins about school and Benjamin and Louis were deep in conversation. Benjamin looked up as Samantha approached. One look at her flushed face and Benjamin knew that something was wrong.

"What is it, Sam?" Benjamin asked as Samantha approached. That got David's attention who was sitting under a nearby tree.

"It's . . ." Samantha began. The sound of her voice brought Louis to his feet. "Yes, yes! I can speak! I know that you are all shocked but that isn't what is important right now. I will explain myself later. Right now, a run-away family is hiding in a cave in the forest that needs your help." Louis was still in shock but he noticed that Benjamin and David didn't seem surprised.

"An entire family? How many?" Benjamin wanted to know.

"An old man and a young woman with a child. I think it's a father with his daughter and grandson. I saw slave catchers in the woods too, but I don't think they are trying to capture them and take them back south."

"How could you know that?" Louis asked.

The small group caught Lillian's attention first, and she came running. Soon the entire family was there, listening to Samantha.

"They were all armed and at least one of them lifted his rifle to shoot. I think he was aiming for the woman. That's when I screamed as loud as I could. Isaac and Joseph heard me and I'm sure those white men heard me too. My scream may have scared them off for a while. They went in one direction and I led the others in the opposite direction. I think it is only a matter of time before they come back to search for that family." She took a breath and searched the faces of the others. "I had no choice but to hide all of them."

"Of course, they are all in danger," Louis said

"Where did you hide them?" Benjamin wanted to know.

"I know those woods pretty well," she said. "I took them deep into the forest to a cave where I use to sleep a few years ago. They're safe for now but I know those men will double back looking for them again."

Everyone just stared at Samantha. It wasn't just that she was speaking. She was speaking perfectly as if she had never been mute. There was no stuttering or hesitation. She was aware that they were all looking at her with anticipation and she knew that they wanted an immediate explanation.

"So, you were able to speak all along," David accused.

"No, no, I couldn't. Really. I never had any intention of deceiving any of you. I really couldn't speak. I tried many times. The words were in my head but they just wouldn't come out of my mouth." The looks on the faces of her newly adopted family were full of doubt.

"And now?" Rebecca asked.

"I didn't plan it. I was high up in a tree when I saw that man lift his rifle and aim at those people. All I wanted to do was warn them. I didn't even think about it. I just screamed. I was just as shocked at the sound of my voice as you all are at this moment. Once I heard my own voice, I tried to speak words. I saw Isaac and Joseph run toward the sound and as I climbed down from the tree, I whispered their names to see if I could actually speak."

"Was that the same thing that happened a few years ago when we all heard you say, yes?"

"I suppose so." She suddenly felt a little embarrassed. "I lived in the woods for a long time. There was no one to talk to, no reason to speak and I guess I just lost my voice."

Mom Cathy came forward and put her amble arms around Samantha's neck. "I understand, child. Life has not always been kind to you." She smiled up at Samantha reassuringly. "You've endured more than your share of suffering. The blessing is that now, you can speak and we are all very grateful for this blessing." Samantha returned Mom Cathy's embrace.

"Thank you, Mom Cathy," Sam whispered. "I really didn't mean to deceive any of you. I wanted to speak many times, even before you took me into your home."

Rebecca was the next to reassure Samantha with a smile and a hug. Then they all surrounded her with love and forgiveness and she was overwhelmed with gratitude.

"You know that we can't move them until nightfall?" Benjamin said.

"Yes, I know."

Louis and Lillian loaded their things into their wagon to leave. The other women took down the tables and chairs to return them to the catering dining room. "I'll be back at sundown," Louis said.

"I don't think that I'll need your help this time, Louis."

Lillian had already climbed into the wagon and sat patiently waiting for her husband. Louis eyed Benjamin suspiciously. "And, why is that, Ben?"

"After church, last Sunday Reverend Evans told me that he and his wife were sheltering a couple of runaways, Earl and Mia Johnson."

"Really?" Louis said as he climbed into the wagon and took his seat beside Lillian. "A couple, you say? Husband and wife? He made no mention to me."

Benjamin chuckled. "I'm pretty sure he knew that I would pass it on. And yes, it is a husband and wife. Evans is planning to escort them to the New York border early Tuesday morning."

"Why Tuesday?"

"Apparently, he and the wife had already planned to visit family in Buffalo. That's an easy enough cover to get the runaways to the border. I'm thinking that if I can get that family to the church by Tuesday, they will be able to go along."

"I see," Louis said. "I'm sure Reverend Evans will gladly oblige. Be careful brother."

"I will. I promise."

Lillian waved to her family as the wagon moved down the road.

It had been an exciting and busy day and the girls were exhausted. They both went right to their rooms. The excitement wasn't over for the adults. Even though none of them knew the couple hidden by Reverend Evans and his wife, or the family that Sam had hidden in a cave in the woods, their hearts were heavy with the knowledge that five people had run away from slavery and were now in need of help to continue their journey to freedom. Benjamin gathered his family around the table. They locked hands and Benjamin began to pray softly. He asked God to watch over the runaways and the Evans and to protect them all from harm through their long journey. When the prayer was over, he kissed his wife and grandmother. "Take care of them until I get back," He said to David.

"Yes, sir," David mumbled.

He and Samantha left the house. He pulled his wagon far enough into the woods as not to be seen from the main road. Samantha led the way.

◆

The young woman was visibly shaking as she slowly untied the fabric that held her child close to her body. The child whimpered a bit and the mother quickly turned her back to the young men as she gave her breast to the hungry child. Isaac and Joseph moved away to give her more privacy.

Joseph could hardly believe that these three had run all the way from Virginia. He remembered his own run for freedom with feelings of gratitude. He would never forget the help he received from Miss. Markel and the Housman's. He now knew that Miss. Markel and the Housman's were not alone. Besides his new family, there were thousands of people, both black and white, from the deep south to as far north as Canada, whose mission it was to help anyone who sought freedom. He would always be grateful to those who helped him and now he was excited to be helping this family in whatever way he could.

"How long since you left the Virginia plantation?" Isaac asked the old man.

He did not answer right away. He tried to answer but it was clear that he was having some difficulty breathing. "Alice and me run away maybe four or five weeks ago." He took a deep breath. "I ain't really sure." Again, he breathed deeply for a few moments. "My name is Wilbur Pearson and this here is Alice, my daughter."

"Mr. Wilbur, this here is Isaac and my name is Joseph." Joseph watched for a few moments as Mr. Wilbur seemed to struggle to breath. "You may be more comfortable over there against that boulder." Joseph and Isaac helped Wilbur to settle himself against the large bolder and Alice came to sit beside her father with the baby in her arms.

"Massa's son got Alice in a family way. Wasn't no secret, everybody knew. He chased after my girl for months, then as soon as he was able to get her alone, he just took what he wanted. There's a whole lot of mulatto children running around the Pearson place. Most of them fathered by Massa. Ruined my girl, like they always do." He spoke quickly and the tumble of words that spilled, seemed to tire him even more. Alice put her arm around her father's fragile shoulders and tried to comfort the old man.

"Everything was all right for a time," Alice said in a small, child-like voice. "Then, somebody goes and tells Massa that his son Charles got me with child. Massa acted like it was all my fault. Called me a slut and a witch. He said I put some kind of spell on his boy." She sniffed back tears before gently moving her son to her other breast. "I didn't put no spell on that boy. He was born evil." No one talked for a few moments. Mr. Pearson was still struggling to breathe and Alice seemed to be trying to push those bad memories from her mind. "I didn't give myself to that monster! He took it. Chased me down and punched me in the face. When I hit the ground, he took what he wanted." Tears spilled from her eyes as she spoke. "I didn't tell a soul, not even my daddy. I hid that I was with child for most of my time but by summer, I was too big to hide." Alice seemed to be remembering. "Some folks just came straight out and asked who the father was and some just suspected Charles, but I told no one. I don't know who told Massa.

"Then one night, Massa comes bustin into our cabin. He snatches the baby right out of my arms and as soon as he looks at him, he knows that his boy is the father."

"Massa decided he didn't want Alice around no more," Wilbur said. "I thought he was gonna sell my Alice and Jason. He got drunk one night and said he was gonna kill my girl and sell the baby."

"I wasn't going let him sell my boy," Alice said. "This here is Jason Wilbur Pearson and he is NOT for sale."

Wilbur's breathing was worrisome to Joseph. "Are you all right?" he asked the old man. "You're looking kind of pale."

"I'm just really tired," Wilbur said.

"So that's why you ran away?" Isaac probed.

"Not me," Wilbur said. "Alice wanted to run. I knew that I was too old for running, but it was either stay there and worry myself to death over Alice and my grandson or help her get to freedom."

Wilbur seemed to have talked himself out. He leaned back and laid his head against the boulder. They waited for what seemed like hours. Eventually, they heard whispers and footsteps. They were all happy to see Samantha and Benjamin. Joseph made the introductions before they were led from the cave to Benjamin's waiting wagon.

Benjamin took Isaac and Samantha home first. Joseph elected to stay with Benjamin until the Pearsons were safely in the church. However, once there, Joseph decided to stay until the group left for New York. Benjamin didn't agree but Joseph was a grown man now and capable of making his own decisions.

Reverend Evans met them at the back of the church and quickly ushered them inside. Benjamin only stayed long enough to make the introductions, say a short prayer, and thank Reverend Evans for his help.

They were ushered into the basement of the church where they met Earl and Mia Johnson. Joseph stayed with the former slaves hoping to give them some comfort. He hoped that he could calm their fears and give them some hope for their uncertain futures.

Just before dawn, the three men that had been tracking the Pearsons, showed up at the door of Reverend Evans Methodist Church. They banged loudly on the door and one man screamed. "Wilbur, we know you're in there! Come on out!" They screamed insults and racial slurs for nearly ten minutes.

The Evan's home was next door to the church and they were awakened by the loud screaming and yelling from the street. In trousers and a nightshirt, Reverend Evans confronted the men. Mrs. Evans followed closely behind her husband.

"Please, please. This is a house of God."

"Reverend we mean you no harm. Just send Wilbur Pearson out and that whore of a daughter, Alice, and we will be on our way."

Reverend wanted to lie and say that Mr. Pearson were not in his church, but instead he said, "This is not right. Why do you want Mr. Pearson and his daughter?"

"Mister?" one of the men yelled. "He ain't no Mister. He's a slave belonging to Mister Charles Pearson of Virginia and we aim to take him and his daughter back where they belong. Send them out and you'll have no more trouble from us."

With his hands shaking like a leaf in the wind, the Reverend unlocked the church doors. Before he could take one step inside, the largest of the three men pushed him aside with one hand. Then, to the Reverend's utter shock, another man steered his horse up the steps and inside the front doors of the church. He galloped up and down the aisles, knocking over chairs and stacks of hymnals and Bibles as he went. He let his horse destroy the pulpit and the podium. As he galloped through the church, he pulled down the heavy drapes that hung at the tall windows. The Reverend, was shocked into silence. He covered his mouth with his hands and ran from the church to stand beside his wife out in the street. They stood there watching as their church was being destroyed.

The people sheltered in an underground room could hear the commotion above their heads and knew what was happening. Joseph gathered them together and led them to a room at the back of the church. "We can't go out the back door yet. They'll see us," Earl said.

"There is no place to go," Joseph said.

"They don't even know about you two. They want me," Wilbur said. "I'll go to them. What could they do to me that they haven't done already?"

"No!" Alice said.

"Baby, I'm dying anyway. I knew I wouldn't make it to the end of this journey but I'll die happy if I know that you and Jason made it to freedom. You got a better chance without me anyway."

"No, Daddy! Please, no."

"Don't worry, baby. I'm going to glory with a smile on my face."

Joseph was the first to notice smoke coming under the door of the sanctuary. "Do you smell that?" he whispered. "They've set fire to the church!"

Without warning, Wilbur pushed pass Joseph and went through the door to the sanctuary. He stood for a moment watching fire climb the drapes and alight the wooden benches. Wilbur could hear the cries of Reverend and Mrs. Evans as they watched their church burn. He also heard the cries of Alice as he slowly walked down the center aisle of the burning church. When he reached the front doors of the church, he pushed them wide open and stood there so that the men who had been tracking him and his daughter could see him. He descended the steps slowly.

"Well, look at this!" one of the men said. "You homesick, old Wilbur? I guess you had enough of this running. An old man like you must be ready to go back to Virginia?"

"I ain't going back to Virginia."

The men laughed. "Is that so?" Wilbur recognized young Charlie's voice. "I had about enough of this shit," Charlie shouted. "Where are Alice and the boy?"

"They're gone. All you got is me," Wilbur lied. "And I'm too old. Your Daddy ain't worried about old Wilbur. He wants to kill my Alice because he doesn't want you to know that the boy could be his as much as it could be yours." Wilbur waited a moment for young Charlie to understand exactly what he was saying. He watched as color seemed to rise to the young man's face.

"You are a lying old fool," Charlie shouted.

At that moment, Wilbur pulled a revolver from the back of his waistband and let off one shot. It hit one of his pursuers in the shoulder. It was pure luck that the next shot hit the other man in the neck. Blood spurted forward in an arc. The man put his hand to his neck in a futile attempt to stop the blood. He soon fell from his horse and quivered a few minutes in the dirt before death stilled him. The men were surprised that the old man was armed and for one split second, there was nothing but the roar of the fire and the cries of the people who watched the fire. In the next moment, the two men began to fire wildly. Wilbur let off two more shots as he staggered forward and was cut down in a barrage of bullets.

The shots stopped when Wilbur fell to the ground in a heap. Young Charlie remembers that his father had sent him on this mission to kill

Alice and the boy. He said he didn't want either of them back and had no use for the old man. Charlie glanced over at his companion. Wesley was the overseer's young son. Blood oozed from his shoulder wound. "We have to get that bullet out of your shoulder before you bleed to death too."

"Charlie, I'm not getting a warm feeling from the folks around here. It seems like they like niggers more than honest white folk."

They turned their horses around and headed out of town. Once they were far enough away, Charlie tried his best to dress the wound. He tore one of his shirts and wrapped Wesley's shoulder to stop the bleeding. "This looks bad," Charlie whispered.

"What about the girl?" Wesley sniffed back tears.

Charlie didn't answer. "What if the old man was telling the truth about your father?"

"What are you saying, Wesley? You think that my father bedded that whore?"

"Wouldn't be the first," Wesley whispered.

Charlie looked away from Wesley's bleeding arm and was quiet for a few moments. He couldn't deny that even he had wondered why his father had been so angry to learn about the baby. After all, he knew that his father had many children on the plantation. Even though in a fit of rage, his father had demanded that Alice be killed, Charlie never thought he was serious until she ran away. Wilbur's words repeated in his head again and he suddenly felt ill.

"What are you thinking?" Wesley asked

"I'm thinking my old man has real feelings for Alice. Think Wesley. Haven't you seen the way my father looks at Alice?"

Wesley was thoughtful for a few moments. "Now that you mention it, I have noticed him staring at Alice."

"Yeah," Charlie said.

"But Alice always seemed like she was afraid your father."

"Yeah," Charlie said again. "Why do you think that is, Wesley?"

Wesley's face flushed as he slowly comprehended what Charlie was saying. "He took her!" He said. "That's why she was afraid of him."

The two men eyed one another for another moment or two. "I think he was in love with her," Charlie said. "He thinks she betrayed him."

"You could be right."

"I'm also thinking that we should just head back to Virginia. We'll tell him we couldn't find them." It all made sense to Charlie now. His father didn't know that he had forced himself on Alice. She hadn't given herself to either of them.

The others heard the shots over the roar of the fire but none stopped to see what happened. Joseph ushered the runaways behind the church and through alleys. He carefully made his way behind several businesses and homes in town that were along Main Street. They could still hear the sound of the fire and the scent of burning wood filled the air for miles.   The town's people began to rally around the church to help put out the fire while Joseph continued to move quickly through town. Alice cried the whole time but she held Jason close to her as she moved quickly to keep up with Joseph and the others. Eventually, he realized that they were close to Althea's boarding house. He left the others huddled in the alley beside the boarding house while he went to the back door and knocked hard.

Althea had already gone to bed. Nan was attending to her needlepoint project while her husband, Jacob was reading the Bible.

They were startled by the knock at the back door. "Who in the world could that be at this hour?" Nan mumbled.

Jacob went to peep through the curtains at the back door. "It's Joseph," he said.

"Oh my God! Joseph!" Jacob said as he opened the door. Nan joined Jacob at the door. As soon as the back door was opened, they were assailed by the smell of burning wood. "There's a fire?" Nan asked.

"Yes. It's the Methodist Church." Joseph explained the situation as quickly as he could and Jacob immediately grabbed the keys to the storeroom at the back of the house. "Come on. They'll be safe in the storeroom until we figure out what's next," Jacob said and Joseph agreed. "Nan, go and tell Althea. Joseph, you go home and let Louis know what's happened. I'll go to Benjamin first thing in the morning."

When Joseph got home, he found Lillian and Louis sitting on the front porch. The Bissett farm was at least 10 miles away but you could still smell burning wood. "Looks like a big fire in town. What the hell is burning?" Louis asked.

"The Methodist Church. Reverend Evans' church," Joseph said.

"Oh my God," Lillian said.

"Yeah! It's even worse than you think,"

Louis noticed the soot that covered Joseph's face and clothing. "You were there?"

"Yes, I went with Benjamin to see that the family that Sam told you about, the Pearsons, got safely to the church. When Benjamin left, I decided to stay and see them safely off to the New York border in the morning. We thought we had lost the three men who were tracking them from Virginia but it turns out that they were pretty good trackers. Tracked us all the way to the church. They waited until Benjamin left to make their move."

"What happened?"

Joseph sat down on the steps and dropped his head in his hands. He was upset. "The men demanded that old man Wilbur come out."

"And, did he?" Lillian wanted to know.

"They set the church on fire to make Wilbur come out. They didn't know that he had already made his peace. Wilbur was going to confront them, no matter what. There was no need to set the church on fire." He shook his head from side to side. "It was all so unnecessary. You have to understand, Wilbur was an old and very sick man. He told me himself that he knew that he was too old to run away. His breathing was shallow and labored from the moment we found them in the forest. He only made the journey for Alice and Jason and he held on for the same reasons. He knew he was dying and he gave himself up to save his daughter and grandson."

"Where are they?" Louis asked.

"I've hidden them in Althea's storeroom until we can figure out what to do."

"What about the couple that was with the Evan's"

"They're in the storeroom too."

Louis went into the house to get his hat and to the barn to get his horse. When he came around to the front of the house, Lillian knew him well enough to know that he would go into town to see if he could be of help. She didn't even try to dissuade him. "Be careful Honey," she yelled as he mounted his horse and headed for town.

He found the Reverend and Mrs. Evans still standing out in the road in front of what was left of their church. "I'm so sorry," he said to Mrs. Evans as he embraced her.

"What happened to the couple who wanted to get to New York?" she whispered to Louis.

"For now, the Johnsons, along with Alice and Jason, are hiding in Althea's storeroom. Don't worry. They will all be taken care of as soon as possible."

"What kind of people would do such a thing?" Reverend Evans asked, though he knew the answer already. He shook his head in despair and Louis leaned over and patted the reverend on the shoulder.

With buckets still in hand and soot covering their faces, the town's people who had come out to help put out the fire were still gathered behind the Evans. "Reverend, we will help you rebuild your church," Louis said emphatically. "As soon as things settle down a bit, we will all help you rebuild the church."

"Yes," someone yelled. "Rebuild." Others also yelled the word, "Rebuild!"

Mrs. Evans was overwhelmed with emotion and began to softly sob.

"Where did the slave catchers go."Louis asked?

"Louis, I have never seen anything like this in my life," Reverend Evans said. "That old man shot one of them in the neck and he died on the spot. He shot wildly and hit another man in the shoulder. No one expected him to pull a gun from his waistband, least of all the men who were chasing him and his daughter. He just walked right through the burning church to confront them head-on. When the doors opened and he came down the steps, you could see the startled look on their faces. Then all hell broke loose. The old man started shooting and it took a minute but they shot him down. He knew he was going to die. It was the price he was willing to pay to save his daughter and grandson." The Reverend cleared his throat and wiped his tear-stained face. "He gave his life to save his daughter and grandson. I think those scoundrels were as shocked as we were, maybe more. They are likely somewhere trying to remove that bullet from the young man's shoulder. I don't think they will be back. I hope they are smart enough to know that they will never find the girl now."

"I hope you're right Reverend."

Reverend and Mrs. Evans kept their plans to visit family in Buffalo, New York and to escort Earl and Mia Johnson to the border. However, Alice and baby Jason decided to stay in Timbuctoo. Alice changed her name from Alice Pearson to Alexis Brown. Six-month-old Jason became Jay Brown. She would be Althea's cousin from Philadelphia. Althea was more than happy to welcome her new cousins and especially little Jay.

The Evans returned the third week of October. The weather was just starting to chill. The leaves were beginning to change from shades of green to a beautiful arrays of oranges and yellows. The sun was still bright most afternoons. When the Evans' buggy neared the town, they could see the church steeple high above all the other buildings just as it had when it was first constructed. "Look!" Mrs. Evans said excitedly to her husband. "They have started to rebuild the church."

The church was not completely rebuilt, but the steeple had been replaced and most of the framework was in place. There was sawing and hammering as a groups of young men were busy rebuilding the pews that would be placed inside the church. They didn't even have pews before the fire. "Look," Mrs. Evans said to her husband. "They have replaced the chairs with pews!" The work of rebuilding was actively underway and Reverend and Mrs. Evans could not be happier. "I knew that this was the right place for us to put down roots," Reverend Evans said. "This town is more like a family than any town I've ever seen."

"Welcome home," Benjamin said as he wiped his hands on his trousers before giving the Reverend a hardy handshake.

"Thank you," The reverend said as he took off his jacket and handed it to his wife. "Where can I be of help?" He asked with a smile.

Benjamin smiled too. He pointed to Louis and Joseph, who were nailing new boards against the frame of the church. Mrs. Evans took the buggy around to the back of the house. Once inside, she immediately began to make refreshments for those who were working to rebuild the church.

Chapter Six
Liberty
1860

"Stand fast therefore in the liberty wherewith Christ hath made us free, and be not entangled again with the yoke of bondage." Galatians 5:1

Alexis and Jay were given a spacious rooms on the top floor of the boarding house, complete with a real bed for her and a crib for Jay. The room also had it's own water closet, the first Alexis had ever seen. Those first couple of days were emotional for Alexis. She knew that her freedom was a blessing. She laughed out loud with over whelming joy every time she thought of being free. However, she cried as much as she laughed. She mourned her father, who had paid the ultimate price for her freedom. She missed her him dearly but found comfort in knowing that he was also finally free. She prayed for her mother Eliza and younger brother Daniel, who were left on the Pearson Virginia plantation. She prayed that they would one day all be together again.

Adjusting to life in Timbuctoo was easier than Alexis could ever have imagined. She liked Althea from the moment they met and was happy to be her cousin from Philadelphia. Alexis reminded Althea of her younger self. She was smart and confident and at times Althea felt as if Alexis really was her cousin.

Alexis was an affable young woman and she got on well with everyone. She smiled frequently and could be heard singing or humming softly as she went about her daily chores. She never complained and always offered to help whenever she could. Nan treated her like a daughter and she and Denny became friends, though Denny was a bit older. Jacob was another story. He didn't talk much but he was always very polite. Everyone loved and looked out for Jay, which gave Alexis time to herself in the evenings.

The work Alexis performed as housekeeper in Althea's Boarding House was nothing compared to the back-braking drudgery of the plantation. She spent most of her time on the upper floors, keeping the floors and furniture free of dust and grime. She also did most of the laundry, making sure the boarding house guests always had clean sheets and towels. After the evening meal was served and the kitchen and dining areas were cleaned, Alexis was free to do as she pleased. She spent most evenings at the Evans' home, where Mrs. Evans taught ex-slaves to read. Before the fire, those classes were held in the church.

Alexis was a small woman with big brown eyes, full lips and a smooth brown complexion. Althea gave her an advance on her salary to help her and Jay get settled into their new lives. Denny quickly volunteered to take Alexis shopping. For the first time in her life, Alexis was able to buy a couple of calico dresses, leather shoes and ribbons for her hair. She loved the dresses but the shoes would take some time to get use to wearing. They were tight on her feet that were use to being free and bare. Her feet were still scared and bruised from the barefoot walk from Virginia. The tight leather shoes seemed to squeeze her toes and heels and became unbearable in a matter of minutes. Denny assured her that the leather would loosen with time. Even though she wanted desperately to go without shoes, since she didn't see anyone else in town walking without shoes, she cringed, but put them on whenever she left the house.

Her hair was thick and dense. After months without brushing or washing, it was matted to her head. Denny helped wash her hair and comb it out. When her hair was dry, Denny soothed her scalp with petroleum jelly and brushed the moisture through her hair to the ends. Then she used a butter knife, heated on the stove, to smooth Alexis' hair until straight. At first, the smell of burning hair made Alexis jerk her head away. "Oh my God," Alexis said in alarm. "Are you burning my hair?"

"No, Silly. I'm straightening your hair. Didn't you ever have your hair straightened before now?"

"No," Alexis said. "I didn't have much time to be worrying about how my hair looked." She relaxed once she knew that Denny wasn't trying to burn her hair out. "We put petroleum on our scalp to keep fleas from biting and most of us kept our hair tied up in a rag, especially the mulattos."

"Why, especially the mulattos?" Denny questioned. Even though she had been a slave herself, mulattos on Gloria did not keep their hair tied up.

"So white folks won't mistake them for white," Alexis answered. "I never even thought about straightening my hair." Denny continued to straighten her hair as Alexis talked. When the straightening was finished, Denny parted her hair down the middle and made two thick cornrows that went past her shoulders. Alexis could hardly believe what she saw in the hand held mirror. One look and her face lit up with a big smile. "Oh my!" She said. "I wouldn't believe it if I didn't see it myself. I never knew that my hair could be straightened out." She smiled at herself in the small mirror and moved her head from side to side, so that she might see it from every angle, all the while smiling. "Thank you Denny. I didn't even know that my hair was this long. Thank you so much."

"You're welcome," Denny said. "Now it's up to you to keep it looking nice."

"I will, I promise."

"Here, I got this for you when we were in town." Denny handed Alexis an old brush. "It's old and used but the lady at the second hand shop said it came all the way from England," Denny said. "I scrubbed it clean for you."

Alexis blinked back tears as she accepted the small gift from her new friend. "Thank you," she whispered.

ॐ

It had been a year since the old Methodist Church burned down and the new church was just weeks from completion. On a sunny afternoon in October 1860, everyone was working hard to put the finishing touches on the new church. Joseph and Isaac were washing the newly installed stained glass windows in the front of the church, when Alexis came into the sanctuary carrying a water bucket and ladle. "Does anyone want a drink of water?" She asked with a smile that was infectious. Both Joseph and Isaac smiled as soon as they saw Alexis. Her good looks did not go unnoticed.

Isaac nearly fell as he scrambled down the ladder. "Yes, Ma'am," he said.

Alexis pretended not to notice as she filled the ladle and handed it to Isaac. He sipped, all the while keeping his eyes on Alexis. "What about you, Joseph? Do you want a drink?"

"Yes, Ma'am," Joseph had already come down from his ladder. He waited patiently for Isaac to finish drinking and hand over the ladle.

"I don't mean to rush you, Mr. Isaac, but I got a lot of hard working people that might want a drink of water."

Isaac acted as if he were in a trance. "Oh, I'm sorry," he said, handing the ladle back to her and never dropping his eyes from her smiling face.

She filled the ladle again and handed it to Joseph. "Thank you, Miss Alexis," he said before downing the water in two big gulps. He handed the ladle back and smiled. "How are you getting along in our little town?"

"I'm getting along just fine," Alexis said. "Everything is so new to me, it's like a dream. I didn't even know a place like Timbuctoo existed."

As Alexis took the ladle from Joseph's hand, he looked into her eyes for the first time since the night he lead her and little Jay to Althea's storage room. "It was the same for me when I first came here," he said. "There is a comfort in seeing your own people free and happy." He smiled at her and found that he couldn't look away. She looked very different from the young woman he remembered from that night. Sure, he had seen her many times when he was in and out of Althea's boarding house, but they were both working and he hadn't paid much attention.

"Every time I go to sleep, I wake up thinking I'm back on the plantation. Then I get up and realize that I'm not on the plantation and a new joy just washes over me. Before I do anything, I take a minute or two to thank God for my freedom." They both laughed. "Well, it's nice talking with you Joseph but I need to move on. You two have a nice day."

As Alexis moved on through the church Isaac and Joseph exchanged glances at her and then back at each other.

"She sure is a good looking woman," Isaac whispered to Joseph.

"She's a fine looking woman," Joseph agreed. "I mean, she is more than just good looking. I think she's beautiful and smart too." He was thoughtful for a moment. "That girl is gonna make some man a real fine wife."

Isaac's eyebrow shot up at that comment. He studied Joseph for a moment with a familiar smirk. "I sure hope you don't think that someone is you, brother?"

"What if I am?" Isaac was speechless for a moment. "I really wasn't thinking about myself but now that you mention it, why not me." Joseph said as he started back up the ladder. "I'm serious, Issac. Why not me?" Isaac stood, still looking up at Joseph as if he were suddenly daft. "Have you ever noticed how Benjamin and Rebecca treat each other when they're together? She's always smiling up at him like he's some sort of God and Benjamin treats her like she's a queen."

They were quiet for a while as they finished the last of the windows. Then the two young men started walking toward the back of the church where the pews were being painted. "They're in love, Joseph, and they've been together for years."

"I know, that's the point. That is exactly what I want. Someone to love and someone to love me."

Isaac gave Joseph a pat on the shoulder. "You got plenty of girls that love you, Joseph. They're always smiling and winking at you wherever we go. Just last week I saw you walking with Miss Lucy's granddaughter. What's her name, Lindy?"

"Linda and that is not what I mean. Yeah, Linda is a cute little girl and it's fun to flirt with her but I want more. I think I want to be a married man. Maybe it's time to settle down with one woman. I want the kind of relationship Benjamin has with Rebecca."

The conversation made Isaac wonder if he should be thinking about settling down too, and Joseph was wondering how and when he could approach Alexis. After a long silence, they began to clean up and get ready to end work for the day. Joseph said, "Christmas is on a Sunday this year. Reverend Evans has chosen that Sunday to be the first church service held in the new Church. Everyone will be here. After service, there is going to be a celebration and new dedication of the church. It's gonna be a really big day. I think they're having an early dinner in the new dining room, too. I'm gonna ask Alexis to go with me."

"I think that is a great idea," Rebecca said as she entered the church from the back door. "I think you two will make a very handsome couple. I got a chance to talk with Alexis and I think she is a lovely young woman. Althea and Nan like her, too. They say that she is cheerful most of the time and she dotes on little Jay."

"Well, that's it then," Joseph said. "I am definitely going to ask her to attend church with me on Christmas Day. We will see where it goes from there." He was quiet for a moment, a reflective expression on his handsome face.

"Is everything all right?" Rebecca asked.

"I've been living like everything is all right, but the truth is, I'm uneasy, always waiting for something to happen that will end these good times." Both Isaac and Jospeh sat with Rebecca. "You know, some stranger comes to town and recognizes me as a fugitive. Or, more slave catchers come looking for me. In the back of my mind, I'm always expecting that slave catchers will catch me and haul me back to Massa Atkins' place or to a prison for runaway slaves."

"No, no!" Rebecca said. "You stop worrying about that. Even if they come for you, your life here will not change. We protect our own here Joseph, and you are one of us now. Didn't anyone ever tell you about Mr. Jimmy?"

Isaac, who had lived in Timbuctoo his entire life, knew Mr. Jimmy's story. "You mean Mr. Jimmy that owns the dry goods store?"

"Yes," Rebecca said. "Well, Mr. Jimmy was a runaway. He ran from a Mississippi plantation almost eleven years ago. About three years ago, slave catchers came to town looking for Mr. Jimmy. He had been here long enough to make a life for himself. He was married with two beautiful little girls. What made those slave catchers come when they did, nobody knows. They must have been watching him for a while because they knew exactly where he lived. They came in the middle of the night and kicked his front door right off of the hinges. Then he was hog tied and dragged from his house while his wife and daughters watched horror. He was thrown into the back of a wagon and off they went. His wife and daughters screaming and crying the whole time. All the commotion and noise brought neighbors out to see what was happening. When the town learned that Mr. Jimmy was taken, they formed a posse, just like they did for young Jesse. They tracked those men down and fought them off. At least one of them was killed. It took three days but, they brought Mr. Jimmy back." Rebecca waited a minute to let her words resonate. "So you see, Joseph, it is time for you to get on with your life and stop worrying about something that may never happen. Slave catchers come and go but we are family here in our little town. This is home for you. No, the only way you are going anywhere is if it is your choice. Do you understand?"

"Yes, Ma'am. Thank you, Rebecca. I needed to hear that story."

Although Joseph had made up his mind to ask Alexis out, it turned out to be a bit harder than he anticipated. Over the next few weeks, the two had come face to face on at least three occasions. Each time, Joseph was unable to ask her to accompany him to church. Her quiet beauty and poise simply took his breath away and left him speechless. He never had trouble talking with a female before now. He wondered why he had so much anxiety when it came to talking with Alexis,. He knew what he wanted to say but the words just would not come.

An overcast, blustery day in October, Joseph was delivering goods to the Althea's boarding house. He tapped on the window of the back door and Nan went to let him inside. As soon as the door opened a crack, a strong wind literally blew the door from Nan's hand and it slammed against the wall. Joseph rushed inside, dropping his bundle to the floor. He had to use all his strength to push the door closed again. "There's a storm coming," he said to Nan. "I think this is a big one too."

"How could you know that? It's just a little windy. The sun is shinning, for God's sake." Nan said with a shrug. "It's just a little windy, that's all," she repeated.

"Yes, I know but I really think a big storm is coming. Look at those dark clouds." He pushed the curtain on the back door aside. "See how they are moving in a wide circle?"

Nan peeped. "Yeah, so. I've seen clouds move in a circle many times. Means nothing."

"Maybe," Joseph said as he piled the bags of grain into a corner of the kitchen. "I was once told that clouds moving in a wide circle could mean that there was a cyclone further down the coast. Those big storms start out over the water but they move up the coast for miles. Believe it or not, it's coming this way. Those dense gray clouds are moving too fast to ignore. Don't ask me how I know. I just know. I've seen this before when I was on the plantation and again when I made my escape. Trust me. A big storm is coming. We need to board up the windows and doors. Is Jacob here?"

"Yes. He's in the storage room. You best take those bags over there because Althea won't want them piled up in the kitchen."

Joseph took the bags of grain and corn and threw them over his shoulder. "Get ready to close the door behind me," he said. He ran the few yards from the house to the storage shed, where he encountered Jacob. He told Jacob of his prediction of a big storm coming up the coast, maybe a hurricane. When they stepped outside, Jacob looked up at the dark swirling clouds. The winds seemed to have calmed and everything seemed eerily quiet.

"I think you might be right, Joseph. I've seen this before, too. Even if it isn't a hurricane, it's a big storm for sure. We have to get the windows boarded up."

Joseph and Jacob boarded up all the windows of the boarding house and then Jacob hitched up the wagon and they headed for town, picking up Isaac along the way. Joseph told Isaac to go and warn Benjamin while he and Jacob headed to the Methodist church. "After all that work on the church, it would be a terrible shame if our new church were to be damaged by this storm," Joseph said. Jacob agreed. In a couple of hours they had boarded up everything and passed the word to other townspeople as they went.

Satisfied that the church was secure, they went to Miss Ida's bakery so they could help Isaac and Jesse board up their establishment. It was fortuitous that Louis was there buying bread. "I think we're in for a big storm in the next couple of hours," Joseph said.

"I'm way ahead of you, Joseph. I felt it early this morning. When we woke up this morning everything just seemed strangely quiet, as if nothing on earth was moving. The sun was shining but it just felt different. Within a couple of hours, the sun vanished for a little while and the wind began to blow. It was like an omen." They all agreed. "That storm may be closer than we think. I need to get back to Lillian," Louis said.

"Won't you need help boarding up?" Joseph asked?

"No. Remember, we've got shutters and a storm cellar. I've already secured the shutters. We'll be fine. You should go to the boarding house, because Althea has guest and may need more help." He shook Jacob's hand, then gave Joseph a look that only the two of them could understand before giving him a hug and a handshake.

"Yeah, going back to Althea's right now. We'll be fine. Don't worry," Joseph said. Louis nodded before mounting his horse and pulling the reins toward home.

As Joseph and Jacob headed back to Althea's Boarding House they noticed that the wind was picking up. Limbs were being torn away from trees and carried on the wind. All manner of debris were being tossed about by the heavy wind.

Inside the front room of the boarding house it was very dark. Althea's few guests were all sitting in front room. An older woman sat reading a book and two younger men were playing a game of chess. Joseph and Jacob bowed their heads in greeting and kept moving toward the kitchen. There, they explained the situation to Althea who quickly went to the front room to inform her guests and workers that they would be moving to the cellar until the storm passed.

The cellar under the boarding house was little more than a crawl space at the back of the house and was mostly used for storage. They brought blankets, pillows, and buckets of water enough to wait out the storm. Althea was thoughtful enough to prepare some sliced ham, bread, cheese and a few boiled eggs in case anyone got hungry. When everyone was comfortably settled in the cellar, Joseph walked through the house to make sure that the windows and doors were properly secured. "Shouldn't you be heading back to the Bissett farmhouse?" Althea questioned.

Joseph looked so startled at the question that Althea knew the answer with one glance at his face. "I thought I'd wait the storm out here, just in case you needed me," he said shyly.

"Ah, so you're staying for me?"

"Well, . . ."

"Oh, don't explain anymore Joseph. We all know that you've got eyes for Alexis."

"Is it that obvious? Do you think she knows?"

"If she ain't blind she knows. Why are you so afraid to talk with her? Never figured you for a shy man."

"Me neither but when I am around Alexis, something weird happens to me."

The kitchen suddenly became very dark and the sound of the wind got even louder. The boards on the front window began to rattle with the force of the wind and you could hear the sound of the wind as it whistled through trees and around buildings. "This is just the beginning," Joseph said. "It's going to get a lot worse before it gets better. We had better get into the cellar."

He took the bundles from Althea's arms before he pulled open the door in the floor of the kitchen. He climbed down after Althea and locked the door behind him.

Alexis had positioned herself against some bags of rice and Joseph was grateful that there was enough room for him in a space between the bags. "Mind if I sit here?" He asked.

"Of course not," she said. Joseph sat down for less than a minute before little Jay came and wiggled into the small space between his mother and Joseph.

"Hey Jay," Joseph said. "How are you doing?"

"Fine."

Joseph noticed that he held a battered stuffed horse. He could tell that the animal had been torn and repaired in several places. "So, you like horses, Jay?"

Two year old Jay shook his head and quickly turned into his mother. She cradled him in her arms and gently stroked his hair. "Yes, he loves horses but this one has seen better days."

"Yeah, I could see that," Joseph said and they both laughed. They were quiet for a while as they listened to the chatter of the others talking in the cellar. Joseph wanted desperately to say something but it seemed like his tongue was stuck in his mouth.

Finally, Alexis said, "Althea says there is gonna be a war. Do you think she's right?"

The question caught Joseph completely off guard and he wasn't able to answer right away. "I have heard some of the men at church talking about war coming."

"But why? This kind of talk scares me."

Joseph wanted tell her not to be afraid but how could he when he had his own apprehensions about the coming war. "Yeah, I know. All we can do is wait and see what happens."

"If there is a war, are you going to fight?"

"I wish I could but they aren't taking Negroes in the Union Army. Benjamin says that it's only a matter of time before they start signing Negroes up to fight. As soon as they do, I'll be the first to sign up."

Again, Joseph was quiet for a moment. "They say that the coming war is over states rights. We are free in some states while others want to keep their slaves. Those Southern states will be fighting to keep their Negro slaves." He looked up to see her big brown eyes looking down on him with anticipation. "I remember what it was like to be a slave. My mother worked her whole life for white folks in Georgia and when she took sick with the fever, they just let her die. They told me and my brother to pray for her and two days after they put her in the ground, they shackled us, put us in a wagon headed for the Atlanta auction house. We winded up in Maryland." Alexis covered his hand with her own. "So if there is a war, and I can avenge my mother and brother, and every other Negro held as a slave, I will definitely fight."

Although he spoke softly, Alexis could not miss the fire in his eyes. She took his hand and gently squeezed it. "You already know most of my story except I still have a mother and younger brother owned by those hateful people. I pray every night that all Negros will one day be free from slavery, but the notion of war is still very scary to me."

"It's good to know that you are a praying woman." At that moment, Alexis gave Joseph the most beautiful smile he'd ever seen. "You know, if this storm doesn't damage the church too much, the first service will be held on Christmas Day."

"I know. The Reverend is planning an all day celebration."

"Will you go with me?" The words rushed from his mouth. Uncomfortable moments passed and Joseph held his breath.

"Do you mind if I call you, Joe?"

"No."

Alexis glanced down at her son, who had fallen asleep. "Joe, I would be happy to go to church with you on Christmas, but there is a lot of days between now and Christmas. I hope we can see each other before the holiday."

Joseph was once again shocked into silence for a moment. But, one look at Alexis and her radiant smile seemed to loosen his tongue. "You can be sure we will see each other soon."

It seemed that they were the only ones talking. Everyone else was dead silent and the only sound was that of the wind. The cellar door was being pulled up by the wind gust and slammed back down when the gust passed. You could hear debris flying around outside. It sounded like a train running right through town. The storm raged for nearly half the day and through the night.

At one point, Alexis got up to get some ham, biscuits, and water for Jay, Joe and herself. After they had eaten, Joseph put his arm around Alexis' shoulder. She made herself comfortable with her head resting against his shoulder. She almost fell asleep but there was a sudden loud clap of thunder, which made everyone sit up a little. Alexis head jerked up and she looked up at Joseph in alarm. He squeezed her softly. "Don't worry. We're safe," he assured her. All they could hear was water rushing. The Delaware River, creeks and streams would have all certainly over-flowed their banks.

Finally, shortly after dawn, the wind began to diminish. Then the rain stopped and everything was calm and quiet. Jacob and Joseph decided to go above ground to judge how safe it might be for the others to leave the cellar.

There was no water damage to the boarding house. The water got no further than the front porch but the wind had blown the front and back doors off the hinges and there was considerable damage to the furniture inside the house from the strong winds.

Joseph helped Althea climb the cellar steps. He kept his arm tightly around her shoulders. "I want you to know that I can repair everything that has been damaged, so don't worry about anything." Everyone thought that Althea would be devastated but she took the loss in stride.

The cupboard doors were hanging from loose hinges, floor board were ripped up in the front room, and most of the furniture had been destroyed. "Praise God!" Althea said. "My boarding house is still standing!" She then lifted the front of her dress and headed up the stairs to see how bad the damage was to the second and third floors. "We can fix this. Yes, Lord. We can fix this," Althea kept saying. "Joseph," she called out, but he was right behind her.

"I'm right here, Althea."

"I'm gonna need you. I know that you a farmer now but never mind that. I'm gonna need Josiah's skills. You hear me?"

"Yes, Ma'am, but you know there ain't no Josiah here, Althea."

She looked dumbfounded for a minute. "Oh, but you know what I mean."

"Yes, I do. Jacob and I will start with the bedrooms so your guests might have a place to sleep. You, Nan, and Alexis should start with the kitchen. Don't worry, we will fix everything in time."

By that time, they had reached the first landing. Althea plopped down in the chair and put her head in her hands and began to weep. Joseph decided to just let her be. She sobbed for a minute or two before she wiped her face with the hem of her apron and stood. Joseph was still standing there waiting for whatever would come next. "Thank you, Joe," she said.

"For what? I didn't do anything."

"Thank you for being here but I'm all right now. I'm fine. Let's get to work."

❦

The rest of the town suffered similar damage, including the Methodist Church. The Bowman's were somehow spared and only suffered minimal damage to the outside of their property. The Catering building and home on the upper floor did not suffer any damage. The wind tossed tables and chairs but there was no real damage. However, the hurricane would affect the Bowman's Catering Company financially. Not too many people could afford to cater an event after suffering such loss. Benjamin and Rebecca were happy to help their family and neighbors through this difficult time.

Louis, and a few other men, joined Constable Willis in surveying the damage beyond the town limits. A massive amount of trees had been felled outside of town and the closer they got to the river, the more damage they saw. There were fishing boats that looked as if they had been dropped from the sky. They even came upon a boat that was wedged between two branches of a large tree.

The water had not yet receded so the men tethered their horses close to the road and trudged into the the soggy, deep mud leading to the river's edge. They soon came across several overturned flat boats, often used for shipping up and down the river.

"Shush," Louis said. "Do you hear that?"

The men stopped walking and began to listen. They all heard more groans and began to run toward the sounds. More groaning and they knew that there were men under a flat boat that the storm had thrown far from the river bank.

They found three white men under that flat boat, buried under layers of mud. One man was already dead and two of the men were badly injured; one with very little hope of recovery. He had been impaled by a tree branch and they knew that his injuries were so severe that he could not be moved. He would die there in the mire of the Delaware River. After the others freed him from under the boat, Louis knelt down in the mud and took the man's hand in his own. The man could barely speak though he tried to say something. "Don't speak," Louis urged.

"I'm dying," the man whispered. "Will you pray with me?" Louis squeezed the man's hand and began to softly pray. His words seemed to console the man and he could feel the tension leave the dying man's body. In a matter of minutes, his hand became slack and he breathed deeply one last time.

The other white man was banged and bruised but did not seem to suffer any life threatening injury. It was obvious that his legs were broken. The men made a makeshift litter to carry the man back into Burlington where he could get medical help.

"Why in the world were you men on the water during such a storm?" The Constable asked.

"We were trying to make a delivery in upstate Pennsylvania. We thought we could dock before the storm came this far north. Guess we just got caught, that's all."

"What's your name, friend," Willis asked as he hitched the litter to the back of his horse.

"Todd. Todd Hunter."

The Constable stopped dead in his tracks. "Hunter, you say?" Now where have I heard that name before, he thought to himself.

Several quiet moments passed and Constable Willis tried to remember if he knew this man and where he had heard the name before. At the hospital, doctors and nurses came out to help Mr. Hunter into the hospital. Don't worry," Louis said. "I think your leg is broken in a couple of places but you're going to be fine. I'm sure."

Mr. Hunter expressed his gratitude and thanked them all for rescuing him. "Think I'll come by and check on you in a few days. Will that be all right with you, Mr. Hunter?" Constable Willis asked.

"Sure," he said but he looked a bit confused.

After the men mounted their horses and headed for home, Louis asked the Constable about that encounter. "What was that about?"

"I think that man might be Samantha's father."

₰

A week after the storm Constable Willis and Louis traveled to Burlington to visit with Todd Hunter. As Louis expected, Hunter's leg was broken in several places and he was in a wheel chair when they entered his hospital room.

"Good morning Mr. Hunter." Constable Willis said. "You're looking a damn site better than the last time we saw you. Hope you're feeling as well."

Hunter looked surprised to see the two men enter his room. "Good morning," he stammered.

"We've come to speak with you about a very sensitive matter."

"Oh?"

"Yes," Louis began. "Nearly a year ago, my daughter and her husband took in a homeless white girl named Samantha."

Hunter's eyes widened in obvious surprise, but he said nothing. "I tried to find out who the child's parents were and where she came from," the Constable said. "I learned that her mother could be a woman named

Caroline, who died in a fire and that her last name is Hunter." Both the Constable and Louis waited to see if that information would have an effect on Mr. Hunter. He gave no indication that this information was meaningful.

"Is Samantha your daughter?" Louis bluntly asked.

"No!" He said a little too loudly. "I can see why you would think I was her father. I was married to her crazy mother for a time but that girl is not mine and she ain't white. The truth is, that child's father could be any man. Her mother was a whore. I always suspected the black man who worked the farm down the road, but I got no proof of those suspicions. I caught Caroline more than once with other men, white and black. I did love her at first, even though I knew she had a problem. She wasn't right in the head but I couldn't help her and after the third time, I couldn't take it anymore. That's when I left her. I never even saw the child come into this world. I was long gone by the time she burned down her house. I was married to Caroline. I guess that's how the girl got my name, but I am not her father." He was reflective for a moment ad Constable Willis and Louis waited to see if he had more to say. He shook his head from side to side. "Poor kid got a real bad start in this world. I'm sorry gentlemen but I can be of no more help to you."

The Constable and Louis exchanged glances. "Well, you've shed some light on the situation, Mr. Hunter. Thank you."

Louis shook his head in agreement. "Good day to you Mr. Hunter."

They rode in silence for the first couple of miles. "So Samantha could be mulatto?" The Constable said. "I guess we'll never know." He shook as if he were confused.

"Why does it matter, Willis?" Louis asked.

"It doesn't matter, my friend. I'm glad we didn't tell Samantha anything about Hunter so there is no need to break her heart with this sad information."

"I agree," Louis said.

Chapter Seven
Love and War

1860/1861

". . . What therefore God hath joined together,
let not man put asunder." Matthew 19:6

Abraham Lincoln is elected President of the United States of America in November 1860. Just one month later, South Carolina secedes from the Union. Mississippi, Florida, Alabama, Georgia, Louisiana, and Texas soon secede from the Union as well.

⁂

The hours Joseph and Alexis spent hunkered down in Althea's cellar turned out to be time they would both cherish for the rest of their lives. For weeks Joseph wanted to spend time with Alexis. He wanted to get to know her, but something or someone always seemed to be keeping them apart. Before that day, he was often speechless in her presence and sometimes found himself just staring at her beautiful face. Sheltering from the storm in Althea's cellar allowed them to finally spend some time together and speak to one another. Talking to Alexis was easier than Joseph anticipated. It didn't take long before they were comfortable with each other. The storm raged for a day and a half and by the time the storm ended and they could leave the cellar, it was clear that Joseph was completely smitten.

Joseph looked forward to spending time with Alexis. They took long walks in the evenings, before the weather became too cold. Sometimes he would sit with her in the kitchen of Althea's boarding house. They would talk for hours. Alexis talked freely about the hardships she endured on the plantation but she also talked about her family. Her mother, Eliza was a small woman like Alexis, who loved music. Alexis smiled and her face brightened as she talked of her family. Joseph could see the love in her eyes. They had both lived lives of suffering and loss and they now seemed grateful to have found each other. Alexis was beautiful, smart, and caring and for the first time in his life, Joseph was falling in love.

By Thanksgiving everyone knew Joseph and Alexis were a couple. People around town rarely saw one without the other unless they were working.

For weeks Joseph had been working on some secret project in the barn. He would work in the barn after he had finished the day's chores on the farm and the work he did for Althea's. When he wasn't spending time with Alexis, he would be in the barn until very late in the evening.

Two days before Christmas Eve, Joseph emerged from the barn with the most beautifully carved wooden rocking horse. It was a Christmas gift for Jay. On the neck of the horse was carved decorative reins which looped up to the wooden handles. He even carved a saddle onto the back of the horse. A red ribbon was tied around the horse's neck. Lillian and Louis marveled at his expert craftsmanship.

"Oh my," Lillian said. "It's beautiful. So this is what you've been working on in the barn?"

"Yes."

"Jay is going to love it."

"I hope so."

♨

Finally, it was Christmas Day 1860 and everyone was excited to celebrate the first service in the new Methodist church. It was a beautiful Christmas morning; cold, but not unbearably so. A light dusting of snow had fallen over night which seemed fitting for the holiday atmosphere.

The rocking horse was placed under the Christmas tree in Althea's parlor. When Alexis and Jay came down to breakfast, the horse was the first thing Jay saw. He was usually a very quiet child, but he took one look at the horse and screamed. "Mine?"

"Yes Jay. The horse is a gift from Joseph."

Joseph, Althea and Nan came in from the kitchen to witness the boy's joy and to wish him a Merry Christmas. "Here," let me help you climb on the horse." Joseph said. He lifted him onto the horse and then gave the horse a little push so that Jay could see that it would rock. It only took a few minutes for Jay to get the hang of rocking and he began to laugh as he rocked his horse back and forth. Smiling from ear to ear, Jay rocked.

"What do you say?" Alexis prompted.

"Thank you, Joseph," Jay said.

"You are very welcome," Joseph said as he lifted Jay from the saddle. "Now, let's go eat breakfast so we can get to church on time.

The large evergreen tree that grew in the church yard, was decorated with small covered candles and red bows adorned the branches. Large wreaths, decorated with gold ribbons hung from the front doors of the church.

It seemed as if the entire town had come out to celebrate the first Christmas in the new Methodist Church. Not only was the sanctuary completely full, even the mezzanine was full. Reverend Evans retold the story of Christ's birth in an inspiring sermon. After the sermon, an early dinner was served in the new dining area.

Alexis was helping Althea and Nan clean up and get ready to go back to the boarding house while Joseph sat with Jay. He noticed a familiar face in the crowd, a stout white man with dark hair and eyes. Joseph was sure he had seen that face before but he just couldn't place him.

In February 1861, Jefferson Davis is elected President of the newly formed Confederate States of America. The continued disagreement over slavery and state's rights seemed to be moving the country quickly toward war.

Beginning April 12, 1861, at 4:30 in the morning, under the command of General Pierre Beauregard, Confederate forces opened fire on the United States Seaport at Fort Sumter in Charleston, South Carolina. The bombardment lasted for two days. The attack was seen as a rebellion and so began the war between the states, the American Civil War. Just five days after the war began, Virginia seceded from the Union. In the coming weeks, more southern states would secede.

The abolition meetings that Louis and Benjamin once attended were now meetings that focused on updates of the war. The Christian Recorder, an African American newspaper published by the African Methodist Episcopal Church in Philadelphia was delivered to the Timbuctoo Methodist Church weekly.

The war was all anyone wanted to talk about. Some folks called it a white man's war, having nothing to do with Negroes. Those folks often said, "Let the white man fight his own war."

Others said, "If this war will free slaves, then let us fight too." Even though Negroes had fought in the Revolutionary war and the war of 1812, President Lincoln refused to accept Negroes into the Union Army. Some Northern, free born African Americans and escaped slaves wanted to fight so badly, that they formed their own militias in the hope that they would be accepted into the Union Army.

According to reports of the Christian Recorder, the war was not going well for the Union, although reports of battles fought and won by Negro Militias were widely spread. These reports seemed to deepen their desire to fight. The North did not suffer as much as the South from supply shortages and blockades, however, the fighting did cause delays in the delivery of certain goods and supplies.

By the summer of 1862, there were more strangers in town than ever before. A good number of those unfortunate souls were too poor for the hotel or boarding house. People were sleeping on the street or in alleys between buildings. Louis said that they were most likely deserters from both armies.

The spring and summer of 1862 were exceptionally wet seasons. New Jersey suffered from one heavy rain storm after another.

Reverend Evans set up rooms in the back of the church for the homeless. It was a rainy June day and the Reverend and Benjamin went out into the storm to coax some of those homeless men to seek shelter in the church and at least have a meal. Some gladly accepted the offer of shelter while a few others flatly refused to shelter in the church.

A young man by the name of Nathaniel Williams, was grateful for the shelter. He looked to be about twenty, tall and thin with unkept blonde hair. Althea brought over a pot of beef stew to help the church in their benevolence to the homeless. The young man appeared to be famished. He thanked the Reverend several times as Althea sat a steaming, hot bowl of beef stew in front of him. He attacked the food with vigor and ate until he just couldn't eat anymore. He thanked Reverend Evans again and was soon fast asleep on one of the pallets laid out for him and the other three homeless men.

It was a rainy Saturday morning when Alexis entered the church to clean and make sure that everything was ready for the Sunday morning service. This was something that she had been doing every Saturday morning. She knew about the homeless men in the room between the sanctuary and the kitchen. Benjamin had said that they were just scared young men, looking to avoid fighting in the war.

She was just finishing up in the kitchen when she noticed a young man watching her from the doorway. "Good morning," she said cheerfully.

"Mornin," he said in a thick southern accent.

"Miss Althea will be bringing breakfast shortly."

Alexis was sweeping the floor and she looked up when she felt the man move close to her. It startled her to see just how close he was and she quickly took a step backward. "Is there something I can do for you?" She asked.

He didn't answer. With one arm swung around Alexis' tiny waist, he pulled her to him. She dropped the broom and pushed at his chest with all of her might. He was stronger than he looked. Alexis could not move him. She began to pound his chest with her fist. "Let me go!" She said. Before she knew it, he swung her around and bent her over the table, intent on raping her from the back. Alexis struggled to free herself as Nathaniel tried to move her petticoat and under garments out of his way, while also trying to undo his trousers.

He smelled bad and the scent of him filled her nose and mouth, making her nauseous. Alexis began to scream as loud as she could and he reached up and grabbed her by her braid, pulling her head back. She felt his rough, calloused hand as he reached between her thighs probing, looking for her sweet spot.

"Please don't do this. You're hurting me." He didn't seem to hear her or even care. His breathing was heavy and hot. All the while, a storm raged outside. There was a loud clap of thunder. Streaks of lightening illuminated the kitchen and Alexis continued to beg him to stop as she struggled hard to free herself. He was able to free his manhood from his britches which made him even more determined to enter her. He fumbled and pushed at her to no avail. The kitchen brightened with a lightning strike and Alexis saw a large ladle on the table just inches away. She had to stretch her arm to reach it. First, she kicked backwards as hard as she could, the heel of those shoes, that she hated so much, caught him in the ass. That seemed to anger him and he became more violent, swinging Alexis around to face him. He was so intent on getting into her clothes that he never saw the attack coming. As soon as her hand was free, she swung that ladle as hard as she could, catching him at his temple. He seemed dazed for a moment, but when he saw blood dripping from his face, he became enraged. Alexis squirmed out of his grip and ran for the door with the ladle still in her hand. He chased after her with his britches still open and his manhood exposed.

She was able to get to the back door first, as Nathaniel tripped over his sagging britches. She opened the back door and ran right into Joseph and Althea bringing breakfast to the homeless. "Alexis?" Joseph said.

A moment later Nathaniel came running out of the church. Alexis ran right into Joseph's arms and he gently moved her out of the way and confronted her pursuer. He knew immediately what was going on and with one punch, Nathaniel lay sprawled in the dirt.

"Did he hurt you?" Joseph asked Alexis.

"No," she said through tears. "But I hurt him."

"Did he . . .?" The question just hung out there without ever being uttered.

"No. He tried. I had to hit him to get him off of me."

Joseph was both worried and proud. "Hit him? With what?"

"I kicked him in the butt first and then I hit him with this big soup ladle." She held the blood stained ladle up for Joseph and Althea to see.

Joseph pulled Alexis to him again, hugging her tightly. Althea smiled and one look at Althea's smiling face and Joseph started to laugh. "I guess he got more than he expected. I'm proud of you." He said. "Are you sure you aren't hurt."

"Who knew that little Alexis would have that kind of courage?" Althea asked.

"I've been raped before," Alexis said to them. "But I was young and stupid. This time I was just determined that he wasn't going to take me. I will never again let anyone take me by force."

Joseph breathed a sign of relief. "Go next door and get Reverend Evans. I will keep an eye on this one while Reverend Evans goes for the Constable. Althea took the food into the kitchen.

Nathaniel was bleeding from his temple and his nose. He sat up as if he had no idea where he was or why he was there. Joseph threw a rag at him. "Get up and get yourself together."

He did as he was told. "So what now?"

"Nothing from me. I'm gonna turn you over to the Constable and he will do whatever he does with people like you."

They were quiet for a few moments. "You mean he is gonna arrest me for trying to have a little fun with a nigger girl?" Nathaniel said. A smug expression lifted the corners of his mouth into a evil smile.

Joseph didn't answer right away. He really could not believe the arrogance of this man trying to rape a black woman in an all black town and stupid enough to boast about it. "You know," Joseph began calmly. "I only hit you one time, but if you keep talking I might have to beat that smile off your ugly face. I mean, not another word."

Constable Willis turned Nathaniel over to the Burlington County Police. Once the four homeless men in the church moved on, there were no more homeless allowed to stay in the church.

When the others heard what happened, they all apologized for Nathaniel. "He wasn't one of us," one said. "We didn't even know where he came from," another said. He just joined our camp one day, long before we got to New Jersey." Even so, the Reverend knew that he would have to be more careful about who he allowed to shelter in the church.

The constant flow of people through town continued. As the war raged on, more slaves left their plantation homes for freedom in the north. More white young men deserted the Confederacy and headed north. The people of Timbuctoo became more wary of strangers in town.

In a meeting held at the church in October, an update in the Christian Recorder reported that the Union was suffering from a manpower shortage. There were less and less volunteers and Lincoln was still opposed to admitting Negroes into the Union Army.

Congress passed the Militia Act in July 1862 which allowed Negros to serve in the Union Army as laborers. Many Negroes were already fighting in militias and in the Union Navy.

The report also sited one of the most horrific battles fought to date. It happened on September 17, 1862 at Antietam, Maryland. President Lincoln was under pressure from abolitionists to allow Negroes into the regular army. Statesman and abolitionist Frederick Douglas wanted Lincoln to make the war about freedom of the enslaved. However, Lincoln steadfastly held to the idea that the war was about preservation of the Union.

As the war raged on, Lincoln's perspective began to change. On September 22, 1862 a preliminary emancipation was issued to take effect in January 1863, however that document only referred to states currently rebelling against the Union. In other words, states that had succeeded from the Union. Lincoln's aim was still to restore the Union. Also, this was more of a military move to increase the number of union soldiers rather than a repudiation of slavery. Still, it opened the door for the recruitment of Negroes into the Union Army.

Recruiting offices began to spring up all over the North and most of the young men in Timbuctoo were eager to sign up and fight. Rebecca and Benjamin were worried for David because they knew that he would sign up at the first opportunity. Isaac was also eager to sign up for the Union army but Joseph was conflicted. Though he wanted to fight as much as anyone, he didn't want to leave Alexis and Jay. He had finally found the love of his life and the thought of leaving her to go south to fight a war was disturbing.

♨

January 1, 1863 President Lincoln issued the final Emancipation Proclamation. This Proclamation did not just free slaves in border states as the previous Emancipation had done. As of this date, all slaves held in Confederate states have been proclaimed free and the enlisting of Negro solders in the Union Army is not only permitted but encouraged. The fight to hold the Union together is now a fight to abolish slavery.

♨

On a cold February day in 1863, Alexis and Joseph sat in front of the fire at Althea's boarding house. Jay, who was now five years old, had fallen in love with his new toys. He was content to play with his toy men, carved and painted by Joseph. Alexis couldn't help smiling to see her son so happy. "He loves those toys," she said to Joseph. "Thank you, again."

"You're welcome." They were both quiet for a while but Joseph knew that he should tell Alexis that he, Isaac, and David had been to the recruiting office in Burlington more than a month ago. They were waiting for a letter from the Army to tell them where and when to report. He took her hand into his own and held it a little tighter than usual. "Alexis, these last few months have been the best of my life. I'm not ashamed to tell you that I'm falling in love with you and little Jay. You are on my mind all through the day and before I go to sleep at night. You are the first person I think of every morning when I wake up. When we are apart, I can't wait until I see your face again. I feel a nervous jitter every time you are close to me." Alexis watched Joseph with wide eyes, though she said nothing. "I want us to be together, Alexis. I don't want to imagine your face in the morning. I want to see your face every morning and before I got to sleep at night. I can't think of anything that would make me happier than waking up to your beautiful face every morning."

Alexis twisted around so that she could look Joseph in the eye. His face held that same nonchalant expression that she had become use to seeing. But his eyes looked different. His eyes seemed to convey his sincerity and his passion. "What does that mean, Joe?"

"It means I am asking you to marry me. I want you to be my wife and I want Jay to be my son."

"I don't know what to say." She never took her eyes away from his face. "We haven't known each other very long. I just don't know what to say."

"I know that we haven't known each other long but I think I have been falling in love with you from the second time I saw you."

"From the second time?" She repeated.

"When I first saw you, I just thought you were a scared little girl. The next time I saw you was in Althea's kitchen and you smiled at me. Do you remember?"

"Yes, I remember."

"Of course, I want you to say yes. I'm sure we will be good for each other. But there is more I must tell you before you give me your answer."

"Is there something wrong?"

"No." He paused as he searched for the right words. "Remember when you asked me if I would fight if there was a war?"

"Yes."

"That's what I need to tell you. I've already signed up." He waited a minute for her to digest that news.

"You mean you've already joined the army?"

"Yes, but I have no idea when they will assign me assigned me to a regiment. It could be as long as a couple of months or longer, but I know that a training camp, Camp William Penn, is being built right outside of Philadelphia. The Recruiter in Burlington told us that unless something happens to end this war, we could be leaving in the spring of 1864."

Alexis' expression could not hide her confusion as she just stared at Joseph for a few seconds before she lowered her head. Joseph lifted her chin with his hand and kissed her lightly on the lips. She did not resist and Joseph quickly pulled her into his embrace and kissed her passionately. "I love you Alexis and I'm really hoping that you feel the same."

"I do love you, Joseph."

"Then say yes, my love. We can be married before I leave."

Alexis leaned into Joseph's embrace. "I will be happy to be your wife, but you have to promise not to make me a widow before I've had time to enjoy being a wife."

With that, Joseph leaped to his feet and lifted Alexis up as he enveloped her in his arms again. "I promise," he whispered. Jay stopped playing to look at his Mommy in Joseph's arms. No way he was going to be left out, so he abandoned the toys and ran right into his mother's dress, wiggling his way in between Joseph and Alexis. Joseph reached down and lifted Jay to his shoulder and the three held on to each other for a few moments.

"I would like for us to be married as soon as possible," Joseph said.

"Why should we rust? You said that it could take some time before your are assigned."

"I don't want to take the chance that the army will call me before we are married."

Alexis just smiled in agreement.

The news of their upcoming marriage was joyously received by the rest of the family. Althea and Lillian were beside themselves with happiness. They didn't mind that they only had a few weeks to plan a wedding. They couldn't wait to make arrangements for the big day.

All the ladies sat around the table in Althea's kitchen making wedding plans. Denny graciously volunteered to decorate a broom for the ceremony.

"There will be no broom jumping," Alexis said softly but emphatic.

Althea had heard of the practice, but she didn't know much about it since she was born free in Philadelphia. The other ladies were surprised at Alexis' words.

"That is what couples did on Gloria, right Lillian?" Nan asked.

"Yes, it is a common practice among slaves on the plantation."

"Yes, I know," Alexis said. "But we are not on the plantation and Joseph and I are free and we're going to walk down the center aisle of the church just like other free people. No broom jumping. I don't want anything that reminds me of my life on the plantation."

Lillian put a protective arm around Alexis' shoulders and gave her an affectionate squeeze. "It is your wedding day dear. It will be as you say."

❧

On March 3, 1863 Congress passed the Conscription Act, which required every male citizen between the ages of 20 and 45 to register for the draft. However, for $300 or a substitute, (usually a slave) one could be exempt from service. This made it easy for wealthy people to get out of war service. Slaves were also exempt from the conscription because many whites didn't want to fight side by side with Negros. The Act was viewed as an affront to poor people and slaves. Poor white people had no desire to free slaves or to unite the fractured country, so why should they be forced to fight. Many slaves, though not part of the regular army, fought because their owners signed them up to fight in their stead or they were eager to take part in their own liberation. Even immigrants just arriving to American shores, were forced to abide by the Conscription Act. However, many Irish and German immigrants willingly volunteered to fight. There were riots against the draft in many of the large cities and especially New York.

᪥

Samantha's speech was improving daily. David took it upon himself to teach her to read, in an effort to help her speak more clearly. After only a few lessons, he realized that she had already been taught quite a bit. It was really a matter of helping her to remember those long ago lessons and taking her a little further. They spent a couple of hours at the table each evening after dinner. She learned quickly and he and Rebecca were proud of her progress. In fact, Rebecca was so proud that she decided to present Samantha with a book at Christmas.

On a cool March evening in 1863, Rebecca and Mom Cathy were helping with the wedding decorations at the church while Catherine was in the catering kitchen helping her father with a large order. David was reading to Samantha from one of the many books his mother had bought he and his sisters over the years. Samantha suddenly seemed very distracted and uninterested. He glanced at her over the book. She was just staring at him. "What is it Sam," he said as he closed the book.

At first she didn't answer and David noticed that her eyes were brimming with unshed tears. "What do you think of Joseph and Alexis as a couple?" She asked. "We don't know anything about this woman. I mean Joseph seems to be in love with Alexis but they haven't even known each other very long."

"Oh, I see," David said. "You're jealous of Alexis."

"No!" She said as she pushed her chair back from the table and stood. "David, you don't see anything at all."

"Yeah? Well I think you're sweet on Joseph. I think you've always had a thing for him." Samantha didn't answer. "I knew it. I remember how you looked at him that day at my Grandmother's house when he came out to meet everyone."

"I am not jealous of Alexis," she said as she rounded the table and grabbed her shawl from the hook on the door. "I like Joseph. He is a very nice person but I am not sweet on him. Like I said, you don't see anything. You are as blind as can be." Uncomfortable silent moments passed as David tried to understand Samantha. She threw her shawl around her shoulders and walked to the door. "It's you, David! It's you. You can't see that I love you," she said as she swept pass him and out of the front door before he could even comprehend that she had just confessed her love.

David sat in stunned silence as her words slowly penetrated his mind. He grabbed his jacket and ran after her. By the time he caught up with her, they were standing in front of the church. The church was aglow with candle light. There was a biting cold in the wind that blew the soft layer of snow from an earlier snow shower across the ground in a swirl. "Samantha," David called but she just kept walking. "Samantha," he yelled again and this time she stopped. Their breath making steam in the cold night air. When David finally caught up to her, he simply put his arms around her, pulled her into a crushing embrace. He kissed her soundly. Big gray eyes stretched open in both shock and happiness. " I love you too," he said. "I always have."

"If you love me, why are you planning to leave me?"

"Leave you?"

"I heard you and Joseph talking about joining the Union Army."

"Yes, I am. I have to do this. If there is a war for the freedom of black folks, I must fight. But believe me, I will get back to you as soon as I can. I promise."

"You have never been a slave. Why do you care so much."

"My grandmother was a slave and my mother was born into slavery. I've heard the stories of my white grandfather's cruelty all of my life and I've listened to the stories of the runaways that have come through our town. I feel for them all."

"But what about me?"

"You will be all right here with my family until I get back." He squeezed her a little tighter. "I promise that I will come back to you, Samantha."

"You better, I'll be waiting."

"Now, can we get out of this cold?"

Arm in arm, they ran back to the house. Once inside, neither missed the fact that they were home alone. David kissed her lightly on the cheek before taking her by the hand and leading her to his room. Samantha did not resist. They slowly undressed each other, taking time to explore each other. David tried to still his eagerness and move slowly but he soon realized that Samantha was just as eager. They made love and it was the first time for Samantha. David did have some experience but this time seemed like the first time because he was in love.

"You know we have to tell the family," he said.

"Not yet. We can tell the family later."

"If that's what you want," he said.

"That is what I want. This is a time to celebrate Joseph and Alexis. I just hope she is the right one for Joseph."

"You're right. We will tell the family later."

❧

The wedding took place at the church on a warm Saturday at the end of March 1863. Reverend and Mrs. Evans, of course, family and a few friends were in attendance. Alexis descended the steps in a high neckline, cream colored muslin dress, accentuated by layers of silk. Denny curled her hair and pinned the curls on the top of her head with tiny little pearls. A few ringlets were allowed to fall around her face. Lillian pinned a broach at her throat and spread a little rouge on her lips and cheeks. Once inside the church door, Louis was there to take Alexis by the arm and guide her down the aisle. She stopped for a moment and smiled at her new family and friends, happy that they all came.

Joseph nervously waited at the front of the church until Lillian signaled that the bride was coming down the aisle. He could hardly believe his eyes. At that moment, he thought that Alexis was the most beautiful woman he had ever seen. The entire room seemed to share his feeling as there was a loud gasp from those who watched Alexis make her way down the aisle. Her eye caught Joseph's eye and they both smiled as if they were oblivious to all who watched in awe.

The ceremony was short and as Joseph took Alexis'

hand to lead her from the church, he again noticed the same white man sitting at the back of the church that he saw on Christmas. When he came to the pew where the man sat, he stopped. Their eyes met and the recognition stopped him in his tacks.

"What is it?" Alexis wanted to know.

Louis noticed Joseph stop before reaching the church doors and he rushed forward. "What is it Joseph?" Joseph didn't answer.

The man stood and extended his hand to Louis for a handshake. "Good day to you. My name is Girard Gale." Louis did not take his hand. "I'm here in your little town searching for a murderer. He's a runaway slave by the name of Josiah Gilbert."

"And you thought you would find this runaway in the church, during a wedding?" His sarcasm was apparent.

"Oh, you would be surprised where these niggers will hide."

Alexis held her breath as she squeezed Joseph's hand tighter. He could feel a slight tremble in her hand.

"No Josiah here, sir." Joseph said. The man stared at Joseph and Joseph stared back hard. Gale wasn't sure if he'd found Josiah or not. Joseph tipped his hat to the stranger. "Good day to you, Mr. Gale," Joseph said as he lead his bride from the church.

Constable Willis overheard the conversation and soon joined the group at the back of the church, as did Benjamin. "Are you a bounty hunter, Mr. Gale?" The Constable asked.

"No. My name is Girard Gale. George Gale was my brother. That nigger killed him and I swear, I'm gonna find him before I leave this earth. He is gonna get what he deserves."

"Oh, I see," Constable Willis said. "Traveling alone, are you?"

The man stood and adjusted his hat on his head. "That's more than you need to know, Mister." Then he hastily left the church.

𝕵𝕤

Alexis' room at the boarding house had been decorated especially for her wedding night. This was not the first time for either of them but it was the first time that they would actually make love with the person with whom they had fallen in love. The room was aglow with candles and a fire burned in the fireplace. Joseph undressed and turned down the bed while Alexis changed into a white lacy night gown, bought especially for her wedding night. She came to him slowly and he rose to meet her, taking her in his arms and pulling her to him. He lifted her and carried her the few feet to the bed, laying her down softly. He helped her out of her nightgown and she undid the buttons on his trousers. For a minute or two, they just admired each other. Then Alexis took his face in her hands and kissed him gently on each cheek. "I love you Mr. Bissett."

"And I love you, Mrs. Bissett.

Joseph made passionate love to his wife, taking time to examine every inch of her beautiful brown body. He nibbled at her ear and placed soft little kisses down her throat and between her breast, carefully tantalizing every inch of her until her passion rose to meet his. They each carried scars from the whippings they received as slaves and neither was ashamed. Joseph kissed the scars on her back, wishing he could have been there to save her from that pain. Their love making did not stop until they were both spent of energy and fully satisfied.

While Joseph and Alexis were enjoying their first night together, Willis, Benjamin, Evans, Louis, and Isaac met in the dining room of the Bowman Catering Company.

"Have any of you seen that guy before today?" Louis asked.

"Yeah." Isaac said. "Joe and I saw him at the back of the church on Christmas."

"Yeah well, him showing up in public places alone, doesn't mean he is here alone." Louis said.

Constable Willis got up from the table and began to pace as he tried to recall anything suspicious happening in town. "There hasn't been any strangers around town since the weather began to cool. Maybe he is alone."

"NO!" Louis said emphatically. "No one would go in search of a murderer alone. Whoever is with this guy, they are staying out of town and we've got to find them."

"All right, then," Constable Willis said. "We'll begin our search in the morning. Say about seven? They must be making camp outside of town. We'll search all the best places to make camp."

"Joseph feared that this day would come and I just kept telling him not to worry," Isaac said.

"You were right," Benjamin offered. "There isn't anything for him to worry about. He and Alexis are fine. This threat will be taken care of one way or another." Isaac nodded, signaling his understanding of Benjamin's words.

The men met early the next morning as planned. They searched all of the known camp sites near Timbuctoo to no avail. There was no sign of anyone camping outside of town. By eleven o'clock the men were back in town and preparing to go to church. As Constable Willis made his way down Main Street toward the church, he saw Mr. Gale walking in the same direction and quickly caught up to him.

"Good morning Mr. Gale."

"Morning.," he said, surprise registering in his face as he turned to look at the Constable.

"I take it that you didn't find what you were looking for in our little town?"

He stopped walking. "No. I haven't found the man I'm looking for yet."

"What makes you think that he came here? Did anyone steer you in this direction."

"I probably shouldn't share this but an old woman named Markel who was an abolitionist was arrested for harboring runaway slaves a few months ago. That old woman kept meticulous records. It seems she gave a boat to three runaway slaves to aide in their escape up the Delaware about the same time that Josiah Gilbert went missing."

"Oh, I see. Well, they could have taken the river all the way to the New York border."

"There was a vicious storm on the river about that time. I doubt if they made it that far."

"Oh, you're right," the Constable said. "They could be at the bottom of the Delaware river."

At that, Gale stopped walking. "I hadn't thought of that possibility."

"This is a small town, Mr. Gale. If there was a Josiah Gilbert here, I'm sure I would know."

"Frankly Mr. Willis, I am tired of looking. I'm not a young man anymore. The story is, my brother beat Josiah's brother to death for laughing. He was told to give him twenty lashes but George has never been one to follow orders. Hateful from the day he was born. Josiah watched his brother being beat to death. I guess he just snapped. I wasn't there but my daddy made me promise, on his death bed, to find and kill the nigger that killed George. I sent my nephew first, but he never came back. The family assumes he met his demise somewhere between Maryland and Pennsylvania. So, I'm here, trying to honor a promise to a dead man."

By this time they were standing right in front of the church. The Constable watched George Gale carefully. The man was likely in his early forties and didn't appear to be the type of person to harbor animosity. "Do you have a family, Mr. Gale?"

"Yes. Married ten years and with three children, boys."

"Have you thought about what you will do if you come across this Josiah Gilbert? You don't strike me as a killer?"

"I would like to say that I would shoot him on sight but the truth is, I don't really want to kill anyone." He seemed to be contemplating the words Constable Willis spoke for a few moments.

"Mr. Gale, you are playing a dangerous game. If this Josiah killed your brother, what makes you think he won't kill you before you are able to shoot him?" Constable Willis didn't wait for an answer. "Besides, there is talk of a coming war. States are arguing over whether to free the slaves. Many people think slavery is an abomination. There are very strong feelings on both sides of this issue and I am of the mind that this war will happen. If this Josiah Gilbert is still alive, chances are, when this war is over Josiah Gilbert will be a free man. Go home Mr. Gale. Your father will not know if you found Josiah Gilbert and I'm sure you would rather be with your family during such trying times."

Gale seemed stunned at the Constable's words. There was a marked silence as the two men stood on the wooden sidewalk in front of the Methodist Church. "I assume you were coming to enjoy our church service this morning? You are certainly welcome." As

Constable Willis watched, Mr. Gale's shoulders seemed to rise before his eyes, as if he was shedding the long carried burden.

Heads turned as the two men entered the church together. Rebecca nudged Benjamin. Louis turned a perplexed look on Lillian but no one said anything and in seconds, all returned their attention to Reverend Evans at the podium.

"This scripture comes from the Book of John, Chapter thirteen, versus 34 and 35 . . ."

A new commandment I give unto you, that ye love one another; as I have loved you, that ye also love one another. By this shall all men know that ye are my disciples, if ye have love one to another."

The Reverend's voice rose and fell in dramatic fashion as he preached love for your fellow man. "God is love! You can't love God if you don't love your fellow man," he yelled. "We are all children of God."

Constable Willis glanced over at Mr. Gale who seemed to be blinking back tears. At the end of the service, the Reverend acknowledged the presence of a visitor. "Will you please stand sir, and tell us your name?"

George Gale reluctantly stood, his hat in his hand and visibly nervous. "My name is George Gale from Maryland," he stammered.

"Welcome George Gale. You are also welcome to join us in the dinning room for brunch this afternoon." There was a benediction and the service ended. Louis couldn't wait to speak with Willis to find out what brought Mr. Gale to their church again.

Constable Willis was the first to shake Mr. Gale's hand. "Thank you," George Gale said. "I am so grateful for our little talk and for the wonderful sermon by your Pastor this morning. I really needed to hear all of it. I never wanted to hurt anyone. I just felt a sense of obligation."

"You are never obligated to do anything against God's Word," the Constable said. They shook hands again and then every person in the church, both black and white, stopped to shake Mr. Gale's hand as they left the church. Louis heard the tail end of their conversation and was amazed. He was the last person to shake Gale's hand and wish him well on his journey back to Maryland.

F. Haywood Glenn

Chapter Eight
The Fight for Freedom

1863 - 1864

"Freedom is never voluntarily given by the oppressor,
it must be demanded by the oppressed." Martin Luther King, Jr.

By the fall of 1863, David and Samantha longed to spend some private time together, but the Bowman household was often too crowded for privacy.

On a cool Sunday afternoon, the Bowman household was bustling as the women prepared their usual Sunday dinner. When Rebecca finally called the family to dinner, Samantha and David sat across from one another. As the family chatted about the current news of the war, town gossip and Bowman business, David and Samantha made eyes at each other across the table. Catherine was the only one to notice but she said nothing.

As soon as the meal was over, Samantha began to help Rebeca with cleaning up the dishes and putting away the food. When her eyes met David's again, he tilted his head slightly toward the door. Moments later, she watched him slip quietly out of the back door unnoticed. As soon as the kitchen was all clean, Samantha also slipped away as quietly as she could. Catherine, again was the only one to notice. They met at the back of the house, far enough away from the window for anyone to see them in the fading day light.

At first, they just started walking toward the river. David took Sam's hand. "Do you remember the first time you held my hand?" She asked David.

He looked down at her with a smile. "No," he answered honestly.

"Your mother told you to take me inside the house and you took my hand. As dirty as it was, as dirty as I was, you took my hand and took me inside the house. Do you remember?"

"Yes, I do remember."

They walked in silence for a while. A gentle wind whistled through the tress as colorful leaves fluttered down from the trees, carpeting the forrest floor. "I think I know a place where we can be alone for a while," Samantha said. David smiled. "Follow me," she said as she took his hand and led him deep into the forrest. In time, they came upon a cave. David could tell that Samantha had been here before now. They gathered some twigs and rocks. After placing the rocks in a circle, David built a fire with the twigs. Soon the cave was nice and warm and the two lovers huddled together.

Feeling warm and comfortable in this quiet intimate space, Samantha felt the need to open up to David. She softly told him everything that she could remember about her life before the fire. "You know David, I do remember my mother."

"Really? I thought you didn't remember anything."

"I remember a lot. Maybe I didn't want to remember. I've tried to forget but memories have been coming back to me slowly. My mother wasn't a bad mother. She was happy most of the time. She was always laughing. I remember playing with her. We would hold hands, sing songs, and dance, even when there was no music." Sam was quiet for a time as more memories came back to her. "I also remembered the men who came to see my mother. Momma would take them into her room and close the door. My bed was in the kitchen and Momma would tell me to stay in my bed and never to come to her room. Back then, I didn't know what was happening in her room. I only knew that it was loud. The wood creaked, the springs squeaked, there was moaning and sometimes screaming and crying. Oh, and there were a lot of men." Samantha put her head down as if the memory was physically painful.

David did not interrupt Samantha. No one knew that she remembered anything. Now he knew that she remembered but was holding all of the bad memories inside. He wanted her to be able to get all those bad memories out.

"On the day of the fire, I remember her being really happy. She was singing when I woke up. We ate grits and biscuits for breakfast. Then a man came. I never saw this man before. He was a really big man and he was angry with my mother. He just kicked the door open and came in, screaming her name, 'Caroline.' She was startled and we jumped at the sound of his voice. He stormed over to her and picked her up by her throat. As he held her up in the air, her feet kicked as he held her too tight around her neck for her to scream. Then, he just threw her against the wall. He called her a bitch and said if she didn't stay away from his family, he would kill her. She struggled to get to her feet. At first she said she was sorry and in the next minute she screamed that she hated him. He left as quickly as he came but after he left, she began to scream and cry. She couldn't stop crying. She took the only oil lamp we had and smashed it against the wall. Orange flames started to crawl up the wall. Then she took me by the hand and we went into her room. She held me tight for a while, crying into my hair. I could hear the fire crackle as it took over the front room of our small house. I could see the smoke under the door.

'Momma, we have to go,' I said but she kept crying. Then she got up and walked into the front room. She walked right into the flames. I screamed at her, begging her to come back but she acted like she couldn't even hear me. She just kept walking. When the flames starting moving toward the bedroom, I climbed out of the window and ran until I couldn't run any more. I ran here. Right here in this cave. I didn't remember this until I heard you all talking about Alexis' father walking through the burning church."

"Do you remember how old you were?"

"I'm not sure. Maybe seven or eight. For a long time, I didn't know what to do or where to go. I just slept and cried. When it got cold, I took a blanket from a clothes line of a house near here."

David was looking at Sam in amazement. He didn't know what to say, so he just squeezed her a little tighter. "I don't know how long I stayed here. I stole food and clothes to keep warm but one day I just started to walk. I saw your mother in the backyard with Cathy and Lilly. I watched her for a long time. I came every couple of days. After a while I began to wish that she was my mother. I even pretended that she was my mother. Then I saw you in the back of the house. I was so hungry, but I was afraid to ask for anything. That day you walked right up to me and I was afraid. You had an apple. You talked to me, I don't remember what you said. I tried to talk but I couldn't. I could think what I wanted to say but the words just wouldn't come out. All I could think of was that apple and I just kept looking at it. Then you gave it to me. I took it and ran away."

She was quiet for a while and they just held each other. David shifted his body so that he could look into Samantha's eyes. He kissed her, suddenly wanting to relieve her of all the pain. He made love to Samantha that night and they stayed in that cave until late in the evening. "I think that I loved you from the moment you gave me that apple," Samantha said.

The family was unaware of the growing love between David and Samantha. It was easy for them to slip away to their special place and they did so as often as they could. However, that winter was one of the coldest winters in recent memory and lying naked in a cave in the woods was no longer a good idea. Their secret rendezvous had to sadly come to an end.

❧

Lillian Bowman had grown into a beautiful, well educated lady in the two years since her arrival at the Institute for Colored Youth. She was an eager learner and her teachers, both black and white, were staunch abolitionist. Community activism was encouraged and Lilly was an ardent participant. During her training, she was able to teach small classes in churches and Negro schools throughout Philadelphia. She loved the work, the lectures, often given by well known abolitionists, and articles in Philadelphia newspapers urging Negro men to join militias and to fight for their fellowman. All of these things shaped the woman Lillian Bowman became. She shared more than a name with her grandmother, Lillian Vance. Lillian Bowman was strong willed and smart.

She planned to go home during the week of Thanksgiving, 1863. However, those plans changed when she met a young seaman from

New York who was scheduled to ship out soon. Lilly and Mary, a classmate, were checking on a family in Philadelphia, whose ten year old little girl had not been to class in three days. It was late fall and the weather was exceptionally cold. It could be that the child was ill or didn't have the proper clothes to venture out in such weather. It was their mission to find out what was keeping her from attending school and do whatever they could to rectify the situation.

Mary knocked hard on the door of the brick row home in Northern Liberties. A tall, thin black woman answered the door. She had a gaunt expression on her face and her dry lips were pursed tightly together as if she tasted something bitter. "Yes," she said curtly.

"Good afternoon Mrs. Young," Lilly began. "I am Lilly Bowman and this is Mary Stern. We're from the Institute for Colored Youth and we are currently student teachers at the Lombard School. The school is concerned because they haven't seen Charlotte in school lately. Is she well?"

Immediately, tears welled in the woman's eyes. "No. My daughter is not well. She is very ill. In fact, we are hoping for a visit from a doctor from the Pennsylvania Hospital but I was told that no one would come. The hospital is over-whelmed with patients from the war. I'm afraid that if Charlotte does not get help soon, she will die."

Mary's face twisted in anguish and she blinked back tears that threatened to spill onto her cheeks. "I'm so sorry," Mary said.

"Look, Mrs. Young," Lilly began "I can't promise you anything but I will go to the hospital and see if I can convince them to send a doctor or a nurse to see your daughter. I'll do my best and I will pray for Charlotte's recovery."

The two young women quickly climbed back into their buggy. As Lilly pulled on the reins to steer the buggy out in the middle of the street, Mary put a hand on her arm. "We have no authority to go to the hospital for this woman. I think that you're going to get us into trouble."

Lilly thought for a moment. "Don't worry. I'll tell the school that it was all my idea. You have nothing to do with my decision. All right?" Mary did not look as if it was alright, but she said no more.

The hospital was just a few blocks away and Mary was content to just wait in the buggy. As Lilly entered the main lobby, she was struck by how beautiful the building was on the inside. A young white man sat at the main desk. His uniform was so formal, it looked like a military uniform. Lilly explained the situation to the young man, who could not hide his surprise. He instructed Lilly to have a seat while he went in search of someone who could help. It was nearly twenty minutes before the young man returned. "I think I found someone who can help," he said before he took his seat behind the desk again.

Within a few minutes, a young very dignified Negro man in a naval uniform approached. He was very tall, dark mahogany skin, with a thin mustache that curved around his full lips. He removed his hat and bowed deeply. "Good afternoon," he said. "I am Lieutenant Hamilton, Theodore Hamilton."

For a moment Lilly just stared up at him. 'This man is beautiful,' she thought. "I, I am Lillian Bowman," she stammered. ". . . and I am very happy to meet you, sir."

He smiled. "No need to call me sir. What can I do for you?"

That brought Lilly back to the situation at hand. "Well, I was hoping to get a doctor to come with me to see a ten year old girl that is very ill. Her mother was told that the hospital could not spare a doctor at this time, but the child is very ill. Her mother doubts that she will survive, if she does not get proper treatment as soon as possible."

"Well, you are in luck. I am free and I would be happy to examine this girl."

"Excuse me, but are you a doctor? I've never heard of a Negro doctor."

"Not exactly. I was a medical student at Trinity Medical College of the University of Toronto for three years. However, I did not graduate. The war began six months before my graduation and I was summoned by the Union Navy to be an on-board ship doctor, officially an Assistant Surgeon. I accepted and here I am." Lilly didn't realize that she was staring up at the Lieutenant. When he stopped speaking, she was still looking up at him with a dazed expression on her pretty face. "Miss Bowman, shouldn't we be going to see the young patient?"

"Yes," she said. After giving the doctor the address, she climbed back into the buggy with Mary.

"Let me get my bag and I'll meet you at this address."

During the ride over to the Young's home, Lilly told Mary about Dr. Hamilton. "Are you sure he's a real doctor?" Mary wanted to know.

"Yes, but it doesn't matter. He is as close to a real doctor as we are going to get. I'll just introduce him to Mrs. Young and then we can be on our way back to the boarding house."

"Good. I'm freezing. I can't wait to get back to my room in the house."

Dr. Hamilton diagnosed young Charlotte with Pneumonia. He gave Mrs. Young medicine and instructions and he promised to look in on them again in a week. Mrs. Young was very grateful.

Lilly was happy that she was able to help Charlotte and she thanked Dr. Hamilton before she turned to leave. Once they were out on the sidewalk, he said, "Charlotte will be fine. She looks more ill than she really is."

"Well, that is good news," Lilly said as she walked toward her buggy.

"I would like to see you again," he whispered. Lilly stopped walking and Dr. Hamilton moved very close to her. "I think I want to get to know you better. Where are you from?"

She glanced at Mary who sat bundled in a blanket, still shivering in the buggy. She smiled up at the doctor. "I was born in New Jersey then I became a student at the Institute for Colored Youth. Right now I'm doing some student teaching which will end at the end of this month."

"I see," he said with a smile.

"As much as I also would like to get to know you better, I think we should choose another time. It is much too cold out here and my classmate has been waiting in that buggy for hours now."

"Oh, I'm sorry." He said as he smiled that beautiful, brilliant smile and Lilly shivered, not from the cold. "Where can I call on you?"

She gave him the address of the boarding house where she was staying in Philadelphia. "I won't be available until after five."

"I'll see you then. Good afternoon, Miss Bowman."

"Goodbye Dr. Hamilton."

"I would like it if you called me Theodore or Theo."

"All right. Goodnight, Theo."

Lilly could hardly contain herself as she rode back to the boarding house. "Oh, Mary. Dr. Hamilton is the most beautiful man I've ever seen."

"Men aren't beautiful, Lilly. They are handsome."

"Not this man. He's beautiful to me, and he is so kind."

"Still, I've never heard of a Negro doctor. You should be careful." Mary warned.

❧

Though the Thanksgiving holiday had been celebrated since the founding of the country, on October 3, 1863, President Lincoln announced that November 26, 1863 would become an official Thanksgiving holiday. It was his way of showing his thankfulness for the great victory of the Union Army at Gettysburg.

Theo and Lilly spent Thanksgiving together in the dinning hall of the boarding house where she and Mary were guests. They told each other stories of their youth, education, and faith. They discovered that they had much in common. They were both Christians, had been educated by Quakers and they both had two siblings. Lilly confessed how much she missed her twin and he was amazed to learn that she lived in an all black town in New Jersey. They laughed and snickered and caught the eye of most everyone at the table, especially Mary.

The Bowmans, Bissetts, and Browns celebrated the Thanksgiving holiday at Althea's Boarding House. The war was the topic of conversation among the men.

"They are going to have to let Negroes fight," Louis said. "Men are deserting left and right. If Lincoln wants to win this war, he has to let the Negro fight."

"I agree," said Benjamin. "Besides, so many young black men want to fight. They want to have a hand in freeing our people."

"I know I want to fight," Joseph said.

"Me too," said David.

"What about you Isaac?" Benjamin asked,

"I guess, I do." Isaac said. He really had no desire to fight. He only went along with Joseph and David because he didn't want them to think he was a coward.

In January 1864 there was one snow storm after another which delayed the date that Theo was to ship out. This allowed Theo and Lilly to spend most of the spring together and Lilly decided to go home after Theo left. She gave him her address in Timbuctoo and he promised to find her after the war was over.

ᴥ

Finally, after months of eagerly waiting for word from the army, a letter arrived for Joseph. It was short and to the point. He had been accepted into the United States Union Army and should report to Camp William Penn, outside Philadelphia on May 15, 1864. He later learned that Isaac and David had received the same letter.

The young men of Timbuctoo, New Jersey left for Army training in early in June 1864. Besides Joseph, Isaac, and David, there were six other young men from their town, and many more from surrounding counties. The families met at Althea's boarding house to say their goodbyes. Louis would take them by wagon to the ferry in Camden. The ferry would take them across the Delaware River and a recruiter would be waiting to take them to the William Penn training camp, which was just outside of Philadelphia.

Miss Ida and Jesse were there to see Isaac off. Benjamin, Rebecca and Sam were there for David, and of course Lillian, Louis and Alexis were there to see Joseph off.

There was lots of kissing, hugging, heartfelt goodbyes and some tears. Alexis didn't want to let Joseph go until he promised to write as often as he was able. Rebecca kissed her son and held him close. "Remember David, we love you and we will be waiting for you to come home to us. I really don't want you to go but I know how much this means to you. Just be safe, honey. No heroics, you are already a hero to us."

"Mother, it is a war. There is no being safe. We are going because we want to fight."

Rebecca just shook her head. "I know, Honey, I know."

Samantha stood away from the crowd and David didn't see her right away. As he shook his father's hand and kissed his mother's cheek, his eyes scanned the crowd looking for Samantha. She was standing in the corner of the porch, with her back against the wall. To everyone's shock, young David quickly ran up the few steps to the porch. He took Samantha in his arms and kissed her soundly. She threw both arms around his neck and he lifted her off her feet as they kissed.

"Oh my!" Rebecca said.

"Don't look so surprised! This relationship has been happening right before your eyes. Even I knew that." Benjamin said.

"Did you know about this?" Lillian asked Louis.

"No. I had no idea." Louis said as he winked at his wife.

"I can't believe you all didn't know. It's no secret that Sam has always been sweet on David." Catherine said

"I can't believe you all knew and not one of you thought to tell me." Rebecca said.

"We thought you knew. It was obvious to everyone else." Catherine said.

There was a mixture of emotions on that day. Parents and lovers were proud of their young men for being brave enough to fight for a cause in which they believed. They were also sad to see them go, knowing that they would worry until they returned.

Chapter Nine
The Fight for Freedom
1863 - 1864

The LORD is near to the brokenhearted
and saves the crushed in spirit. Psalms 34:18 (ESV)

David had been gone only a couple of weeks, but Samantha ached for him. She missed his husky voice softly whispering just how much he loved her in her ear. She missed laying securely and comfortably in his arms. He was all she thought of day and night. Unable to share her feelings with anyone else, she spent less and less time with the family. However, with a family as close as the Bowmans, there wasn't much that could go unnoticed. They all knew that Samantha really missed David.

One evening when all three Bowman women were in the kitchen preparing supper, Rebecca asked the question that they all were thinking. "I wonder where Samantha goes when she leaves the house."

"I've seen her helping Reverend and Mrs. Evans at the church a few times," Mom Cathy offered.

"I think she still goes to that cave in the woods where she was living," Catherine said.

"Why on earth would she go there?" Rebecca asked.

"I don't know. I just know she really misses David."

Rebecca was quiet after that comment. She hadn't yet come to terms with Samantha and David as a couple. Just seeing them together made her wonder if David were truly in love with the girl or was this just an infatuation with her because she is white. Even so, she believed that if they ever to left Timbuctoo, they would face prejudice and racism everywhere they went.

The food was ready and the table was set when Samantha came in. All eyes turned toward her but Rebecca was the only one to speak. "Samantha! We were just talking about you."

Samantha looked from face to face. They all looked worried. "Why were you talking about me? Did I do something wrong?"

"No, Honey." Mom Cathy said. " It's just that we are worried about you because you have been so quiet. You don't spend much time with the family any more and we just want to know that you are all right."

"Why?"

"Because you've been so sad since David left." Rebecca said. "We know that you miss him but we all miss him."

Samantha sat down with a thud. "There is no need to worry about me. I've just been feeling a little sick. I can't seem to keep any food down, especially in the morning."

Mom Cathy's and Rebecca's eyes met over the table. Serving bowls and plates were passed around and no one said another word. They ate in silence for the entire meal. Benjamin was clueless. He hardly noticed the quiet as he ate his beef and potatoes with gusto. As soon as the meal was over, Catherine said, "Samantha and I will clean the dishes, Mother."

At that Benjamin gave Catherine, who never volunteered for kitchen clean-up at home, a questioning look. He glanced at his wife, who looked as if she had swallowed something very unpleasant. Her lips were pressed tightly together and her eyes were stretched wide open. It was obvious to Benjamin that there was something hidden behind those twinkling green eyes. "Thank you," she said to Catherine and she nodded her head toward Samantha.

"What's going on?" Benjamin asked his wife.

"I'm not sure," she whispered.

When her parents and grandmother finally left the room, Catherine began to chatter about the most mundane things she could think of and Samantha just looked confused and uninterested.

Finally, Catherine brought up the issue that they had all been thinking about. "Sam, I know that you love David, we all do."

Samantha was washing the dishes as Catherine dried them and stacked them to be put away. She gave no indication that she knew what Catherine was talking about. "Is your love for David like mine, like a sister's love for her brother, or is there something more that we should know about?"

Sam stopped washing dishes and turned to face Catherine. "I do not love him like a brother," she said bluntly. "David is much more than a brother to me. I just love him. I always have. I loved him even before I could say it, but I didn't know what it was I was feeling. Now that I know, and I can say what I feel, I love him even more. When I was all alone, sleeping in the woods, David was the only one to talk to me. He brought me food. He didn't care what I looked like or how I smelled. He was the kindest person I had ever met. I think that I loved him even back then."

Catherine put her arm around Samantha's shoulders. "Have you and David been intimate?" Sam just stared in confusion. "Have you had sex with David?"

Samantha smiled sheepishly. "Yes," she whispered. "We spent time together a couple of weeks before he left." Samantha hoped that Cat would ask her more about the time she and David spent together.

"How long have you been feeling sick?"

"I don't know. A while. Why?"

"Samantha, I think that you might be with child." Again, Samantha just looked confused. "I think that you might be carrying a baby. You could be getting sick in the morning because you're pregnant."

"Pregnant," Samantha repeated.

"Yes. I think that you are going to have a baby and you have to tell Mother and father."

Samantha just stared, wide eyed and speechless. "Pregnant," she repeated again. "Do you think Rebecca and Benjamin will be angry with me?"

"I don't think that they will be pleased, but what does it matter now? You are carrying their grandchild. They will just have to accept it."

"I might be having a baby?" She asked. Then she began to smile as the idea started to appeal to her. She threw her arms around Catherine's neck. "I will tell Rebecca and Benjamin right now. Will you go with me?"

"Yes, but let us finish the dishes first and then we will tell the family together."

Benjamin was in his favorite chair reading the paper, Rebecca was knitting socks and Mom Cathy was reading her Bible when Catherine and Samantha came into the front room. "Mother, Samantha has something to tell all of you," Catherine said and then she stepped back to give Samantha the floor.

Samantha was not nervous at all. In fact, she was beaming. She stepped forward, smiling and proudly announced, "I think that I'm having a baby." Because they all suspected as much, her statement did not illicit the reaction that she expected. They all just looked at her as if they expected more. "It's David's baby," she added. "David and I are having a baby!"

"Does David know?" Rebecca asked.

"No, but I'm sure he is going to be very happy when he finds out."

There was a marked silence. Again, it was Mom Cathy who first offered congratulations. Then they all came to congratulate Samantha and give her a hug. "You really are a part of the family now, Samantha," Catherine said. Benjamin kissed Sam on the cheek. "Welcome to the family," he said before he left the room.

Later, when Mom Cathy and Rebecca were alone, Rebecca expressed her displeasure with Sam's pregnancy. "David is just a boy. What does he know of relationships or having a child? She must have seduced him. I should have seen this coming," she said angrily. "I knew that David had eyes for her but I didn't expect that they would lie together."

"Why not?" Mom Cathy asked. "Believe me, Samantha didn't have to seduce David. He was a willing partner."

"How would you know that?"

"Huh," Mom Cathy smirked. "Our David isn't as innocent as you want to believe. I am quite sure that Samantha is not his first relationship with a girl."

"Again, how would you know that?"

"I pay attention to these children. We have all watched them grow up. They aren't children anymore, Rebecca."

"I know, but . . ." Rebecca's voice trailed off as Mom Cathy continued to speak.

"I pay attention to what they say to each other, where they go, and who they choose to spend their time with." She waited to see if Rebecca accepted what she was saying. "Rebecca, you are still thinking of David as a little boy. He is a grown man and he has been a grown man for a very long time."

Rebecca was quiet for a time as she tried understand how Mom Cathy knew so much about David and Samantha. "I am just not comfortable with this relationship." She finally said.

"Who says the you have to be comfortable with David's relationship? Don't get too self-righteous, Rebecca. Remember, you have a past that isn't so virtuous."

Rebecca was stunned. Mom Cathy had never brought up her past. They were quiet for a time but Rebecca was seething, even though she knew that Mom Cathy was right. She kept her thoughts to herself and focused her attention on the sock in her lap.

"Have you ever considered telling David that Benjamin in not his father?"

"No! Absolutely not. What would he think of me? You know that I was young and stupid. I just wanted a better life and I stupidly thought that a white man would make life easier for me." She stood abruptly, dropping the sock and yarn to the floor. "I pray every day that God will forgive that terrible indiscretion but I will never tell David and I'm begging you not to tell him."

"Don't worry. I would never do anything to hurt my family, especially David. I accepted him as my grandson as soon as I found out just how much my Benjamin loved you. Just as I accepted you because of my grandson's love for you, you must likewise accept Samantha because of David's love for her. Don't make this into a race thing. What has you so uncomfortable is the fact that she is white. You're thinking about what happened with David's father. Put it out of your head. That girl is as comfortable with us as if we were her family and as of now, we are."

Rebecca was silent for a long time. Finally, she said, "Thank you, Mom. I needed to hear that. You always know just what to say. I love you so much, Mom Cathy."

Later that evening, when she and Benjamin were alone in their bedroom, Rebecca repeated the entire conversation to Benjamin. He just smiled as Rebecca rattled on and on about how she didn't want David to be hurt by this relationship with a white girl. Benjamin let her finish because he knew that she had to get her feelings out before she could let this go. Finally, and very calmly, Benjamin said, "She isn't white Rebecca. She is mulatto just like your mother and David."

"What? How do you know that?"

"After the hurricane, we rescued a man that matched Constable Willis' description of the man he was sure was Sam's father. He was hurt, but not badly. He had a couple of broken bones but he was conscious. After leaving him at the hospital in Burlington, we went back the next day and confronted him about being Sam's father. He admitted to being married to Caroline, her mother, but according to Mr. Hunter, besides being promiscuous, Caroline was not mentally stable. She slept around. After catching her with several men, both white and black, he just left her. Never even saw the child. He suspects that Samantha's father is a black man who lived close by and was known to spend a lot of time with Caroline, but he has no proof. Apparently, Caroline burned her own house down in an effort to kill both herself and the child but Samantha escaped the fire and hid in the woods, where she lived until we took her into our home."

Rebecca sat on the bed stunned into silence. She couldn't help but wonder, for the second time, just how long that child was living like an animal in the woods. "Oh my," she said. "Aren't you surprised that David would lie with her?"

"No," Benjamin said emphatically. "David is a healthy young man. I'm surprised they haven't been together before now. You could see that they cared for each other as far back as Joseph's freedom celebration. Don't you remember.?"

"Yes, I do. You and Mom Cathy are right as usual. I will write David and tell him the good news."

"No. Let Samantha write to tell David. Of course, she will need help with her letter writing."

"Yes, as soon as possible."

✒️

After months of somewhat meager training, each man was assigned a regiment. There were black volunteers from Philadelphia, New Jersey, New York and Delaware; all very eager to join the Union Army. Joseph and David were able to stay together and were assigned to the 127th Colored Infantry Regiment. Following training, they joined the 10th Corps. Isaac was assigned to the 45th Colored Infantry which left Philadelphia for Washington, D. C. soon as his training ended.

Joseph and David couldn't wait to fight but instead of fighting, they spent their time marching and drilling. They were called upon to dig sinks, trenches, and graves. They were sometimes ordered to guard abandoned railroad depots. Their letters home were few but those that reached Rebecca and Lillian, were full of complaints of their current situation. It was rumored that the colored troops would never fight and since they had not been able to engage the enemy, they began to believe those rumors. The only reason that they were eager to join the army was so that they could fight. They wanted to be a part of the fight for freedom.

In the mean time, as the war between the states raged on, the young men were fighting another war. They were fighting a war against racism and prejudice in the Union Army. It wasn't long before they realized that their superiors were determined to use them only for menial labor and had no intentions of letting any of them fight. Although most of the young men were from northern states, free born, and educated, some of the generals treated the recruits as if they were uneducated and unqualified for military service. They were often openly hostile to the young Negro men. White soldiers spat at them and called them monkey or other derogatory names. It was clear that white soldiers did not want to fight along side of Negro soldiers. Some even had the notion that Negroes were the cause of the war and bore resentment against the Negro soldiers. Only determination and pure grit forced Joseph to hold his tongue and his fist. It was his strength that stilled the rage that boiled inside young David.

The Negro soldiers were paid $10 a month while white soldiers were paid $13 a month. Negro soldiers were charged $3.00 per month for clothing, reducing their pay to $7.00 per month, while white soldiers were paid an additional $3.50 a month clothing allowance. In an act of solidarity, the Negro soldiers decided to protest this unfair treatment by not to taking any pay until their pay was equal to the pay white soldiers received.

Things began to change when they started moving officers around. Even though the officers were all white, the new officers appeared not to be as racist. These officers were patriots. They cared more about winning the war than they cared about the race of the soldiers who were fighting the war. This made for much less tension in the company.

Finally, they were marching south again. When they marched through Maryland, even though it had been almost seven years since Josiah, now Joseph, had run away from the Atkins plantation, Joseph felt a knot in the pit of his stomach as they came closer to the plantation. The tension that he felt began to build as they passed sights that were very familiar to him. It was a very hot day and Joseph was sweating heavily. It seemed that they had been marching for hours before the order was given to stop and rest. He took a rag from his pocket and mopped the perspiration from his neck and face as did some of the other men.

Joseph and David sat on the ground with their back against a tree. Other soldiers just stretched out on the grass from pure exhaustion. The rest lasted for about twenty minutes before they were ordered to prepare to march again.

The sun was high in the sky and it felt like it was right over their heads. Joseph was not only exhausted, he was nauseous.

"You don't look so good," David said.

"I'm alright. It's just so hot."

When they stopped again, David poured water from his canteen over Joseph's head and neck. Joseph jumped when the cool water first touched his skin but he breathed deeply as the water ran down his face and neck. He wiped his face and smiled up at David. "Thank you. I needed that."

David shrugged. They both drank from their canteens. Joseph took several deep breaths and began to feel better.

"Look," David said. "Who would build a house out here? A lone house out in the middle of nowhere?"

Joseph looked up. His gaze following where David pointed. That lone house was Miss. Markel's house. You could see it from the road. It looked abandoned. Wood planks had been nailed over the windows and doors and Joseph couldn't help wondering what ever happened to the old woman. He remembered something about her being arrested. As he marched, he silently prayed that the woman who had helped him escape slavery had survived her ordeal and was somewhere peacefully living out her years with God's blessings.

David had never been out of New Jersey and what he witnessed was shocking. Slaves who were too old or physically infirm to be drafted into the Confederate Army, used the unrest as an opportunity to run away. Women, children, and old men left the cotton and tobacco fields, hoping to find freedom with the Union Army. They began to follow the Company. Some wore ragged clothes and carried bundles. Others had nothing but the clothes on their backs. Very few wore shoes. They cheered when they saw the Negro troops. At night they slept in the fields near the camp.

The first real battle Joseph and David faced came in late August in Petersburg, Virginia. It was nothing like the young men expected. Gunfire from so many guns was loud, and the cannons were even louder. The air was filled with smoke which burned their eyes and throat, making it difficult to breath. There were bodies, dead and dying, black and white, strewn across the blood soaked landscape. At one point, a fellow soldier was standing not more than a foot away from David, when he took a bullet right between his eyes. The soldier's blood splattered over David's face. The blast shook him to his core. He blinked and began to tremble as he watched the soldier's body fall to the ground. A perfect hole in the man's skull began to slowly ooze dark blood. David began to tremble from his shoulders down. Joseph put his arm around David's shoulders and held him tight to still the trembling as he led him away from the scene. "It's all right David."

"All right? What is all right?" David's voice was louder than he realized and heads turned in his direction. "None of this is all right," David said.

"It is all right to be afraid, David. We're all afraid."

David nodded his head slowly as if he understood, but in truth, he did not understand at all. He gathered himself though, loaded his rifle, and moved in to engage the enemy again. The battle seemed to go on forever. The sound of gunfire seemed to get louder and louder. Men's voices cried out as they were wounded, while other men screamed out as they attacked the enemy. When it was finally over, they all breathed a sigh of relief, collapsing on the ground from tension and exhaustion. Though they had won their first major battle, they did not feel a sense of victory or honor. Both were struck by the horror of it all. Joseph prayed out loud, thanking God for their survival. They spent nine months in Petersburg, Virginia, during which time there were six major battles.

In late September General Grant ordered an attack on Confederate fortifications near Richmond. Though it was late September, it was still scorchingly hot. Even in early morning, you could feel the heat before the sun rose. The extreme weather made the battle even more difficult. At one point, David lay in the trench, listening to screams of soldiers and the sound of bullets whizzing over head. For the first time since leaving home, he whispered a prayer. He asked God to end this madness.

He was in the trench for so long that his legs began to cramp. As he carefully lifted his head, he saw that a line of Confederate troops were moving far left of their line. At first, David was confused but it soon became very clear that they intended to swing around and come up behind the Union line. That would put the company in a crossfire. They were already outnumbered, making this a deadly situation. David crouched down as low as he could get and crawled over to the Major. The gunfire was so loud that he knew that he could not be heard. He used his hands to motion to the Major, making him aware of the confederate line moving to the left. The Major instructed David to lead about thirty men behind that Confederate line. When the Confederates began to fire on the Union Army, they did not expect an attack to come from their rear. There was no where for them to run. They were surrounded. Union forces won that battle and took many prisoners of war. David and the soldiers who followed him behind the Confederate line were awarded for their bravery.

It never got any easier. Every battle was worse than the one before, but they fought bravely, prayed often and both young men couldn't wait until the war came to an end and they were allowed to return to home.

In late October 1864, the Union Army attacked Confederate forces in Henrico County, Virginia. The battle raged for two days and the Union took a grave loss. One morning, fifty men were missing from their post. By the end of the day they were presumed deserted. Moral began to wane.

Upon entering their tent that evening, Joseph began to pray out loud again as he settled himself on his pallet. "Why are you always praying?" David wanted to know.

"I pray because prayer works and I believe in Jesus Christ. Don't you pray?"

"Yeah, but not as much as you and not out loud. You been praying since the first battle and we are still fighting and watching men die every day. When is this war is gonna end? "

Joseph mopped the sweat from his face and neck and laid down to go to sleep. "Remember David, we signed up for this. Every night that we drag ourselves back to this here raggedy tent and take a breath of what little bit of air there is in this sweltering state, I know that God has answered my prayers. We have survived another day, another battle."

David didn't say anything else. He made himself comfortable on his own pallet and tried to read the letter that was given to him on his return to camp. The moon provided only a sliver of light shining through the tent flap. David assumed that the letter was from his mother, and made up his mind to put it away until morning. Then he saw Samantha's name on the envelope and he bolted upright and darted from the tent. The letter was written in Samantha's untrained hand but the words were, more than likely, his mother's.

He began to smile as he read. The more he read, the broader his smile became until he gave a loud shout of joy. Back into the tent he yelled for Joseph to wake up. "Samantha is going to have a baby!" He shouted. "Can you believe it? She is going to have a baby sometime in May."

Joseph raised on one elbow. "Of course I can believe it. Don't tell me that I have to explain to you just how this works," Joseph said with a smile before he embraced David. "Congratulations man," he said. "Did she say how your Mom and Dad are taking this bit of news?"

"No, but I'm sure they will be fine with Sam giving them a grandchild."

"Yeah, I guess."

"Don't worry Rev, I plan to marry Samantha as soon as I get back home. She also says that Isaac is home. He was injured and they sent him home."

"You don't say!" Joseph silently prayed for Isaac and Samantha. He and David were both quiet for a few minutes. He thought he heard David whisper a prayer and they soon fell asleep.

◆

Isaac did not fare as well as Joseph and David. He was injured by a canon blast that blew off his left foot. The only reason he didn't bleed to death was that he was also captured by Confederate forces.

His ankle was wrapped tightly to stop the bleeding before taking him from the battlefield. He and five other men were chained together and transported by wagon to a prison tent in a Confederate camp. They were there for four days. During that time, Isaac's wound kept bleeding and the pain was unbearable. The loss of much blood made him so weak that he could hardly sit upright to eat. A Confederate doctor came into the prison tent to treat the wounded. He was given a strong drink before the doctor cauterized his wound to stop the bleeding. The pain of that procedure caused Isaac to loose consciousness. The doctor also gave him medication to prevent infection and to help with the pain.

The men were supposed to be transported to a prison camp in North Carolina. It was August and the heat was dreadful. The prison tent was stifling and the stench of blood, medication, and unwashed bodies was smothering. Isaac slept a lot and was plagued by terrible nightmares. He would awake screaming and lashing out. The other prisoners were in no better shape. The injured soldiers were often wailing and screaming throughout the night.

It was just one of those sweltering August nights when the prisoners were awaken by gunfire. Light flashed outside the tent and they could hear men yelling back and forth. The prisoners soon realized that the camp was being attacked by Union forces and they all began to cheer.

Isaac was soon treated by a Union doctor and told the he would be sent home as soon as possible. He wasted no time in writing to his mother to tell her of his injury and that he would be coming home.

♨

A few weeks after the young men left, Lillian was surprised when Louis handed her a letter from the day's stack of delivered envelopes. "For me?" She asked.

"Yeah. You got a letter from Beth in Philadelphia."

Lillian's eyes brightened at the thought of a letter from Elizabeth. The war had changed all of their lives in one way or another, especially the mail service. Though she and Elizabeth kept regular communication, it had been quite a while since she had heard from her friend.

Lillian took the envelope and sat down to in the rocking chair in front of the fire to read.

September 07, 1864

My Dearest Lillian,

I hope this letter finds you and your family well.

I regret to inform you that after a long bout with pneumonia this past fall, my dearest husband, Jefferson has passed on. His physician did everything he could, but the infection seemed to hang on and Jefferson was not strong enough to fight it through. He went quietly in his sleep two days after Thanksgiving, Saturday, November 28, 1863.

I apologize for not writing sooner but my life has not been the same since Jefferson's passing. I don't mind telling you that I have been overcome with grief. It has taken this long for me to come to terms with Jefferson's death.

Things are even move complicated by the war. The atmosphere here in Philadelphia is perilous at best. There has been an influx of Union soldiers, Abolitionists, and Confederate deserters in the city. There has even been some rioting in the streets.

Though I would like nothing better than to visit you and the family, I believe that travel at this time is much too dangerous under such circumstances.

I can't tell you how much I miss your companionship. I take pleasure in reminiscing of those cold winter days when we sat in my parlor, you reading from the scriptures while my attention was taken by my latest needlepoint project. We've come along way, you and I; from slave and mistress, rivals in love, to genuine friends as close as family.

I promise to travel to New Jersey as soon as it is safe to do so. I miss you all so very much and with Jefferson gone, there is nothing to keep me here in Philadelphia.

Until then, stay safe my friend. You are continually in my prayers.

Yours Sincerely,
Elizabeth Vance Martin

Lillian read Beth's letter with a heavy heart. She regretted that they had not been in touch as often as she thought they should, however they both understood that these were complicated times. She was sad for her friend, who had now buried a second husband.

"You don't look happy," Louis observed.

"I'm not happy. This is a very sad letter. Jefferson has died and now Beth is all alone."

"Really?"

"Yeah, apparently he died of pneumonia back in November." Lillian was quiet as she said a silent prayer for her friend. "She says that when the war is over, she might be coming to New Jersey for a visit."

Louis looked surprised but he said nothing for a minute or two. "I'm sorry Jefferson has passed on and your friend is all alone but things will work out for her, I'm sure. She is certainly welcome to visit at any time." By then, Lillian was deep in thought, imagining life with Beth there in New Jersey. Louis just kissed her forehead and left the house by the backdoor.

❧

Isaac returned to Timbuctoo in September 1864. Louis was happy to pick Isaac up from the ferry. He happily greeted him with a big smile, a big bear hug and a hand shake, but Isaac did not look happy. Louis watched as he struggled to carry his bag while leaning heavily on his crutches. He quickly offered to help but Isaac waved him away. "This is my life now, Mr. Bissett. I better get used to walking with only one foot."

Although it made him sad, Louis understood. Once they were in the wagon and heading home, he tried talking to Isaac again. He asked a few questions about the war but, he quickly realized that Isaac was in no mood for conversation. From that point on, they rode in relative silence. It was obvious to Louis that Isaac's injuries were having more than a physical effect on the young man. He also realized that Isaac needed time to come to terms with his disability. Everyone would have to give Isaac all the time he needed. They would talk when Isaac was ready to talk.

Miss Ida and Jesse planed a welcome home celebration and invited practically the entire town. The Bissetts, Bowmans, and Evans were all there to welcome him. All his favorite foods were prepared and set out on a long table. He was welcomed home with hugs and hearty hand shakes and pats on the back. Most of the men assured Isaac that he would learn to get on fine with one foot. He couldn't help feeling that it might have been better if he had lost his entire leg. He had seen soldiers with artificial legs but there was nothing to be done about a missing foot.

Isaac had known most of the people who came to celebrate his homecoming all of his life. He also knew that they were genuinely happy that he made it back alive and they would not love him less because his right foot was missing. The problem was, he was having a hard time loving himself. They were having a good time but Isaac couldn't wait until they all left. He wanted nothing more than to be alone with his misery.

The celebration lasted well into the evening, but eventually everyone except Catherine left. She was helping Miss Ida clear the dishes and food away when Isaac hobbled into the kitchen, his crutches thumping on the floor. It was as if he was seeing Catherine for the first time. He asked himself why he had never noticed what a beautiful girl Cathrine had become? David's little sister was no longer little. Catherine was tall, poised, and very pretty. She was beautifully brown with light brown eyes and full lips. How did she grow into such a beauty without him ever noticing her? He really wanted to say something to her but it was like his tongue was stuck in his mouth.

Finally he said, "Ma says that you helped with the cooking."

"I did. I hope you enjoyed the food."

"I did."

"Good." For a moment or two they just looked at each other without saying a word. "It's getting late. I should go," Catherine said.

"Yeah, I would offer to walk you home but that might be a problem." He regretted those pitiful words as soon as they left his mouth but Catherine just smiled at him.

"I'm sure we will be able to have that walk one day. It will just take some time." Isaac was so shocked at Catherine's response that he just stood there staring at her. *'I'm an idiot,'* he told himself.

"I'm gonna go. Sam is waiting for me outside," Catherine said. Isaac just waved. He didn't trust himself to speak again.

His leg was still very painful. The pain would come on suddenly, like a sharp knife being plunged into the foot that was no longer there. He saw the entire incident in his dreams almost every night since it happened. It had gotten so bad that he was sometimes afraid to go to sleep. He got into the habit of drinking until the liquor had dulled his brain so much that he could sleep without dreaming. It wouldn't be so easy to do now that he was back home. He had a bottle of whiskey in his bag and as soon as Catherine closed the door behind her, he wanted nothing more than to drink until he passed out. Jesse offered to help him up to his old room, but he refused.

"Mother, if it is all right with you, I really don't want to bother with the steps just yet. I want to sleep down here."

"I don't think you will be very comfortable on this old sofa but it will be all right for tonight. Tomorrow we will find something more comfortable. You can sleep down here as long as you like."

For the first couple of months after Isaac's return home, he was sad and dispirited. Jesse helped by buying the alcohol for him and they kept it from their mother as best they could. He knew that his mother would never stand for a drunk son, laying around feeling sorry for himself. He had to shake this thing off.

&s

Catherine and Sam had begun to spend a great deal of time together. Catherine was happy to fill in for her brother, helping Samantha with reading and writing. The two girls were close in age and with David and Lilly gone, Samantha seemed more open to the friendship. Catherine had always felt that Sam was like a sister and when she first came into the family, the twins were fascinated with Samantha. A mute girl living all alone in the woods was like a story from one of the books they read as children. Now, six years later, Samantha was definitely a part of the family.

It was late August when Samantha received her first letter from David. She struggled through it but was very proud that she was able to read his letter to the family. They were in Virginia and he wrote that there was a battle almost every day. He didn't say much more than that about the war, except that he and Joseph were fine and could hardly wait until the war was over. "Your good news is what keeps me fighting as hard as I can, so that I can come back to you." He was sorry to hear about Isaac and planned to write to him soon.

When she finished reading the letter, she noticed tears in Rebecca's eyes. Benjamin put his arms around his wife and held her for a few moments.

That night, when Catherine and Samantha were alone in their bedroom, Sam blurted out the question that she had wanted to ask Catherine for some time. "Cat, why don't you have a beau?"

In the weeks since David had been gone, Samantha and Catherine had become very close. Catherine was amazed at how much Sam loved their family and especially her parents.

Catherine just glared at her in shock. Once Samantha began talking, she had a habit of just blurting out whatever was on her mind. You never knew what she would say. "I don't know, Samantha. I think I just haven't met a man that I liked very much."

Samantha made a face, twisting her mouth.

"What?" Catherine asked

"You do like a man and I know who."

"Then you know more than me."

"I saw the way you looked at Isaac when we went to Miss Ida's the other day. You're sweet on Isaac."

"No! I just feel sorry for him. He goes off to the war and he comes back in a matter of months without a foot."

"He seems to move around pretty good with one foot. Plus, I also caught him staring at you. You might feel sorry for him but he's got eyes for you."

Catherine was quiet. She knew that Samantha was right. She had a crush on Isaac since she was a little girl, but she was surprised that

Samantha was able to figure that out. "All right Samantha, but how did you know?"

Sam shrugged. "I don't know. I just watched the way he looked at you and the way you looked at him and turned your head every time you thought he was going to look your way. I saw it even before he went off to fight in the war."

Catherine pretended not to hear as she slipped her nightgown over her head. Samantha did the same. After Catherine turned out the lamp and climbed into bed, again she said in a very low voice, "You were right, Samantha. I think I've liked Isaac for as long as I can remember but he always treated me like a little girl. Sometimes he acted as if he didn't even know that I was around."

"Well, maybe that was when you were just David's little sister. Believe me Cat, Isaac has noticed you and I think that he likes what he is seeing," Samantha said sleepily.

They were both quiet for a few minutes. Catherine was beginning to fall asleep when Samantha said, "David thought that I was in love with Joseph and jealous of Alexis."

"Really?" This bit of news jolted Catherine awake and she leaned up, propping herself on one elbow.

"Yes, so I had to tell him that it was him that I loved. I'm thinking that you are gonna have to tell Isaac how you feel, especially now."

"Why especially now?"

"I don't think he's feeling really good about himself right now, being that his foot has been blown off. He could use a friend."

Catherine thought about that for a few moments. Samantha's breathing soon took on the soft cadence of sleep, but Catherine was wide awake now. 'When did Samantha get to be so wise,' she silently questioned. Samantha was a lot smarter than any of them knew. Catherine thought, maybe all those years of listening and not speaking gave her some sort of insight. I'm going to take her advice and pay more attention to Isaac.

Catherine would get the opportunity to spend time with Isaac on a warm September afternoon. Rebecca noticed that Isaac had not attended church since he came home and she suggested that they pay a visit to Miss Ida's to see just how he was getting on. Miss Ida and Jesse were in the bakery. The house was just next door. It just so happened that Rebecca and Catherine came into the bakery just as Miss Ida was about to take her son a prepared lunch. "I'd be happy to take Isaac his lunch. Catherine and I wanted to look in on him and see just how he's doing," Rebecca said.

"Oh, thank you. I was waiting for a free moment but today I have been just so busy. I appreciate this Rebecca. I left the door unlocked because I didn't want Isaac to have to get up to open it. Just knock first."

There was no answer to Rebecca's soft knock. She waited a minute and knocked again before opening the door. Isaac was stretched out on the sofa and he jumped at the sound of the door opening. "Hello, Isaac," Rebecca said as she slowly walked into the house with Catherine right behind her.

"Hello, Isaac," Catherine said.

"Hello." Isaac sat up wiping at his sleepy eyes.

"We just wanted to see how you were getting on." No answer. "We haven't seen you in church lately."

"I am getting on as well as anyone could with a missing foot!"

Rebecca's eyes opened wide in surprise at Isaac's curt response. "Look, I know that you may be feeling a little down because of your accident but now is the time for you to be strong. There are people, soldiers who have not come home from this war at all. Fathers, brothers, and husbands did not come home. Many buried in mass graves in southern towns that they never knew. They have left wives, children and parents that will never see them again. You came home, Isaac. Yes, your foot was blown off and I can't tell you how sorry I am that you have experienced such loss but God spared you. I don't know why but he spared your life. Now it is up to you to do something with that life." Rebecca stopped talking and just watched Isaac for a few moments.

"I know that it won't be easy, Isaac. You are going to have to learn to live as your are now and not as you were before the war. The good thing is that we are all here to help in anyway you need," said Catherine.

For a moment Isaac just sat there stone faced and then tears began to spill from his eyes. Rebecca immediately went to sit beside him on the sofa. She wrapped her arms around him and he cried on her shoulder while Catherine stood by watching. For a few moments, no one said anything. When he finally sniffed back his tears and lifted his head from Rebecca's shoulder, and very softly said, "Thank you."

"I smell the whiskey." Rebecca whispered. "Whiskey will heal you. Whiskey will not help you walk or feel better about yourself. You may have to use one or two crutches for the rest of your life, I don't really know. So I think it is time for you to start learning just how you will do that. You have to start somewhere."

"I will help you," Catherine said. "I'll come by whenever I get the chance so that we can walk together."

Isaac's face lit up. "I would really like that. Is that a promise?"

"Yes," Catherine said. That is a promise."

Rebecca gave Isaac the lunch that his mother had prepared for him and then she went to the kitchen to make tea. They spent the rest of the afternoon drinking tea and chatting. Isaac told of some of his experiences in the war before the accident and Catherine and Rebecca caught him up on town gossip. When they finally left, Isaac had a smile on his face.

Catherine kept her word   and went by Miss Ida's whenever she got the chance. During some of her visits, Isaac said very little. She would not pressure him to talk if he wasn't in the mood. Sometimes she would just take his hand in hers and they would just sit for a while. He was in pain much of the time and would complain that the foot that was no longer there gave him pain. The Confederate Surgeon who had stitched close the bottom of Isaac's leg to stop the bleeding and prevent infection, had done a magnificent job. The stump had healed smoothly but Isaac still found it difficult to put any pressure on the end of his leg. Even so, there was continued progress. He had learned how to walk more easily on his crutches, which meant that he could do for himself and be more independent.

Later that September, Isaac received a letter from Joseph. He told Isaac how sorry he and David were to hear about his injury. He also promised that once the war was over and they were all together again, they would help Isaac in anyway possible. Hearing from his friends seemed to lift Isaac's spirits.

When the weather finally began to chill in late October, Isaac finally asked Catherine to walk with him. "Where shall we walk?" She asked.

"Let us walk to Miss Althea's. I haven't seen her since I came home and the boarding house isn't that far away."

"That's a great idea."

He used the one crutch and Catherine held the other hand. The walk was slow but Isaac seemed in good spirits and Catherine felt that they were becoming closer. Althea was happy to see them both and served them tea and cake. The whole thing took no more than an hour but the walk to and from the boarding house, seemed to tire Isaac.

Even so, their walks continued and they walked further every couple of days.

F. Haywood Glenn

Chapter Ten
Fall 1864

Jealousy and revenge, are fodder for an evil heart!

There were very few new residents in Timbuctoo since the war broke out. The hotel and Althea's boarding house were experiencing some financial loss as fewer and fewer people were looking for rooms. Althea had always been good with managing her property. She had diligently saved to prepare for the uncertain times she knew that the war was likely to bring. She wasn't yet at the point where she needed to worry about money. She currently had only three residents. A young couple who had planned to move to Maryland, but the war altered their travel plans. They decided that it would be better to stay at the boarding house until it was safe to move further south. An older black gentleman also moved in after the war began. He was on his way to

New York, where at the time, the city was plagued by riots over the Conscription Act. The rents were minimal but Althea was able to manage.

It was a very hot July when a young white man showed up at the office to rent a room. He said that he had come from Vermont and planned to cross the Delaware and move into Philadelphia where a new job awaited him. He only needed a room for a few days. The young man was tall and thin with blond hair and ice blue eyes. He was clean shaven and well dressed. He volunteered information not asked of him. He told Althea that he was applying for employment as a clerk in the legal profession. In fact, he was so well dressed that Althea did not recognize him. "May I have your name, sir?"

"Williams," he said. "Nathaniel Williams"

Althea wrote his name down without a second thought. He requested a room in the back of the house where he would be far enough away from the sounds of a bustling town. She took him to a room facing the back of the house on the second floor. All of the rooms in the boarding house were large rooms with large windows. Red Oak trees shaded the back of the house so those rooms were much cooler than those on the front of the house. Althea briefly went over the rules of the house before she handed him a key to his room.

"Don't I get a key to the front door?"

Althea chuckled a little. "No sir," she said. "The front door is open until nine o'clock in the evening. You only get a key to your room. Have a nice day, Mr. Williams."

Later that day, Alexis went to take fresh linen to the new guest. She tapped on the door and waited for a response. No one answered so she took her key and opened the door. "Hello," she softly called. There was no answer. The room appeared to be empty so she took a few steps into the room to place clean towels on the wash stand. "Here is your linen," she softly said. When she turned to leave, her way was blocked by the tall blond man. Alexis recognized him immediately.

"Well, hello, pretty lady. Surprised to see me, I guess?"

Alexis tried to step around him but he blocked her way again. "You know, I was in that wretched prison for an entire year and I thought of you every single day. I kept thinking that I should not have gone to prison at all. I didn't actually do anything. You are the one that should have been arrested. You assaulted me, remember? You assaulted a white man and I'm sure that you think that you got away with it."

Alexis tried to slowly move around him again and toward the door but as soon as he saw her move, he moved to block her way again. "Aren't you going to say anything? I think that I deserve an apology. I don't even know your name, but you know mine, don't you?"

"Let me pass," she said through clinched teeth.

"You remember that day in the church? I can't forget that day, I got a nice little scar, right here to remind me." He pointed to a tiny scar at his temple where she had struck him with the soup ladle. "You know," he paused, letting his eyes roll up and down Alexis' body. "I wanted you real bad that day. I watched you moving around, swaying your hips and smiling down at everyone like you were above us all. I don't think I ever stopped wanting you. For a year, you were all that I could think about."

Alexis leaped for the door but he quickly kicked it shut and grabbed her around the waist in one swift move. She fought as hard as she could but he was as strong as he was determined. He swung her away from the door, then without warning he punched her hard in the face. The punch dazed Alexis and she felt herself slowly falling toward the floor. He caught her before she hit the floor and lifted her off of her feet. He punched her again before throwing her onto the bed. She tasted the blood that oozed from the corner of her mouth. When she looked up, she saw him just standing there staring down at her with an evil smile on his thin face. In the next moment, he was on her and when she tried to push him away, he hit her again. She was not only dazed by that punch but lost her breath. She tried with all her might to push him off, but she just couldn't move him. He would not budge. He became like a ravenous animal, crazed with revenge and desire. He didn't just pull her skirts up, he violently ripped her clothes away. The fabric tore through her flesh as he pulled and yanked at her clothes. "Please don't," she pleaded as she still fought as hard as she could. He forced her legs open with his feet and she brought her knee up as hard as she could, trying to stop his vindictive assault, but he moved away too quickly for her knee to reach him. She was no match for this kind of evil intent. He punched her again and again, before he plunged into her, taking her hard and violently. Alexis cried out for help and he quickly put a hand over her mouth as he slammed into her, over and over, moaning and groaning with pleasure. Tears began to stream from her eyes and her screams became muffled whispers. Every so often, he would punch her again. It seemed to go on forever. Eventually, she stopped fighting and just lay there, all her resolve falling away. He punched her one last time before he turned her on her stomach and continued his assault from the back. She lost consciousness with the last punch. Her lifeless body just laid there and even that did not stop him. When he was finally finished his brutal assault and pulled away from her, he smiled as he looked down on her bruised and battered body.

"That will teach you that with all your airs about being free, you still just a nigger wench." He gathered all of his things and left Alexis sprawled on the bed naked, bloodied and unconscious.

It was hours later when Nan noticed that Alexis had not been seen for an hour or more. "Where is Alexis?" Nan asked Althea.

"I don't know. The last I saw of her, she was taking fresh linen to our new guest." Althea and Nan looked into each other's eyes and they somehow knew that something was wrong. Both women hurried up the steps to the room that Althea had rented to the new guest. "Oh my God!" Althea whispered as she entered the room.

Alexis was still unconscious. Nan immediately sent for the doctor. Dr. Benson, a Quaker who moved to New Jersey from Philadelphia more than thirty years ago. It took the doctor about thirty minutes to arrive and Nan began to clean the dried blood from Alexis face as they waited.

After examining Alexis, the doctor assured Althea and Nan that although the attack was vicious and cruel, Alexis suffered no lasting damage. Her bruises would eventually heal. The man had pummeled her face and both her lips were swollen and distorted. She had been cruelly brutalized. Her entire body was marked with bruises on her arms, chest, back, eyes and her cheeks. One cheek was so swollen, Althea was sure it was likely fractured. Her eyes were swollen shut. When she finally regained consciousness some hours later, she mumbled, "It was him."

"Who?" Althea asked. "Who did this to you?"

"It was the same man who tried to rape me in the church."

Althea was stunned into silence. Why hadn't she recognized that white boy. She looked him right in the face but did not see the same homeless boy that had taken shelter in the church a year ago. She couldn't help feeling that she was somewhat to blame for what happened to Alexis. Nan and Jacob assured her that it wasn't her fault but every time she looked at Alexis' battered face, she became consumed with guilt. She gave Alexis time to recover. She made it her business to personally nurse Alexis back to health. Althea brought

Alexis' meals to her room. She washed and bandaged her wounds every afternoon.

Denny took on the responsibility of caring for Jay. After a couple of days had passed, Denny took Jay to visit his mother at least once a day during her recovery.

Alexis cried every day. Every part of her body ached. She kept wondering if she could have done anything different that would have avoided such a confrontation with that man. She asked herself how could a person who really didn't know her, harbor such hate for her. She did strike him, but only because he attacked her in the church. Though these questions weighed heavily on her heart, she knew that there were no satisfying answers.

At first Alexis was afraid to look in the mirror. It was nearly two weeks later when she finally looked at herself. Her face was healing and she was sure that in time, it would heal completely. But she would never be the same.

Alexis was afraid most of the time. She would jump in fear at the slightest sound. She also began to spend much of her time alone. She stopped going to Sunday service and attending the weekly dinners held by Rebecca, Lillian, or Althea. She missed Joseph more than anything but she did not want to tell him what happened while he was away. She spent countless hours pondering just how she would tell him and how this would effect their marriage.

ॐ

The winter of 1865 was not as bad as 1864 but the Northeast was beset by plummeting temperatures and one snow storm after another. In mid-February the east coast was hit by a snow storm of at least ten to twelve inches and temperatures that hovered between fourteen and nineteen. No one ventured outside.

At the end of January, Althea celebrated her sixtieth birthday. That same month, she developed a persistent cough. Lillian was not only worried for Althea's physical health, but her friend had not been the same since Alexis was assaulted. The depression that had claimed so much of Althea's life almost eight years ago had returned. Moving to Timbuctoo had allowed her to escape that first bout with depression. Now, Lillian wasn't sure that anything would lift her depression.

She moved around the house in a haze of guilt and sorrow, as if she were all alone. That jovial, welcoming personality had vanished. She rarely spoke to anyone in the house, but she was constantly talking to someone. She cleaned the house obsessively while she incoherently mumbled under her breath much of the time. Occasionally, her voice would rise as if she were angry with someone. No one knew who she was talking to but it was clear that Althea was suffering mentally.

She did all of the cooking as usual and gave orders for the management of the house but nothing more. When the work was over, Althea quickly escaped to her room and was often not seen again until the next morning.

Nan slowly began to take over the running of the house, which was relatively easy because there were so few guests in the house.

Lillian spent more time with Althea in the hope that she could help her friend get over her feelings of guilt. She tried to convince her that she could not have known of the evil lurking in that young man's heart. Althea acted as if she hadn't heard a word. No matter what anyone said, she had convinced herself that she could have somehow prevented the assault.

In the middle of February, the east coast was hit with another snow storm that dumped over a foot of snow. All movement on the river came to a complete stop and nothing moved in Timbuctoo. Althea caught a chill, which brought back the alarming cough she had contracted earlier that winter. The storm kept Lillian from getting to the boarding house for a few days. Nan and Alexis did the best that they could to nurse Althea back to health.

Alexis fed Althea chicken soup and lots of honey tea. Despite all of her efforts, Althea woke one morning with a fever. When Nan came to check on Althea, she found her sitting in front of the fire wrapped in a blanket. The room was stiflingly hot and Althea was sweating profusely. Nan knew she had a fever even before she put her palm on Althea's forehead. She and Alexis tucked Althea into bed and began to take turns bathing her brow with cool water in an attempt to break the fever. It took weeks, but the fever finally broke. Nan and Alexis were both hopeful that Althea would recover but Althea began to refuse meals. It seemed to Nan that Althea had just given up. She drank a lot of tea but she rarely took her meals. Her weight loss was striking.

When Lillian was finally able to visit, she was struck by how different her friend looked. The broad smile that usually welcomed everyone, was gone. Her skin looked dull and sallow. Her hair had started to fall out, leaving her hairline thin and wiry. Lillian sat and drank tea with Althea for more than an hour but Althea hardly said a word. When she left Althea that evening, she had a bad feeling churning in the bottom of her stomach. She kissed Althea on the head and promised that she would be back in a few days. Althea simply nodded.

It was very cold evening and Alexis went to Althea's room to bring her supper, Althea refused the meal. The fire had almost gone out and the room was freezing. Alexis left the tray on the bedside table and threw a couple of pieces of wood on the fire. When she turned to leave, she heard Althea's weak and raspy voice call her name. She went and sat on the side of the bed, taking Althea's hand in her own. "What is it, Althea?"

"I want you to know that I really did not recognize that white boy. I was so interested in renting the room that I never really looked at him. I am so sorry for what happened to you. Alexis, please say that you forgive me. I have been miserable about it every since it happened. I need to know that you forgive me."

"Althea, there is nothing to forgive. You didn't do anything wrong. I never blamed you, in the first place. If anyone is to blame, I blame myself. If I had let him take what he wanted in the church, he wouldn't have harbored such revenge against me for an entire year. Maybe he wouldn't have wanted to hurt me so bad."

"That isn't true, Alexis. He is an evil man. If it wasn't you, it would have been some other young woman. The man is just pure evil."

"Yes. If that is true, then there is no reason for you to feel guilty. I don't want to think about it anymore, Althea. I don't blame you and you have to get over this. You're my big cousin from Philadelphia, remember. I need you to get over this." Both women had tears in their eyes. Alexis bent down and placed a kiss on Althea's head before she left the room. Althea died in her sleep that night.

Lillian was beyond distraught. Althea was Lillian's first and only friend for years. Of course, she and Beth grew to be friends but when she had no one, there was Althea.

Althea was gone but Lillian couldn't stop thinking of her friend. Memories of their relationship from their first meeting in Philadelphia right up to the day of her death flooded Lillian's every waking moment. She told Louis about the time she had fought off Althea's husband, who would beat her and steal her money whenever he was drunk. Visions of Althea in the Pennsylvania Hospital Mental Ward kept coming to Lillian in dreams.

"Now, don't you go getting depressed on me." Louis said one morning.

"I'm not depressed. I'm just really sad. Althea was closer to me than any other person in the world besides my daughter and then you."

"What about Beth?" Louis wanted to know.

"Beth and I grew to love each other. Remember, she was my mistress and I hated her. Just our stations in life made us at odds with each other besides the part David Vance played in our lives." She paused to wipe new tears from her cheek. "Althea and I became friends from the moment we met. I feel like I've lost a part me."

"Everything that lives also dies, Lillian. Althea is at peace now."

For two days Althea's body was laid out on a long table in the parlor of her boarding house. Lillian and Louis were there to greet the people as they came to express their condolences. Apparently, Althea was more well known and liked than anyone knew. People even came from some neighboring towns. Some came empty handed and some brought food.

Lillian had been strong but by the end of the second day, she could take no more. She ordered that Althea's body be placed in a pine box coffin and prepared for burial. Althea was buried on a cold day at the end of February.

After the burial the people gathered back at the boarding house. Lillian watched Alexis who seemed to be taking Althea's death very hard. She knew that Althea blamed herself for the assault that Alexis suffered but she didn't know if Alexis blamed Althea.

"How are you holding up?" Lillian asked Alexis.

She seemed startled by the question. "I'm fine," she whispered. She tried to step away but Lillian stepped with her and they both moved toward the kitchen.

"I hope you don't blame Althea for what happened to you."

Alexis stopped walking and turned to face Lillian. "No!" She said a little too loud. "I told Althea over and over that I didn't blame her but she blamed herself and no one could talk her out of how she felt."

"I know that. I just wanted to make sure that you weren't holding on to bad feelings about any of this."

"Do I feel bad? Yes, I am feeling awful. I'm sorry that Althea died and I'm really not over what happened to me. I think that she gave up on life because of what happened to me but I didn't know how to make it right and I don't know how to move on. I feel so damaged."

"Have you written to Joseph?" Lillian asked. "Have you told him about the assault?"

Alexis was suddenly unsteady on her feet and quickly took a seat. "No," she whispered. "I couldn't bear to tell him. I'm afraid of what he will think of me if I tell him."

Lillian put her hand on Alexis shoulder. "It was not your fault and Joseph will not think less of you, I'm sure. You must tell him."

"It is such a horrible thing that I'm not sure I should give him such bad news while he is away."

"So you think it will be better to tell him when he comes home?"

Both women were silent for a few moments. Finally, Alexis said, "I don't know what to do, Lillian. I'm afraid to tell Joseph."

"Alexis, you must get over this and Joseph has a right to know what has happened to his wife." Lillian didn't agree and she made up her mind at that moment that she would write to Joseph and tell what his wife had gone through in his absence. "You don't have to tell him. I will tell him for you but you must be strong for Jay. I promise you, Joseph will love you more for your strength through this terrible time in your life."

♨

Joseph hadn't gotten a letter from Alexis since late summer and he was beginning to worry that she may not be well. Later that same month, Joseph got a disturbing letter from Lillian.

March 10, 1865

My Dearest Joseph,

It pains me to write this letter but I would not have you in the dark about something that I know would greatly concern you. Unfortunately, your wife was attacked by the same man that attempted to rape her more than a year ago in the church kitchen. It is with great sadness that I inform you that Alexis has suffered a sever beating and a brutal rape.

You need not know the details of this vile and evil act. You only need to know that she is well now. Her physical scars have healed and she is as beautiful as she was the day you left.

Be that as it may, emotionally she is not the same woman. Her scars are hidden behind that beautiful smile.
I know that she has not written to you because she does not want to tell what has happened. I am writing to you because I believe that a word from you could make all the difference in her emotional well-being. It is not enough

*for us to all tell her that you will love her no less after
this horrible incident.*

*Joseph, please know that we all miss you and pray for
your safe return everyday. Don't worry too much about
Alexis. We will take care of her and little Jay for you. I
can't tell how sorry we all are that these things have
happened.*

*Also, I must inform you that my dearest friend Althea
has passed on at the end of February. Although she had
been ill most of the winter, I feel as if the guilt she felt
after Alexis was attacked, caused her to give up her will
to live.*

*Again, I implore you to write to your wife and let her
be assured of your love and devotion. Until we see each
other again, I remain,*

Yours Sincerely,
Lillian Bissett

Joseph's eyes filled with tears and his free hand clinched into a fist
as he read Lillian's letter. He didn't fold the letter. He crumbled it into
his fist and sank down on his pallet in the tent he shared with David
and two other soldiers. He pulled his knees toward his chest and
dropped his head as tears began to well in his eyes.

"What's wrong?" David wanted to know.

Joseph just shook his head. He had no desire to air his private
grievance in the presence of the other soldiers. The men chatted
amicably among each other but Joseph and David remained quiet. It
wasn't long before everyone except Joseph slept. Besides being

heartsick over the bad news in Lillian's letter, he felt helpless. Without warning, he jumped to his feet and threw off the woolen blanket. He stormed out of the tent. Fires burned around the camp as March nights could be very cold. Joseph seemed not to even notice the cold as he walked away from the camp site. He needed to be alone to work out his frustration. Tears that he'd held back while in the tent, now came forward. His fist were thrown through the air as his mind's eye saw the face of the young man who had assaulted his beloved Alexis more than a year ago.

When David realized that Joseph had left the tent, he went looking for him. He found Joseph sitting with his back against a tree, a mile or so away from the camp. His face was wet with fresh tears and his hands trembled from the rage that he held in check. "What on earth has gotten into you?" David asked.

"Alexis was beaten and raped," he stammered through clinched teeth.

"What?"

"It was the same white man that tried to rape her last year."

"Oh my God!" David exclaimed. He helped Joseph to stand. "I know how upset you must be, but you can't stay out here, Joseph." David could see that he was still very distraught. "Come on man. You have to get it together because we need to get back to camp."

"I need to go home. Alexis needs me."

"You can't go home, Joseph. You know that, at least not until this war is over." David put his arm around Joseph's shoulders. "I want to go home as much as you do. I even miss my sisters. But we signed up to fight this war. We signed up to fight for freedom and we can't go home yet."

They stood close to one of the camp fires as Joseph wiped the tears from his face and they warmed up as much as they could before going back into their own tent. Joseph didn't sleep that night and it didn't get any better in the coming months. He barely slept at all and when he did, David could tell that his soul was tortured by what happened to his wife.

Something changed in Joseph after he read Lillian's letter. He was always brave, but now he was ferocious. Every Confederate he saw wore Nathaniel's face and Joseph killed him over and over again in his mind's eye.

David marveled at how their roles had changed. He was the younger of the two of them and more naive. When they first joined the army, Joseph acted as an elder brother, protecting and advising David whenever necessary. Now, it was David that had to often pull Joseph back and stop him from running headlong into danger. He was determined that both he and Joseph would make it back to the people that they loved.

Early that April, Confederate forces under the command of General Lee, camped outside the village of Appomattox Court House. They expected to meet a supply train and wagons, however an unanticipated attack from Union forces were upon them before they could retreat. At first, it looked as if they would survive the attack but under General Grant's leadership, thousands of Union Infantry and Calvary Units converged in a brutal attack that left Confederate forces in tatters and led to the eventual surrender of General Robert E. Lee. The war would soon be over.

There were celebrations in many Northern states and especially Washington, D.C. On April 14, 1865 the United States Flag, the stars and stripes, was raised over Fort Sumter, where the conflict that led to the Civil War began. Ironically, that same evening, President Lincoln and his wife attended a play at the Ford's Theater in Washington. An actor, John Wilkes Booth, who was convinced that the President planned to overthrow the Confederacy and the freeing of slaves would destroy the south, assassinated President Lincoln.

There were no battles on the arising. The mood in the camp quickly moved from the heightened tensions of the battlefield and the sheer weariness of battle worn soldiers, to a more lighthearted spirited atmosphere. The war was ending and joy rained throughout the camp. The men sang and danced, played cards, and joked. They all knew that they would be going home soon.

It was a warm day in May and Joseph and David heard a commotion out in the camp outside of their tent. There was a woman speaking from a platform in the middle of the camp. Both Joseph and David joined the other Negro soldiers as they moved toward the platform to listen to this woman. She was a woman of small stature but she spoke with authority, and knowledge. The men stood mesmerized as they listened to this woman. They called her Moses and said that she had single handedly freed hundreds of slaves. Her name was Harriet Tubman.

Joseph had often told Isaac and David of his experience of running away from Master Akins plantation. However, it wasn't until they heard miss Tubman speak that David really understood. The first time Joseph mentioned the Underground Railroad, David remembered that he and Isaac just looked at each other before they both began to laugh. They couldn't grasp the concept of an Underground Railroad and thought their new friend was just exaggerating, until he met Harriet Tubman.

She knew a great deal about the Underground Railroad and was able to help David understand exactly what Joseph had been trying to tell him and Isaac. She talked a lot about surviving slavery, escaping slavery and the strength of the Negro family and they all felt blessed at having met this courageous woman.

◌

On the evening of May 17, 1865 Catherine and Samantha were in the Bowman kitchen preparing for supper when Samantha was gripped with a pain in the bottom of her belly. She grabbed her belly and dropped to her knees. "What is it?" Catherine asked. "Is it time?"

"Yes. I think it is time."

"Mother," Catherine screamed for Rebecca.

Rebecca came running. She knew immediately what was happening. "Go and get Mrs. Kenny." Mrs Kenny was the town Midwife, as was her mother before her. Mrs. Kenny had delivered scores of babies in the twenty years since her mother passed. Catherine grabbed her shawl and darted out of the back door.

It took over sixteen hours for Kira Rebecca Bowman to come into the world. Everyone in the room was surprised to see the beautiful brown baby girl that emerged from Samantha's womb. The shock on the faces of the women who stood around her bed alarmed Samantha. "What is it? What's the matter?" She questioned.

"Nothing," Rebecca said. "You have a beautiful baby girl."

"Then why do you all look so shocked?"

"Your baby looks just like David, except . . ."

"Except what? Let me see her."

"She is beautifully brown, Samantha," Rebecca said softly. "Your daughter has the coloring of a Negro." She wiped the sweat from Samantha's head and sat down beside her on the bed. Mrs. Kenny took the baby away to wash and swaddle her. Catherine stood near the door. She had no idea what her mother was going to say but Rebecca knew that the truth that she wanted so desperately to keep secret, would now have to be told. "You see, Samantha, David is half white. He is mulatto."

Catherine gasped.

"I was in a relationship with a white man before Benjamin and I got married. We all thought that you were white."

"I am, but why does that matter?"

"It matters because you have a little girl that doesn't have the coloring of either parent. We know that I am of mixed blood, both my parents were mulatto. But the off spring of a mulatto and a white, will usually produce a very light child, sometimes even light enough to pass for white, like me and David's father. Your daughter looks like a Negro. That means that you may have some Negro blood also. That's the only way you could have a child with Kira's skin color. It is likely that your father was a dark skin Negro like Benjamin."

Mrs. Kenny returned with the child and placed the baby in Samantha's arms. Samantha looked down at her baby girl and smiled. "She's beautiful. She is the same color as Cat and Lilly." She snuggled her nose into the folds of the baby's neck. "Mom," she said. "I know that I've never called you that before but you are the only person that has actually been a mother to me." The emotion that Rebecca had been able to hold back, now came forth as tears began to stream down her face. "Mom," Samantha began again. She was also unable to hold back her tears. "I want you to know that I never knew who my father was or anyone else in my family. I saw my mother with all kinds of men. My father could be a black man but I don't care about any of that. I love David and we will both love our daughter. I will be the kind of mother I never had. I will be the kind of mother I've watched you be to Cat, Lilly and David."

Rebecca leaned down and kissed Samantha's cheek before she took the baby from her arms. "Get some sleep, Samantha. You will need it, I promise."

Later, as Catherine and Rebecca watched little Kira sleep in the small basket Catherine had decorated in layers of white and pink lace ruffles, Catherine asked her mother about David's father. Tears welled in her eyes as she looked at her daughter. She reached over and took both of Catherine's hands in her own. "I never wanted to tell this story to any of my children but, I guess the time has come for me to stop hiding the truth. "When my mother and I left the plantation and moved to Philadelphia, we took jobs as housekeepers for some rich white family in Overbrook farms, outside of Philadelphia. At first I was treated well, special even. The mistress of that house thought I looked like her dead daughter. She gave me books and treated me better than any of the others servants. I use to look into those full length mirrors in her room and what I saw was a white girl. I got to thinking that if I were white, everyone would treat me special. When we left the Wallingford House, we went to live with Miss Beth, who use to be our mistress on the plantation."

Catherine frowned. "Oh no honey, that is a story for another day. Our neighbors had a servant girl near my age and we became friends. One day when her employer's accountant came to visit, he thought that I was white. He flirted and I flirted back. I really believed that if I could make him fall in love with me and marry me, I could just live the privileged life of a white woman. I thought that I could actually pass for white and that would solve all my problems, but I was wrong. I was so wrong."

"What happened?" Catherine wanted to know.

"Because I was young and stupid, a country girl in the big city, I thought that by giving myself to him, he would love me in return. I gave myself but he did not fall in love with me. In fact, when he found out that I was a Negro, he wanted nothing more than to kill me. I didn't know that I was with child when he attacked me and beat me, leaving me to die out on an ice covered sidewalk in the middle of winter."

"Oh my."

"Your father found me and carried me all the way to Mom Cathy's house. No one knew where I was but I was with your Grandmother. Mom Cathy and your father nursed me back to health. After David was born, we married and moved here."

"Oh Mama, I'm so sorry for what you went through. I promise that I will not tell Lilly or David."

"You don't have to make such a promise. I will tell them myself, when the time is right."

Chapter Eleven
May 1865
The End of the War

General Lee's surrender virtually ended the war, although there were reports that intense fighting continued west of the Mississippi. The Union attacks had interrupted all supply lines leaving the Confederate soldiers of Virginia broken and starving. Even before the surrender, many Confederate Officers began to flee to safety in states further south.

Union soldiers were charged with providing medical aide and food to Virginia's confederate army. They had also been charged with the reconstruction of an abandoned plantation house into a military hospital for wounded soldiers, both Union and Confederate. The large bedrooms were converted into wards. Cots were separated by the remnants of the heavy drapes that were once all the rage in those beautiful plantation homes. The first floor was gutted and turned into small offices where officers, doctors, and nurses could keep track of their patients. It was a lot of work and almost every soldier and infantryman was called into this service.

It didn't take long for David to notice that Joseph had some expertise in this field. "You seem to know a lot about construction, Joe."

"More than you could imagine. I was a carpenter on the plantation. After I ran, Louis and I decided that I would give up carpentry so as not to call attention to myself by slave catchers. They were looking for a carpenter so I became a farmer."

"Wow, I never knew that."

"You were too young at the time but you are right. I know a good deal about building houses."

"Now that I think about it, you were pretty good rebuilding the church too." David was quiet for a long time. He was thinking about Joseph's skill and their future. Later that night when the two of them had bedded down for the night, he brought up the subject again. "Hey Joe, what would you say to starting a carpentry business?" Joseph sat up and gave David a curious look. "No need to worry about slave patrollers and slave catchers anymore. You can be who you really are, a carpenter, a damn good carpenter."

"You're right. I hadn't thought of that before. I can be a carpenter again."

"Yeah, and I can be your apprentice until I learn the business."

"That is a wonderful idea, David. Thank you."

Both men sat up and shook hands. "It's a deal," Joseph said. That night Joseph dreamed of he and William on the Atkins plantation. Those dreams usually disturbed him and left him feeling sad and lonely. This dream was different. He and William were making furniture, interior doors, and laying new floors. William was laughing and joking as usual and '*Josiah*' was urging him to get serious and get back to work. Joseph woke up with a smile on his face and happier than he had been in a very long time.

As they worked that day, David was right at Joseph's side. He asked a lot of questions but did exactly as he was instructed without question. Joseph watched David closely. By the end of the day, he was feeling that David might make a pretty good carpenter with a little more experience. '*I guess David is now my little brother now,*' he thought.

♨

Days later, David could hardly keep his mind on the task at hand. He had not received a letter from Samantha in months. He knew that she should have delivered the baby by now and worried that something may have gone wrong with the delivery. All of the men knew that they would be discharged from service soon but as yet there were no orders.

Joseph tried to reassure David that if anything had happened at home, someone would notify them and they could do nothing but wait for discharge orders. David finally agreed but it did not stop him from worrying.

It was a very hot day in May and all the soldiers were working hard on the new hospital. They were chopping wood, painting, and cleaning. David was replacing a shattered windowpane in the front of the house when he saw the postman striding across the grass toward the house. He nearly dropped the glass as he tried to gently lean it against a nearby wall before running to meet the postman. He was not alone. The war had slowed mail delivery and many of the men were anxious for a word from home. Almost all of the soldiers working on the hospital that day, dropped what they were doing and rushed to meet the postman. Finally, after months of silence, there was a letter from Samantha. David ripped the envelope away and sat down on the steps to read.

Joseph. Looking over his shoulder said, "That isn't a letter. It is barely a note," he joked.

David unfolded the single sheet of paper.

May 25, 1865

My Dearest David,

I am pleased to announce the birth of our daughter, Kira Rebecca Bowman. She was born on May 5, 1865 and she is the most beautiful baby girl that anyone has ever seen. I can hardly wait until you come home and meet your daughter.

You'll be interested to know that your friend Isaac and your sister Catherine have become an item. They seem to really like each other. Isaac was in a bad way when he came home, and now everyone agrees that Catherine has been good for him.

Yours Always
Sam

David was elated at the news of his daughter's birth. Joseph gave him a big hug and other fellow soldiers patted him on the back in congratulations. To their great surprise, the soldiers who had been working on the new hospital for the past week, were given a few hours of leave that evening. The timing was perfect for David and Joseph to celebrate the birth of his daughter. It was also their good fortune that some of the local families wanted to celebrate the end of the war and invited many of the Negro soldiers to share their evening meal. At least ten of them would be dining with the Johnsons.

The Johnsons were a large family. Jed Johnson, a man in his late fifties, had bought his freedom over ten years ago. His former master helped him to buy a couple of acres of land, which he farmed and expanded over time. Eventually, Jed was able to buy and free his wife and five children. They were a happy family and seemed to be overjoyed to celebrate the end of the war with the Negro soldiers. They drank white liquor and ate fried chicken, collard greens, and homemade buttermilk biscuits. Other Negro families had also opened their doors to the soldiers.

The rations that the soldiers would have eaten, were being given to the starving Confederate soldiers and the run-away slaves who had been following the Union Army for months.

They stumbled back to their tents in the wee hours of the morning with their bellies full of good food and their spirits lightened by moonshine. Joseph blindly fell onto his pallet and did not notice the letter that had been placed there while he was away from his tent.

David saw a letter on his own pallet right away. Seeing the familiar Union Army Seal, he ripped the envelope open straight away. "Joe," he said hesitantly, as he slowly read. "Joseph," he said again, more loudly this time. "We're going home!" He yelped. They had finally received their discharge orders. They would be home before the end of the summer.

They spent the next couple of weeks finishing the hospital. There were parts of the south where fighting continued even after the surrender and the wounded were coming by the wagon full. Soldier's wounds were stitched up, bullets removed and limbs were amputated. No sooner than they were discharged, another wagon full of wounded arrived.

When the hospital was finally finished, union soldiers helped with transporting patients, making beds, emptying chamber pots, and any other duties assigned by their commanding officer. But just knowing that they were going home enabled them to take it all in stride.

June was hot and rainy in Virginia. When they weren't working, they sat around playing cards, checkers and chess. The men wrote more letters home and received more letters from home.

Finally, their discharge day was upon them. They received their separation documents on July 30, 1865. They were headed home.

Trains heading north left from the city of Richmond. They would have to walk to Richmond to meet the next train north. It was a twenty-one mile walk and they knew that if they broke camp at sunrise, they could make it to Richmond by afternoon. Knowing that they were going home put new vigor in their steps as the men moved toward Richmond under the hot Virginia sun.

They walked past tobacco and cotton plantations. Some were still being worked by slaves that had no idea that they were free. Most were abandoned, dilapidated from gun fire or sometimes from just sheer neglect. One of those dilapidated plantations caught David's eye.

There were no slaves in the tobacco field. In fact the planting field and much of the property was overgrown with weeds and wild shrubbery. The main gate was some distance from the road but it still caught David's attention. They were walking at a leisurely pace when

David suddenly stopped walking. He glanced to his left and stood there for a moment. Joseph kept walking for a minute.

A large iron gate enclosed the property and just beyond the gate there was an enormous live oak tree. Live oak trees surrounded the property. Moss hung from their limbs and the weeds that covered the grounds were so high that you could hardly see beyond the front gate. David left the road and walked up to the gate for a closer look. He could see the main house.

Joseph stopped walking and just watched David for a moment. "What are you doing, David?" Joseph wanted to know.

"I'm not sure."

"Let's go. We don't want to miss our train. Besides, I don't want us to be too far from the company."

"We have time. Besides, if we miss one, another will come along shortly."

"Yes, you're right but, being caught out here on the road at night doesn't seem like a good idea."

"The war is over, Joe. What are you so worried about?"

"Look, little brother, the war may be over but it did not do away with all the racist white people the run this part of the country. It just isn't safe."

"All right. We will just have a quick look and then we can catch up with the company went they break for a rest."

Against his better judgement, Joseph joined David at the gate. The two men stood there looking through the iron gate, not knowing what they were looking for, what they expected to see, or why this particular property had so captured David's attention.

"Look!" Joseph said as he pointed to the top of the gate. At the very top of the wrought iron gate was a very decorative 'G.' The letter was hanging, as it's supports had long ago rusted and fell away. Joseph shook the gate, hoping that the letter would fall to the ground. David looked up, still confused by his reaction to this property. Joseph shook the gate again but the letter did not fall.

"Let's go in." David said.

"Why?" Joseph wanted to know.

"I think that this may be the plantation where my mother and grandmother were born. They were born

on a plantation named Gloria in Virginia, just outside of Richmond and near the James River."

"No," Joseph said in surprise. "Really? You think that this could be the place."

"If that G stands for Gloria, this is the place. Let's go in."

Joseph just stared for a few moments before he put an arm around David's shoulders and the two slowly moved onto the property. The house looked as if it had been abandoned years ago. Shutters were hanging, the elaborate iron railings that surrounded the balconies were now rusty and pealing. Termites had eaten away at the wood on the wrap around porch, leaving big gapping holes in the floor boards. Even the base of the tall wooden pillars that held up balconies were destroyed by termites and dampness. "No one has lived here for a very long time," Joseph said. "You can certainly tell that this was once a beautiful and elegant southern home."

The front door was unlocked and David pushed it open. Rusty hinges squeaked as the door swung open onto a large foyer with marble floors. The room was circular. There were several doors around the foyer and between each door hung a large portrait. David walked to the the center of the room and slowly turned as he looked at the face of each portrait. The first portrait was that of a large, robust white man. His skin had the color of someone who spent much time out in the sun.

Large green eyes dominated his face and David recognized those eyes. He stared at that face for a long time.

"I can see the family resemblance," Joseph jokingly said. But David saw it also and did not find it funny.

"This is definitely the Vance house," David whispered. "I think this portrait is my great grandfather. I've heard about this man my entire life, Big Bill Vance."

David stared at that face for a moment. "My grandmother talked about this man as if he were the devil himself. Everything about him was evil. That was all I could ever get out of her. It was as if she were afraid to even speak his name." He was quiet for a moment. "I can see it."

"What can you see?"

"The evil. I see a dark shadow behind those eerie green eyes. Even a portrait as grand as this could not hide the evil of their man."

The other male portrait was an older white man with a stern face and a long gray beard. *'This is probably Big Bill's father,'* David thought. The one woman whose portrait hung in the foyer was a very pale, thin woman. She had thin blond hair the color of corn silk and it was pulled tightly back. She wore tiny pearl earrings. Her pale blue eyes seemed too big for her small face. He stared up at that face for a few minutes. Remembering the stories Rebecca had told him, he knew that this woman was Gloria Vance and that he had no blood relation to this woman.

He slowly walked through the ground floor of the house with Joseph close behind. On the second floor, doors were off the hinges, trunks had been ransacked, furniture was broken. Some rooms were piled high with destroyed furniture and portraits. Back in the foyer again, David stopped. "There are ghosts in this house. Don't you feel it, Joseph?"

"Do you mean the ghosts of the people who once lived in this house?"

"No. I mean like spirits. I feel like bad things have happened in this house. It feels dark and heavy in here."

"I don't know if I would call what I'm feeling a ghost but there is definitely a heaviness here."

They were quiet for a time as David continued to stare at the portraits that hung in the foyer. "I can't really say what it is I'm feeling but it seems unnatural and wanton. I think we best be on our way," he finally said. "Let's get out of here. This place gives me the willies."

They did not run but they did make hast away from the Gloria Plantation. They left Gloria with all its secrets, lies, and its dark legacy behind them forever.

"Whatever died here, God, please let it stay dead here," David said as they moved through the front gate and back onto the road to Richmond.

⚜

The city of Richmond was nearly burned to the ground as Confederates fleeing their Capital City set fire to the armory, bridges, and warehouses. They destroyed the sources of whiskey hoping to keep it out of Yankee hands. They destroyed cotton, tobacco, and other food stuffs for the same reasons. Confederate documents were also set on fire. The fires burned unchecked for days until Union soldiers arrived to put them out. Gun and artillery fire had decimated the capital city. The Fourth Massachusetts Calvary entered the city on the morning of April 3, 1865. The American flag, the stars and stripes was hoisted over the capital soon after the Calvary arrived.

The men from the 127th Colored Infantry Regiment arrived in Richmond at the end of May 1865. Though the city had been virtually destroyed, it was now swarming with Union soldiers. The men were lucky enough to find several boarding houses throughout the city, some even owned by Negros. Joseph and David were lucky enough to find rooms quickly and they spent a couple of days in Richmond as they waited for train passage to Philadelphia.

It was at supper one evening when Joseph met a fellow soldier named Paris Ledger. He was a very tall man with a dark complexion and a friendly smile. Paris had lost his leg from the knee down in a battle in Tennessee and was now on his way to Philadelphia. "Are you from Philadelphia," Joseph inquired.

"No." He said with a smiled. He looked as if he had a secret to tell. "I'm a southern boy. I ran away as soon as I heard that the war started. I didn't want to be dragged into the Confederate army so I ran all the way from South Carolina to Maryland to join the Union Army. Then they shipped me back south again. Can you believe that?" They all laughed. "I'm going to Philadelphia because they tell me that there is a company up there that can give me a leg. An artificial leg, of course. They call it a prosthetic."

"Really?" Both Joseph and David were interested now. They were both thinking of Issac.

"Yeah, they make artificial limbs all over but the doctor that cut off my leg told me about a couple of guys in Philadelphia that are the best at making prosthetics."

"I'm sure there must be a big cost for such a thing, right?" David asked.

"Naw," Paris answered. "I don't really know. I just know that whatever the cost, it will be worth it. I just have to get to Philadelphia."

"What is the name of this company?"

"Whitley and Sons Prosthetics."

"Would you mind if we traveled with you to see someone at this company? We have a friend who lost a foot in the war. It would be really nice if we could take him some good news."

"Sure. Always willing to help a fellow soldier."

&s

Philadelphia had always been seen as a very vibrant city with its diversity and industrial leaning, but now it was not just crowded, it was surging with vitality. Besides its vast diverse neighborhoods, there was a large military presence. The sidewalks were crowded with new businesses opening, street vendors and markets soaring. Philadelphia had more Military Hospitals than any city in the country.

The three young soldiers hired a hack to take them from the train to the Satterlee Military Hospital at 46th Street and Baltimore Avenue. It was a short ride and David stayed in the hack while Paris and Joseph inquired at the front desk for the address of the Whitley and Sons Prosthetics.

They were directed to an elegant three story town house on the 900 block of Spruce Street. Tall buildings lined both sides of the street, blocking out much of the sun. All three young men went inside this time and were greeted by a handsome young man who informed them that because they had not scheduled an appointment, they would have to wait to see Mr. Whitley.

After about forty minutes, they were invited into a spacious office, with very tall windows. The heavy drapes were pulled back to let in what little sunlight they could. The prosthetics that had brought the company fame and fortune were on display in glass cases around the building and especially in the office. They expected to see wooden legs and hooks for hands but this particular field of medicine had far outgrown those archaic forms of artificial limbs.

It was the younger Whitley that came out to greet the men.

"Good afternoon gentlemen." He surveyed the three young men before him, taking special notice of Paris who leaned heavily on his crutches, his empty pant let pinned up behind him. "I am sure you have come to the right place," he said as he ushered Paris into his private office.

Joseph and David waited patiently, their interest occupied by the different prosthetics displayed around the room. One case in particular displayed what looked like a leather boot. It was tall and probably created to connect to the leg of a tall person whose leg was removed at the knee. "Look," David said. He could hardly contain his excitement. It looks like its made for an entire leg but I imagine it could be cut down."

Just then, Mr. Whitley and Paris came out of the office. Paris was thanking Mr. Whitley and promised to return in two weeks time.

"Mr. Whitley," Joseph said. "Mind if I ask you a few questions about these limbs."

"Sure, what can I help you with."

"A friend of ours lost his foot in the war and I was wondering if one of these prosthetics might serve him?

"If you know your friend's shoe size, I'm sure I can make something for him. Mind you, it will not replace his foot, but he doesn't have to look like he has no foot. Which foot is missing?"

Joseph and David looked at each other with stunned expressions. They did not know what size shoe Isaac wore or which foot had been blown off. "We don't know," Joseph said.

Both Joseph and David felt a little foolish for thinking that buying an artificial limb would be as easy as buying a new pair of shoes. They looked at each other and smiled, silently acknowledging their lack of knowledge of prosthetics.

"How much does something like this cost."

"That would depend on exactly what suits the patient." Mr. Whitley could see that his answer did not seem to satisfy the young men. "I'll tell you what," he began as he presented both men with his card. "Tell your friend to contact me. Send me a note and we will set up a meeting so that I can understand exactly what he expects and what he needs. Then I will take the proper measurements, and we will work from that point. The one thing you don't want, is a prosthetic that doesn't fit properly."

They thanked Mr. Whitley and promised to be in touch before the three left his office.

It was late and they were all tired. They decided to have dinner together before finding a place to sleep for the night. Paris was lucky enough to find a room in a boarding house on a small street close to the Whitley office. The house was run by a nurse that worked at the Military Hospital and often rented to Union soldiers. Paris would like to have offered Joseph and David to spend the night with him but that would have been against house rules. The men said their goodbyes, exchanged addresses and promised to keep in touch.

Joseph thought it best to find something close to the river as they planned to catch the ferry to Camden in the morning. They began to walk south on Spruce Street. The closer they came to the river the more the neighborhood changed. They walked as far as Fifth Street before they turned north looking for a "Rooms For Rent" sign. One block away from the docks they came across a Tavern that rented rooms above. Joseph went in to secure a room. He was back in a matter of minutes with the key to a room.

"That was fast." David said.

"Yeah but I am not really tired. How about you?"

"I'm not tired."

"Let's take a walk through the city before we turn in for the night. What do you say?"

"Sounds good."

They began to walk down toward the waterfront. There was a commotion on the docks. A man was being chased. The crowd was yelling and screaming. Some of them carried sticks and bats. "A riot?" David asked.

"I don't think so. One man is being chased."

The man was soon caught and a crowd of men began to gather around. The man was screaming for help as the crowd jeered. As Joseph and David came closer, they could see that a rope had been tied into a noose and swung over a lamp post. Joseph's first thought was that the crowd was attempting to lynch a black man. He and David exchanged looks before the two of them ran into the crowd.

But it wasn't a crowd of white people. The people were of all races. There were blacks and whites and foreigners. "String him up!" Someone yelled.

Joseph and David waded through the crowd to the front of the commotion. The man had already been beaten to a pulp and three men were attempting to get the noose around his neck. Suddenly the sound of whistles and bells rang out and Philadelphia Police moved in to take control of the situation.

The three men thought to be the agitators were shackled, arrested and taken away. Police then tried to disperse the crowd and make room for the ambulance that would soon come for the injured man. As the crowd moved away, Joseph stepped forward. Even through the blood that poured from the man's mouth and nose, Joseph recognized him immediately. The man was Nathaniel Williams. Joseph froze. Unable to speak or move as he looked down on the man who had haunted his dreams for months. The man who had raped and beat his new wife. He bent down close enough for the man to look into his face.

"Remember me?" He asked.

The man tried to open one of his rapidly swelling eyes before he shook his head indicating that he did not know Joseph. "The good people of Timbuctoo gave you shelter in our church. I was there when my wife hit you with a ladle. Remember? She gave you that little scar on your head."

Recognition lightened in his one opened eye. Joseph could tell that he now recognized him and he remembered. "You couldn't let go, even after spending a year in prison. You came back to our little town and raped my wife."

At that moment, Joseph noticed that there was another man standing by and he was watching closely. He looked up at this sizable, red faced white man. His clothes were dirty and his hands were both clinched into fists. One of those fists held a knife. The sound of the coming ambulance could be heard by all four men and Nathaniel thought that the bells ringing would save him from further harm.

"I remember your wife." Nathaniel said before he spit a stream of blood and mucus at Joseph's feet. "Haughty little bitch but I was able to bring her low." He laughed and his raspy voice sounded like a growl. Before Joseph thought, he threw a punch that hit Nathaniel hard in the jaw and his body fell to one side.

The man who had been watching suddenly stepped forward. "It would seem that this little runt likes taking advantage of women. He raped my little girl just a couple of hours ago, but he ain't getting away with it this time." The man moved quickly. He bent over Nathaniel as if to whisper something to the rapist, but in one swift movement, his knife sliced through Nathaniel's neck. Blood spurted from Nathaniel's neck as his hands went instinctively to the wound in an effort to staunch the blood flow. Gurgling sounds came from his throat as he choked on his own blood.

When Joseph looked up, the man was gone. The bells on the ambulance became louder and they knew that it was close. "Joe, we gotta go," David pleaded. Joseph's knuckles were red with Nathaniel's blood. "Put your hand in your pocket and let's get out of here." David urged

They did not run away as David wanted to do. "We aren't running." Joseph said. "We did not stab him. Running will make it look like we did something wrong."

"Alright," David whispered. "Just put that bloodied hand in your pocket and let us move away."

Joseph thrust his fist into his pocket and stood back and watched the scene before him. There were still on-lookers standing close by when the horse drawn ambulance arrived. Men in white hospital uniforms examined Nathaniel. "He's gone," one of them said. Nathaniel's dead body was lifted onto a stretcher and taken away.

Joseph and David went back to the Tavern where they ordered beer and was quickly served by a very friendly and voluptuous waitress.

"There was a time when a black man would not be served any kind of alcohol in such an establishment." Joseph told David. They sipped their beer without the need for conversation. The beer was served in big glass mugs. It was cold and strong and more satisfying than any

Joseph could remember drinking. He and David watched the waitress as she went about her job, swaying her hips, smiling, and flirting with her customers.

When at last Joseph swallowed the last drop of that cold beer, he breathed a sigh of relief. It was a long sign, almost as satisfying as the beer had been. He was able to release the rage and anxiety that had consumed him since learning of the attack on Alexis in his absence.

Nathaniel William was dead and Joseph couldn't help thinking that the man deserved his fate.

Chapter Twelve
Timbuctoo, New Jersey
Homecoming

Althea's passing left a shroud of gloom over the Bowman and Bissett families. Everyone went about their normal lives but with a sense of foreboding. The boarding house was practically empty which meant that there wasn't much Jacob and the women could do to occupy their time. They cleaned and cooked as usual, but with so few residents, even that did not take much time.

Jacob's age was beginning to slow him down. His joints ached and it was harder for him to move around. He spent less and less time out at the Bissett farm and there simply wasn't much for him to do around the boarding house. He started to spend more time on the porch with one of the male residents with whom he had become friends. Nan worried about him, but what could she do? Jacob was a big man but he now seemed smaller. His shoulders slumped and he took slow, small steps. Nan noticed that his breathing was shallow when he slept, Jacob was seventy years old and fading fast.

Denny and Alexis use to spend a lot of time together but Denny, who rarely showed any interest in men, finally met a young man from church.

Luke Hansen was a local farmer and a widower, but he had no children. He was older than Denny by ten years, which made no difference to her. She was smitten from the moment they met. He was a tall, lean man with a medium complexion and big brown eyes. His arms and chest were muscular from hard work. Luke Hansen could bring a smile to Denny's face with just the tip of his hat. For weeks they stared at each other from opposite sides of the church sanctuary. Alexis urged Denny to at least speak with the man. "A friendly, 'hello,' couldn't hurt." She told Denny. Finally, it was Luke who made the first move.

He waited for Denny after service one Sunday. He tipped his hat and gave a friendly greeting to she and Alexis as they left the church. "Good afternoon, ladies," he said. They each nodded their heads in greeting, but Alexis took the hint and hurried to catch up with Nan, leaving Denny to walk with Luke.

"I'd like to walk with you, if you don't mimd."

"I don't mind," she answered shyly.

From that moment on, they became a couple. Luke cared deeply for Denny and treated her well. At his urging, Denny finally decided to learned to read and write, taking classes at the church.

With Denny out of the house more, Alexis had plenty of time to brood over Althea's passing and Joseph's absence. She put all of her energy into taking care of little Jay and teaching him all that she could. Jay was the only one able to bring a smile to that pretty face. She still felt damaged, used, unworthy and continued to worry about telling Joseph the whole sorted story. Lillian and Rebecca did what they could to help her purge such damaging notions but in the end, they knew that Joseph was the only one who could bring her back to herself.

⚜

It was the first Sunday in June 1865. The Bowman's and Bissett's had planned a special celebration for after church that afternoon. They would welcome home Catherine's twin sister Lillian and Kira would meet her Aunt for the very first time.

Kira Rebecca Bowman was a very happy, beautiful, honey brown baby girl, with striking green eyes and sandy blond, curly hair. From the womb, she looked as if she had been kissed by the sun. Her toothless smile melted hearts and her baby giggle brought smiles to the faces of all who heard her. She was simply adorable. Samantha dressed two month old Kira in a daisy yellow and white dress and booties, knitted by her namesake and grandmother.

The church was packed that June morning. The weather was so pleasant that the church windows and doors were opened. A refreshingly gentle breeze wafted through the sanctuary. Reverend Evans preached a rousing sermon on family and forgiveness. Louis held Lillian's hand and Benjamin's arm rested on Rebecca's shoulders. As the service began to wind down, the congregation took notice of Samantha and her new baby girl. Kira cooed, giggled, and sometimes screeched loudly, gaining the attention of everyone who sat close enough to hear her babble.

At the end of the sermon, a young man came and handed Reverend Evans a note. His eyes quickly scanned the note before he stepped to the podium again. "Church," he said loudly enough to quiet the people. "I am happy to report that the War between the States is over. Apparently, General Robert E. Lee of the Confederacy surrendered to General Ulysses S. Grant in Appomattox Court House in Virginia early this April. The Civil War is over."

There was a collective sigh of relief. You could hear people as they exhaled, relieving the tension and emotional unrest that the people felt since the onset of the war. Then a great shout went out among the people and they began to scream their joy at this news. They hugged and kissed one another and began to jump for joy in celebration. Even though they had celebrated the emancipation more than a year ago, this seemed like a grand turning point for the entire country.

The whole town was celebrating. Harmonicas and banjos were suddenly heard from every corner of town. People were dancing in the street and singing. Some of the young men lit fire crackers. The celebration went on until very late in the evening.

The families returned to the Bowman house after church to continue their private celebration. The entire family was there. Catherine had even been able to convince Isaac to come out to welcome her sister home. This was one of the more pleasant days Rebecca could remember enjoying in recent years. The past couple of years had been plagued by one tragedy after another but not this day. Today Rebecca was excited to welcome her daughter home and show off her beautiful granddaughter.

The kitchen was full of Lilly's favorite foods. Apple pie and Chocolate layer cake, prepared by Catherine in the Bowman Catering Company ovens. Lillian's fried chicken, baked sweet potatoes and buttermilk biscuits. Rebecca made corn pudding and collards to add to the feast. The food was set out on the buffet in Rebecca's dinning room. Benjamin took the company wagon to the ferry landing to pick up Lilly while everyone else waited impatiently for his return.

Samantha had been watching the road from her usual perch at the front window. Finally, after what seemed like half the day, she saw the Bowman Catering Company wagon turn off the main road and move toward the house.

"They're here!" She yelled. "Lilly has come home."

Samantha watched as Benjamin helped Lilly step down from the wagon. "Oh my," Samantha said. "Lilly looks like a lady, a real sophisticated lady."

Catherine joined Samantha at the window to watch. Benjamin handed Lilly one of her traveling bags as he took the other two. Lilly saw Samantha and Catherine watching from the window and she smiled and waved. "Wow," Catherine said. "She looks so different."

Lilly was met at the door with hugs and kisses from her family and neighbors. She was introduced to Alexis, Jay, and two month old Kira. After all of the greetings, Lilly and Catherine came face to face. Catherine embraced her sister. "I missed you so much," Catherine said.

"I missed all of you."

"Why didn't you write?"

"I did. I wrote mother a few times. Maybe I should have written more but there wasn't much time to think about home. Besides going to class every day, our school was very active in the community. Once the war broke out, the school became even more active in the community. But I did miss you all very much."

"I'm glad you're home Lilly." Catherine said.

"Me too," Samantha said as she lifted Kira from Catherine's arms and placed her in Lilly's arms. "Say hello to your Auntie, Kira."

Samantha said. Kira giggled a little and then gave her new Aunt a big toothless smile, which filled the three women with laughter.

"She is beautiful," Lillian said.

"Before you ask, her complexion probably comes from my father, whom I have never met. We think he may be a Negro."

"Oh my, Sam. When did you learn to speak so well? When I left you were hardly speaking at all."

"I have learned a lot of things since you left, Lilly."

"I guess so. You speak as if you never had a problem at all."

"Thank you," Sam said with a smile.

"Your daughter is adorable. Who is her father?"

There was the slightest moment of quiet as the girls look from one face to the other, but Samantha quickly filled in the blanks. "Why, your brother David, of course."

If Lilly was surprised at that answer, she did not let on. "You and David? I never would have guessed." She smiled as she bounced Kira on her hip. Kira giggled up at her Aunt. "She is a gorgeous baby and I am very happy for you and David."

The welcome home and end of the war celebrations went on well into the evening. While the rest of the family was fawning over Lilly and Kira, Catherine and Isaac were able to sneak away. Catherine led the way from the back of the house into the dining area of the catering company. They sat on the parlor sofa in the front dining room, where guests usually sat while waiting to be seated.

"You seem a little tired," Catherine said.

"I am. Trying to walk with one leg is harder than you think."

Catherine snickered but she helped Isaac to lift his leg onto the sofa. She was quiet for a few moments as she massaged his swollen leg at its stump. Isaac leaned his head back and took a deep breath.

"Cat," he whispered.

"Yes," Catherine answered softly.

"I'm falling in love with you." She didn't immediately answer. She let out a long breath. "You are so kind to me. You are all I think about these days. I am grateful for every moment we spend together."

"Isaac, did you know that I had the biggest crush on you when I was just a girl? I think that maybe I've always loved you, but when you came home injured, I felt that you needed me. I was determined to help you learn to accept your disability and move on with your life, no matter if we were together or not."

"Catherine, I'm not sure that we are talking about the same thing." Confusion shown on her face. Isaac cleared his throat and took Catherine's hands in his. "As I said, I am in love with you. I'm not talking about a school boy crush. I am asking you to be my wife. I don't have a ring, and I am a cripple with nothing to offer you except my love. I want to be with you always. I know that I am asking a lot. Being married to a cripple will probably be difficult but I think that we are good for each other. Please say that you will marry me."

Tears welled in Catherine's eyes. "Yes, Isaac. I will marry you. I love you too, but I am not as naive as you may think."

"What are you talking about?"

"I'm talking about your drinking. Do you think that I don't smell the liquor when we are together? When you first came home, I knew you needed the drink to ease your pain and to cope with your disability. Now, it is time to stop. I will help as much as I can, but I will not marry you until you can give up the drinking."

"I will. I promise to stop drinking. I'll do whatever it takes."

"One more thing. I am not ready to share this news with the family just yet. Are you alright with that?"

"Yes. I'm not sure why but, we will wait until you are ready."

"The reason is simple. I want you to be well and whole when we tell our families. As I said, I will do whatever it takes to help you, but you have to help yourself as well." She leaned over and kissed him on the cheek. Isaac slid his arms around Catherine's waist and pulled her to him. For the first time, he kissed her passionately.

⁂

Denny had left with Luke earlier in the afternoon. Louis and Lillian offered to take Nan and Alexis back to the boarding house but they refused. It was such a pleasant afternoon that they decided take their time and walk. They stopped at the bakery to visit with Miss. Ida for a few minutes before they walked the few blocks to the boarding house. It was close to six in the evening when they finally arrived home. They found Jacob slumped in the rocking chair on the front porch. "Have you heard, honey? The war is over." Nan said as she mounted the steps. Jacob did not answer. As she slowly walked toward him, she could see his arm hanging over the arm of the chair and his chin resting on his chest. She stopped walking. "Jacob," she whispered even as she knew that he was dead. For a moment she seemed not to know what to do next. She slowly mounted the steps and walked to the rocking chair where Jacob sat. Wrapping her arms around his shoulders, she pulled him into her embrace. They had been together since she was just a slave girl on the Gloria plantation. Forty years she had been with this man. They had shared all of life's joys and tribulations together, hand in hand. Now Jacob was gone. Nan did not cry. She simply held her husband to her breast. "Goodbye, my love," she whispered. "Rest in God's peaceful arms. We will meet again in paradise, my love." Minutes passed and Nan held on to Jacob.

Alexis stood by, not knowing what she could do. "I'll get help," she said as she turned and walked away.

"It's too late for help Alexis. Jacob is gone."

Nan and Alexis got help from their neighbor to carry Jacob's body into the house. He was laid out on the same table where Althea had laid months earlier. Alexis sat close and watched as Nan washed her husband's body and changed his clothes.

"Why is it that you and Jacob never had children?" She asked.

Nan smiled as she glanced at Alexis. "Jacob and I had a son years ago."

"Where is he?"

"I don't know." She stopped dressing Jacob and seemed to ponder Alexis question. "My son's name was Christopher. He was a big boy, just like his dad. He was real smart too. We loved him more than anything."

"What happened to him?"

Nan continued to wash and cloth Jacob as she spoke. "One summer day he was fishing in the river. Big Bill wanted him for some chore and sent another boy to fetch him. Christopher came quickly but he couldn't hide the fact that he was annoyed at having to leave the river. He sassed Massa Vance. I grabbed him to shut his mouth before he said something that would get him into more trouble." She sat down as if sitting would help her recall the painful memory. "He didn't mean no harm, Massa, I said. Christopher is a good boy. He just loved fishing so much." Nan clear her throat and blinked back the tears that filled her eyes. "Massa just smiled that evil smile that let you know something real bad was going to happen. Then he just walked away." She stood and went back to preparing her dead husband for the wake that would start it the morning. "Big Bill sold my boy the next day. Didn't even have the decency to tell me. Our cook, Bell, saw from the window that Christopher was shackled and loaded onto a wagon. I was washing in the barrel when I heard Bell scream. I looked up to see them loading my boy onto the wagon. I screamed and begged for Big Bill not to sell him but he just pushed me down in the dirt. Jacob came and helped me up." Nan was quiet for a moment as she buttoned the tiny little buttons on Jacobs shirt. "Christopher was eleven years old, big for his age. He cried and called out for me and his dad but we could do nothing. I broke away from Jacobs arms and ran after the wagon. The next thing I knew, I was stopped because the Overseer's whip sliced through my cheek. It stung like being cut with a sharpe knife. I fell to my knees and watched and cried as my boy was taken away."

Neither of the women spoke for some time. "Why didn't you and Jacob have other children?"

"Jacob said no more children until we see freedom. By the time Massa James died and Louis freed us, we were just too old to even think about children." Nan looked down on Jacob. His face appeared to be so peaceful. "I'm just grateful that Jacob was able to enjoy many years of freedom. Goodbye my love," she said again.

The next day, word of Jacob's passing spread throughout the town and people came to express their sympathies and condolences. Nan greeting her neighbors warmly. Her face gave no indication of how she was feeling and she did not cry.

Jacob's body laid out for three days in the boarding house parlor before the wake. Reverend Evans came to do the eulogy and everyone piled into that small room to say their goodbyes and prayers. Nan was stoic right up until Jacob's body was placed into the coffin and lowered into the ground. Tears streamed down her face but she didn't say a word until the very end. "Goodbye Jacob. You have been the love of my life but God has called you home. I will miss you, my love." She wiped her face before she turned and walked away.

🪝

That evening after the celebrations ended and the rest of the family and had gone to bed, the twins and Samantha sat in the back of the house chatting.

"You look so different, Lillian." Catherine said. "You look too sophisticated for our little town."

"Well, Philadelphia is a big city and all the women dress as I do. Besides, I'm not working on a farm or in a kitchen. I was a student and then a student teacher. I was looking forward to teaching, right here in Timbuctoo."

"Was?" Samantha said. "Your plans have changed?"

"Not exactly but I am hoping that they might."

"What does that mean?" Catherine asked.

"It means that I met a wonderful man and if things move the way I expect, I might not be settling down here in town." She paused a second. "The truth is I don't know if he will have me but if he wants me I will settle anywhere he wants to put down roots."

"Well, are you going to tell us about him?" Samantha asked.

"His name is Lieutenant Theodore Hamilton and he is the most handsome man that I have ever known. He is kind hearted and thoughtful and I just adore him."

"How did you two meet?" Samantha wanted to know.

Lilly told the story with dramatic flourish. "Are you saying that he is a doctor?" Catherine asked. "I've never heard of a Negro doctor."

"Well, although he has been serving in the Navy as an Assistant Surgeon, he had some training in medicine at Trinity Medical College of the University of Toronto. He has completed three years. He needs one more year to get his Doctor of Medicine degree. Once he has been discharged from the Navy, he will return to Toronto to finish his education."

"Wow," Catherine said. "You actually snagged a doctor."

"Well, I wish. I haven't snagged him yet. I'll have to wait and see if he contacts me now that the war is over. I don't even know if he will share his plans after graduation with me. In the meantime, I plan to help at the school and maybe teach until I hear from Dr. Hamilton."

"Why didn't you tell us before now? Why haven't you told mother?"

"I don't know. I guess I wanted more to tell before I said anything but I will tell everyone soon."

＊

On the morning of August 10, 1865 Joseph and David took the ferry across the Delaware River arriving in Camden mid-morning. They left the ferry and bought two horses to continue their journey home. It was a beautiful August day and they rode leisurely toward Timbuctoo. Not much had changed as they passed familiar landmarks. Finally, they came to that crude wooden sign stuck in the mud at the beginning of Main Street.

"We're home, Joe," David said with a bright smile. "We made it. We went to war, we won the war and we made it back home, heathy and safe."

Joseph just smiled. He was thinking of how mature David had grown over the past year. "The Bissett farm is just a few miles away. I'll come with you to see Louis and Lillian before we move into town." David said. Joseph nodded in agreement.

Louis was shirtless and wet with perspiration as he pounded a wooden steak into the ground to repair a fence. He was so intent on his task that he hardly heard the two horses as they approached. "Need some help, old man?" Joseph yelled.

Louis swung around. "Joseph!!" He yelled. "My God, it is you." He ran toward them. Joseph jumped down and he and Louis embraced. "Oh David," he said. "I hardly recognize you with that beard. You look so grown up." He and David embraced. "Why didn't you let us know that you were coming home?"

"We wanted to surprise everyone," David said.

"Well, you have certainly surprised me. Lillian is going to be surprised too. Let me go in the house first."

The young men tied the horses up and walked around to the back of the house. Louis went into the kitchen first. He slipped his arm around Lillian's waist and kissed her on the cheek. With her back to the door, he motioned for Joseph and David to quietly come into the kitchen.

"What's that for?" Lillian questioned.

"No reason. I just love you."

She gave Louis a curious look. "What are you up to?"

"Nothing. As I said, I just love you." He kissed her again. "Got a couple of other men with me who love you too."

"What?" Lillian said as she pushed Louis away and turned around. At first, it was as if she had seen a ghost. She was too stunned for words. It was about 20 seconds before she screamed out. "David! Oh my God, you're here." Lillian opened her arms and her grandson ran into her embrace. She squeezed him and he lifted her off her feet and swung her around. No sooner than her feet touched the floor then Joseph lifted her in the same way. "Oh my God! I've missed both you so much."

Lillian prepared lunch for the four of them. As they ate, Lillian and Louis explained the things that had gone on in their absence. They were full of questions about the war. David showed his grandmother the accommodation he won for his bravery in the Petersburg battle. Lillian couldn't have been more proud. Louis gave David a hearty handshake and pat on the back.

There was a pause in the conversation while David debated with himself whether he should reveal his encounter with the Gloria Plantation. Finally, after a few quiet moments, David said, "I saw his portrait." More silence but, somehow Lillian knew.

"You went to the Gloria Plantation and saw the portrait of Big Bill?"

"Yes. We walked through the plantation house."

Joseph blew breath through pursed lips and shook his head. "You could tell that it was once a magnificent house, but now it's just an old, rundown and eerie mansion."

"Yes," David said. "It almost felt like the house wanted to tell me some secrets. It felt alive."

Lillian took a cake from the oven and placed it on a rack to cool. She dusted the flour from her hands on her apron before she turned to face David. "That house is not alive, although if it were alive, it could really tell some secrets." She kissed her grandson on the head. "Joseph is right. It is just an old mansion. Whatever secrets that house held, died with James. He was the only one left who knew anything." She glanced at Louis as she spoke and he shook his head as if to say no.

They stayed a while longer, enjoying cake and coffee and just chatting. Finally, Joseph told them of his encounter with Nathaniel Williams. "I really wanted to squeeze the life out of the man with my bare hands but I just couldn't bring myself to kill him. I thought that I would feel some sort of satisfaction when my fist plunged into his face, but I felt nothing. He sat there on the ground, blood oozing from his face and under all that blood, I saw an arrogant, insolent white boy. Yeah, he was a grown man but his evil was just boyish rebellion. I couldn't hate him anymore than he hated himself."

"Apparently," David said. "He had just raped another young woman and it was her father who killed him. The crowd had already beat him senseless and then Joseph punched him. That old man came out of nowhere and just slashed his throat."

Lillian winced. "I can't say that I know how you feel but I do think that it is good that you did not kill him. You wouldn't want that on your conscious." Joseph nodded in agreement.

By the time Joseph and David left the farm, it was already late afternoon. Louis and Lillian waved their goodbyes from the porch. "Why did you give me that look when David was talking about the Gloria Plantation?" Louis asked.

"As I was telling David that the secrets of that house and the Vance family died with James, I was also thinking of Big Bill's journals hidden away in the attic. The secrets outlined in those journals are what set me free and lead David to take his own life."

Lillian leaned against the porch bannister and Louis came to stand behind her. He wrapped his arm around her and kissed her behind her ear. "When James was very ill and he knew that he was dying, he told me all about those journals. He urged me to get them down and read them for myself. He said the details of my own birth was recorded in one of the journals."

"Did you read them?" Lillian asked.

"Yes. I read each journal." Louis took Lillian by the hand and they went into the house. "James also told me to destroy those journals. After reading them, I was happy to destroy every one of them."

Lillian was quiet and Louis knew that some of those memories had come to mind and she suddenly looked very sad. "William Vance was a vile and evil man," Louis said. "I was lucky that my mother was sold away from Gloria and raised me away from that man." Louis was quiet for a moment, remembering his mother.

"He wasn't all bad," Lillian offered. "He loved one woman his entire life and some of his most despicable deeds were done to keep her happy."

"I don't understand."

"Well," Lillian began. She made herself comfortable in one of the rocking chairs. "According to Bell, the plantation cook, his wife's son was stillborn. He replaced that child with David to keep Gloria from knowing that her own son was stillborn."

Louis sat in the other rocking chair. "Yeah, I read that but I didn't see anything noble or honorable in his actions. In fact, that doesn't change anything. Look how many lives such a lie has destroyed. It was a cruel lie."

They were both quiet for a while. "It is strange though that you and I would find love. You and David Vance shared a mother and Me and David shared a father."

"I'm happy that you burned those journals. I never want to think of Gloria again."

"You will, though. Gloria is part of who you are, it is what made you the woman you've become in spite of what you have suffered."

Lillian turned to face Louis. "I love you Louis Bissett," she said with a smile.

Chapter Thirteen
Timbuctoo, New Jersey

A Heart Rejoices

The smell of fresh linen wafted through the air as Joseph and David came close to the back of the boarding house. A soft wind billowed the clean sheets and towels that had been hung from the clothes lines strung behind the house. A canvas bag full of clothes pins was slung over Alexis' shoulder as she quietly went about her work. Joseph left his horse at the the edge of the road with David and walked across the grass. Alexis removed the pins from one of the sheets and dropped the pins into her bag. When she removed the next few pins the sheet fell into her arms and Joseph was standing behind the sheet. He stood there with a broad smile on his face and his arms were outstretched to receive her. Alexis did not immediately move. It was as if she hadn't recognized him in his dress blue uniform. She just stood there looking into his eyes as if he were an apparition.

"Joseph?" she whispered.

"Yes, it's me. I'm home, Alexis.

She slowly, hesitantly, moved into his arms and Joseph wrapped his arms around her tightly. "I'm here," he whispered against her head. "I am here and I will never leave you again."

Alexis held him as tight as she could and her eyes filled with tears. "Oh my God, Joseph I missed you so much," she cried.

He bent his head and kissed her long and passionately. When their bodies finally separated, Alexis began to run her hands up and down his arms and chest looking for wounds. "I'm fine, he said. No wounds. I am absolutely fine."

Nan heard the commotion and came to investigate. "Oh my God," she screamed. "You're home." She said to Joseph.

David joined them as he came from behind one of the sheet. "Yes, Nan. We both came home."

Nan was overjoyed to see the young men. She hugged them both and they expressed their sympathy at the passing of Althea and Jacob. Nan told them about Denny's new beau and they both expressed their happiness that Denny found someone to love and to love her.

The plan was that once Joseph saw Alexis, he would ride with David to see the Bowmans, but Joseph found it hard to leave Alexis at that time. She seemed smaller, more vulnerable and unsteady. Although she appeared to be overjoyed at Joseph's return, he couldn't help noticing a slight tremble in her hands. He wanted to stay with her now. He felt as if she needed him. David assured him that he could travel the rest of the way alone. They promised to meet the next day at Miss Ida's to pay Isaac a visit. They embraced and David rode off, waving to Joseph, Alexis, and Nan.

Alexis and Nan prepared the evening meal while Joseph went to change out of his uniform. After changing, he went to the front porch where Jay was busy playing with his toy soldiers. "Hello," Joseph said.

"Hello," Jay said without even looking up.

"I see you have gotten a little taller since the last time I saw you."

Jay was now five years old and very talkative. Finally, he recognized Joseph's voice. He dropped his toys and sprung into Joseph's arms. They embraced for little while. "I missed you," Joseph said.

Jay was too overwhelmed to say anything. His eyes filled with tears and he hugged Joseph even tighter. Joseph swung little Jay onto his shoulder and the two of them joined the women in the kitchen and even helped by setting the table in the small dining room. The boarding house had only three guests at this time.

When the meal was over and the guests left the dining room, Nan sensed that Joseph and Alexis wanted to be alone. She politely excused herself and went to the front porch.

Joseph couldn't help but notice that Alexis was still very nervous. The tremble in her hands became more prominent. As soon as Nan left the room, Alexis stood and started to clean away the dishes. Joseph came and stood behind her, wrapping his arms around her tiny waist. "What is it?" He softly asked.

"Nothing," she said as she twisted out of his embrace and continued to clear the table.

"Alexis, I can tell that something is bothering you. Whatever it is, you can tell me."

As she turned to face him, she began to cry. "Oh, Joseph. There is so much. I wanted to tell you but I was afraid. I'm still afraid. I don't know what you will think of me. I don't know if our marriage can survive something so horrible." The words tumbled from her mouth and seemed to make it difficult for her to stand.

Joseph led her to a chair. She sat with her head down sobbing uncontrollably. He stooped down in front of her and took her hands into his own. "Alice," he said. The mention of her given name brought her head up suddenly.

"You called me Alice."

"Yes, Alice. We no longer have to be Joseph and Alexis unless we want to be Joseph and Alexis. We can now use the names our mothers chose for us. We are Josiah and Alice. The emancipation freed the slaves and the war changed a lot of things. No one is searching for us anymore. We are truly free."

Although she smiled at knowing that they were free, she was still holding on to something that was damaging to her spirit. Josiah knew that it was about Nathaniel Williams. At first he wanted her to trust him enough to tell him herself but he now knew that just remembering the attack was for her a torment. "I already know that Nathaniel Williams' attacked you here in the house. Lillian wrote to me about the rape and beating that you suffered at the hands of that degenerate. Finding out that someone hurt you, and I could not be here to protect you, was the hardest thing I have ever had to endure but I did endure. I took all the anger and rage that I felt for the man that hurt you and used it to fight the enemy. As horrible as the attack was, it will not destroy our marriage. It can only make our marriage stronger. I am home now, and I will never let anyone hurt you again."

Alexis practically fell into his arms. He cradled her as he told her just how much he loved and missed her. Later that evening, in their own room at the boarding house, Josiah made love to his wife Alice with slow deliberate patience. Their coming together after so long a separation and the pain that they each suffered, made their love making special. When it was over and they lay in each other's arms relaxing, Josiah kissed her lightly. "Nathaniel Williams is dead," he said.Alexis raised herself on her elbow and looked into Josiah's eyes. "Tell me that you didn't kill him,"

"I didn't. I did however, lay a perfect punch on his jaw. Turns out, he had raped some white man's daughter. The people on the Philadelphia waterfront were ready to hang him from a lamp post but the man whose daughter he raped came a long and stabbed him to death."

"Oh my," she said.

"I struggled with the thought of killing him even before his throat was slashed. I wanted to kill him myself, with my bare hands but that one commandment, 'thou shall not kill,' kept coming to my mind. In the end, I didn't have to kill him. Someone else killed him and he died instantly."

"Well," Alexis said as she snuggled closer to her husband and rested her head on his chest. "I'm glad that you didn't kill him. You wouldn't want that on your conscious, but I am also glad that he is dead. He was such an evil man." They were quiet for a while. "Joe," Alexis whispered.

"Yeah."

"If it's all the same to you, I got use to our new names. I like being Joseph and Alexis. Besides, changing again might be to confusing for Jay."

"Joseph and Alexis it is," he said sleepily.

❧

It was dusk by the time David came close to the Bowman house. It was a warm evening and the house was ablaze with light. David walked his horse into the barn and lead him into a stall before walking back to the house. He stood in the yard for a while just watching his family through the window. It occurred to him that this was exactly what Sam use to do, watch his family through this very same window.

He was surprised to see Lilly. She and Sam were setting the table for the evening meal and apparently sharing something that they both thought was very funny. Lilly put her hand over her mouth as she tried to stifle a giggle but Samantha threw her head back and bellowed a loud strong, belly shaking laugh. He smiled to himself realizing that they had not changed much since they were teens. Finally, he opened the door into the kitchen. The entire family stopped and looked his way. No one said anything for a couple of seconds. It was as if they couldn't believe their eyes.

"David!" Rebecca screamed as she ran into her son's arms. One by one, the women came and hugged David and welcomed him home. Finally, it was Samantha standing in front of him. He picked her up and swung her around, just as he had done with his grandmother. He kissed her and she cried tears of joy. "Oh David, I can't believe that you are finally here."

"I'm here, and I'm never going away again, at least not without you."

When the lovers finally moved away from each other, Rebecca came and placed Kira into David's arms. "Meet Kira Rebecca Bowman, your daughter," Rebecca said.

He gazed down at his baby girl and marveled that he and Samantha could have made such a beautiful child. He smiled at first but that smile soon gave way to a very nervous giggle. "She is so beautiful,

Sam." Kira giggled and cooed as she wrapped her tiny hand around her father's finger. "I think she looks like my mother."

"I agree. She is a beauty," Benjamin said as he came through the door.

David handed the baby over to Samantha as he embraced his father. "Dad, I missed you but your voice was in my head the whole time."

Benjamin embraced David and they held on to each other for a few moments. "I'm so glad you made it back to us in one piece."

"I am so happy to be back home. I missed all of you.

With the table set and the food ready, the family sat down to eat. Mom Cathy was the last to join the family. She screamed the second she opened the back door and saw David sitting at the table. "My prayers have been answered." She screamed. "God brought you home safe and sound," she said as she embraced her great grandson.

"I missed you, Mom Cathy."

"We all missed you," she said. "You and Lillian are both back home. It's like a miracle. I am so happy the entire family is home again and we got a beautiful addition in little Kira."

"Amen!" Rebecca said.

Plates and serving dishes were passed back and forth as the meal progressed and the family chatted. "Lilly, you look so grown up that I hardly recognized you. You are as beautiful as ever." David said.

"Thank you," Cat said with a laugh. "We are twins, after all." Everyone laughed at that comment.

"Oh, I didn't mean that you were not pretty. You are both pretty. It's just that Lilly has changed. Her hair, the lip rouge, and her clothes."

"We all know what you meant, David." Samantha said. Everyone laughed and David winked at Samantha.

Rebecca and Benjamin were happier than they had been in quite a long time. Their family was whole and well and they couldn't be happier. David told them of his visit to the Gloria Plantation. His sisters and Samantha listened with rapt attention. Rebecca shuttered just thinking about that place. Then David cleared his throat and sat up straight. "Oh yeah," he said. "I almost forgot to tell you all that I won an accommodation for bravery while fighting in Petersburg, Virginia."

"Really?" Sam said.

David pointed to the metal on his lapel and then slowly and dramatically explained how he, with the help of his fellow soldiers, foiled the Confederates attempt to attack Union troops from behind. "The army gave me a medal and some extra cash."

"I'm proud of you son." Benjamin said. They all seemed impressed but Sam more than anyone else.

Cat told him about Isaac and even confessed that he had asked her to marry him. The rest of the family was unaware of the proposal and they were surprised that Catherine was able to keep such a secret.

When the meal was over, Cat and Samantha began to clean the kitchen while Lilly attended to Kira. Mom Cathy and Rebecca took their usual places in the front room and Benjamin in his chair.

"So," Benjamin began. "What are your plans? A young man back from the war with a little money, you must now plan a future for you, Samantha, and Kira."

"I know. I have been thinking about it."

"Well?"

"While we were in Virginia, Joseph and I helped to reconstruct an old plantation mansion into a military hospital for wounded soldiers. Did you know that Joseph was a carpenter when he was a slave?"

"Yes, I did."

"Joseph was very skilled and I learned a great deal about carpentry while reconstructing that mansion into a hospital. I thought I might put some of that knowledge to good use here in Timbuctoo."

"Sounds good," Benjamin said.

"First, I want to marry Samantha." Approving ah's went through the family. "After that, my first job will be to buy us a plot of land and build a little farm house. I plan to do a little farming between carpentry jobs."

"Well, I am happy to know that you have plans. It will all work out, I'm sure."

"Yeah, well I plan to give it my best and Joseph will be there to help me. We are going to start a carpentry business."

"Your own business?" Benjamin said.

"Yes. I thought about this for some time."

"And you never even considered joining me in the catering business?"

"No disrespect Dad, but cooking has never been something that interested me. Besides, you and Catherine love being in the kitchen. I can't say that I do."

"Well, I am disappointed but I'm also impressed that you and Joseph are going to start a business."

"That sounds very promising," Rebecca said. They were all quiet for a few minutes and Rebecca could see that David was tired. "You must be very tired, honey."

"Yeah, well it has been a really long day. I hope you won't mind if I turn in for the night?" David said.

"Not at all," his mother said. "Goodnight David."

He was a little worried about the sleeping arrangements now that Samantha had a baby. However, Samantha had moved into David's room after Kira was born so the sleeping arrangements had already been set. David was not surprised to see a cradle in his room and all the pink and yellow decorations. He was surprised that his parents did not have a problem with him and Sam sleeping in the same room and in the same bed, but after all, they already had a baby, he thought.

⁂

The next day Joseph and David met at Miss Ida's as planned. Cat came with David. Isaac was happy to see his friends. The young men laughed and talked for a few hours before Joseph told Isaac of the Whitley's in Philadelphia. At first Isaac couldn't believe his ears. "You are joking, right?" He asked Joseph.

"No. We were there. They have prosthetics of all kinds and the doctor assured me that he would be able to make you a foot. You just have to save your money and get to Philadelphia."

Isaac was more than delighted at that news. Miss Ida and Jesse were also excited to hear that news. After Joseph and David left and Catherine and Isaac were alone, Catherine said she hoped Isaac could get his prosthetic by the time they planned a wedding. He agreed.

⁂

Many things changed after the Civil War ended. The state of New Jersey lost 6300 troops to the Civil War. Many New Jersey slaves moved to Philadelphia, New York and Delaware looking for paid employment, not knowing that in the months ahead, the Industrial Revolution would boom in most northern states, including New Jersey. Those who accepted the promise of a living wage stayed on working at New Jersey plantations. However, freed slaves migrating north provided industry labor. Factories sprang up throughout the state. People, black and white, began to migrate through Timbuctoo again. The hotel and boarding house began to fill. Church congregations increased as more people came and decided to settle in the small town.

Louis had not decided what to do with the boarding house. When he bought it, he assumed that Althea would be there to run the business. The boarding house actually belonged to Althea but he did list himself as co-owner for security purposes. Now he would have to decide who would own the boarding house business. Lillian suggested Joseph and Alexis but Louis thought that he should at least make an offer to Nan. She had been faithful to him on Gloria and again here in New Jersey.

However, Nan had no desire to own the business. She promised to help as much as she could but she wanted no part of the responsibility of a business. Nan wasn't quite as old as Jacob but she was coming to an age where work was more of a challenge than it was in her younger years.

Louis then offered the business to Joseph and Alexis. However, Joseph declined the offer. He did agree to run the boarding house temporarily. He informed Louis the he and David had agreed to start a carpentry business together. He offered to renovate the boarding house and make the property ready for sale and Louis agreed.In the coming weeks Joseph, David, and Louis worked on updating the boarding house. The kitchen was updated with a modern cast iron wood stove with a spacious oven.

Joseph repaired or rebuilt much of the furniture while David and Louis painted the walls and cupboards. Alexis recovered chairs and made curtains for all of the windows. It was all finished and ready for sale by the end of September Nan, Lillian, and Alexis were very impressed with the transformation. Louis ran advertisements in the local newspapers and in Philadelphia and New York newspapers. All he could do now was wait. In the meantime, Alexis, Nan, and Joseph ran the house.

David bought a small plot of land on the outskirts of town and he and Joseph began working on his house late that same summer. They hoped to at least lay the foundation and build the outer walls before the weather became too cold. He and Sam planned to be married the first Saturday in October. Samantha didn't want a large wedding and she tried to talk the family down about a big celebration. She wanted to be married in the back of the house and have tables set up on the grass as they often did during the summer months. At first, Rebecca wouldn't hear of it. She thought Samantha and David should be married in the church. It took Cat to take her mother aside and explain why Samantha didn't want the fanfare of a large church wedding.

"Mother, she and David already have a baby. A big church wedding would make Sam uncomfortable."

"I don't understand. Why would she feel uncomfortable? It doesn't matter what other people think of her and David." Rebecca argued.

"What doesn't matter, Mother, is how you or I feel. It is Samantha's wedding and her feelings are the only ones that matter."

Rebecca thought for a moment. "I guess you're right. We will do it her way."

David and Samantha were married on October 3, 1865 in the dinning room of the Bowman Catering Company. Though it was supposed to be a small celebration, almost the entire town turned out to celebrate their union. Samantha was radiant in her ivory dress. She carried a bouquet of pale pink tulips. Cat had curled Samantha's long sandy blond hair and soft spiral curls framed her face. David smiled broadly as Sam slowly walked down the isle between the folding chairs to the podium where he stood waiting with Reverend Evans. David hardly heard the Reverend speak the wedding vows until he heard that he could now kiss his bride. He took Samantha into his arms and kissed her as the crowd roared their approval.

Samantha felt as if she were living a dream. When her new husband released her, she turned to Rebecca and threw her arms around Rebecca's neck. "This is all because of you, Mom. You loved me and took me in when I had no one. I would never have met David if it were not for you. Thank you, Mom. Thank you so much." Rebecca was too emotional to speak so she just nodded her head in agreement and hugged her new daughter-in-law tightly.

Joseph, Alexis and Jay were in attendance. Alexis and Joseph decided to keep their new names in public because it might be to confusing for some people and especially little Jay. Alexis looked better than she had for nearly a year. You could tell that Joseph's return helped her to work through her anxiety. She even seemed to have gained some weight and that did not go unnoticed.

"I see you have gained a little weight," Lillian said.

"Oh," Alexis responded in surprise.

"Oh, don't mind me. No harm intended. I just noticed that you look a little different. You are as beautiful as ever, though."

"My weight," Alexis said with a wink. "Is because Joe and I are going to have a baby." She waited to see Lillian's reaction.

"Oh my God," Lillian whispered. "When?"

"Probably about April next year. I really hope it is another boy. Joseph wants a boy too. If it is a boy, his name will be William Josiah Bissett and this boy will not be for sale. He will never be for sale."

"Amen!" Lillian said. "Are you going to tell the rest of the family?"

"Not today. This is Sam and David's day."

Chapter Fourteen
Epilogue

The Reunion

William Josiah Bissett was born on April 13, 1866 to Joseph and Alexis Bissett, (a.k.a. Josiah and Alice). Joseph and David had finished building a farm house for David and Samantha and they expected to move into their new home in May.

Although Joseph and Alexis declined to be business owners, it was mostly Nan and Alexis who ran the house as usual. Joseph and David had their hands filled with their carpentry work. As more people migrated to Timbuctoo their carpentry business increased and they were building new homes and furniture at an astounding rate.

With two children now, Alexis thought it was time for her and Joseph to move into their own place. However, Joseph was so busy that he couldn't find the time to build his own house. He bought a small four bedroom house in town, not far from the boarding house. "Why four bedrooms?" Lillian wanted to know.

"Jay and little William are going to have a brother or sister early this winter." Joseph said with a smile.

"Oh Lord! You're pregnant again?"

"Yes," Alexis said.

"Who knows?"

"No one. Joe and I are gonna have a dinner for everyone in the big dinning room of the boarding house and Joe will announce it then."

Lillian hugged Alexis. "When is this dinner?"

"After church this Sunday."

Isaac and Catherine traveled to Philadelphia in March. They had been gone three months and Miss Ida was beginning to wonder if they intended to return to Timbuctoo.

Isaac was fitted with a perfect prosthetic. He still needed to use a cane but the prosthetic gave him balance and more importantly, he felt better about himself. Catherine immediately noticed the change in Isaac. He was happier, more assertive more free spirited, and most importantly, sober. Catherine thanked God for these changes.

Since neither wanted the fanfare of a large wedding in town, they married in a civil service while in Philadelphia and wrote to Miss Ida promising to be home in July.

Lilly finally heard from Dr. Hamilton. He wrote that he had completed his studies at the Trinity Medical College and planned to visit her in her hometown in early July. This news both excited and scared Lilly. She wanted more than anything to reconnect with Dr. Hamilton but she had not yet prepared her family meet him. She wished that Cat was home so that she could talk to her about things. Since Samantha and David moved out there was no one to talk to except her mother and grandmother and she doubted if she could make them understand how much she felt for this man that she hardly knew. It would all be settled one June evening.

Rebecca had summoned her, David and Samantha to the house. She only said that she had something of importance to share with the family. Her mother, father and grandmother sat around the kitchen table when Lilly came in and sat down warily. "What is this about?" She asked.

David and Samantha came in and they greeted one another with worried smiles. After everyone was seated, Rebecca stood. "I asked you all here because there is a secret that I have been keeping from you all of your lives. Your father and I have decided that the time has come for you all to know the truth. I love you all and this secret has been a heavy on my heart. I just don't want to carry this burden any longer. The secret must be revealed."

With the exception of Kira's tiny whimpers, the room was dead silent. "David," Rebecca continued. "This is about you. Because we thought that it was just easier for everyone, we have let you believe that Benjamin is your father."

David's eyes immediately went to Benjamin's face which was stoic and gave nothing away. "Although Benjamin has been a father to you in every conceivable way, he is not your real father. Your father was a white man with whom I had a short relationship. The truth is, I was young and stupid. I thought that I could pass for white. I also thought that if I could get a white man to fall in love with me and marry me, I could live as a white woman."

Lilly covered her mouth with her hand but David sat wide eyed looking at his mother. "As I said, I was young and stupid. When the white man found out that I wasn't white, he tried to kill me even though I was carrying his child. You are that child, David. In fact, knowing that I was carrying his child enraged him even more. He beat me, kicked me in my stomach, and back, broke my legs and left me to die on an ice covered sidewalk in Philadelphia. It was Benjamin who found me that night. He carried me all the way to his grandmother's house, five or more blocks. It was Mom Cathy who set my broken legs and nursed me back to health. Benjamin and I were married shortly after these things happened."

"I am sorry that I didn't tell you about these things earlier but I was ashamed. I thought that if you knew, you would lose respect for me. I know now how wrong it was for me to keep this from you and I am so sorry. I don't expect you to understand but I do hope that you will forgive me."

"Oh my," Lilly said. "Mother, I am so sorry you went through something so horrible."

The room was still quiet for a time. "If ye forgive not men their trespasses, neither will your Father forgive your trespasses,. . ." David said as he looked into his mother's eyes, which quickly filled with tears. It was a familiar scripture.

"Amen!" Mom Cathy said.

"David, as far as I am concerned, you have been my son since the moment you were born. Nothing will ever change that and I love you as a father loves his son," Benjamin said. David rose and hugged both his parents one at a time. When they all seated again, Rebecca breathed a sigh of relief.

Now it was Lilly's turn for confession. "Mom, Dad, I have something to tell you." They all looked expectantly at Lilly. "When I was in Philadelphia I met a man. A beautiful man. He is a doctor and he is interested in me."

"Wow, that is great," David said.

"A doctor, eh?" Benjamin said skeptically.

"A black doctor? Rebecca questioned. "I've never heard of a black doctor."

"Yes Mother, he is black and he studied at Trinity Medical College in Canada. When we met he was about to go back to finish his studies. He will be coming here in a couple of weeks to see me."

"So why haven't you told us about your doctor?" Rebecca asked.

"It may sound crazy but I think I'm in love with this man. We only spent a few days together but he is all that I think of and I can't wait to see him again."

"And he is coming all the way here from Canada?" That was Sam's question.

"He wouldn't be traveling all this way unless he was also feeling something for you," said David.

Lilly smiled. Rebecca put her arms around Lilly's shoulders. "I am so happy for you. I'm happy for all of you."

❧

Dr. Theodore Hamilton arrived in Timbuctoo the first Saturday in June. He showed up at the boarding house in his dressed Naval Uniform and took a room on the second floor. Later that day, he called at the Bowman residence. Rebecca answered the knock at the door. She took one look at this tall, dark, and distinguished gentleman and knew that it was Dr. Hamilton.

"You must be Dr. Hamilton," she said.

"At your service," he said as he bowed deeply. "I am looking for Lillian Bowman. Does she reside here?"

"Most certainly. I am her mother, Rebecca. Please come in."

Rebecca directed him to a seat in the front room while she went to retrieve Lilly from the back of the house where she was hanging laundry. "He's here," Rebecca said.

"Who?"

"Your beau, the very dignified Dr. Hamilton."

"Here? Now?"

"Waiting for you in the front room."

Lilly striped off her apron and swiped misplaced hair from her face before she went in to see Dr. Hamilton. "Theodore," she said as she came into the room.

He stood and went to her. Without a moment's hesitation, he lifted her chin with his finger and kissed her lightly on the lips. "I've missed you," he said.

"But you didn't write me as you promised."

"I'm sorry. I spent my time studying to take my final exams. I couldn't afford any distractions. I am all finished now. I have my medical degree."

"That is wonderful."

"I told you that I would come for you and I am here."

"How long will you be here?"

"I took a room at the boarding house. I'll be staying there for as long as it takes for you decide if you will be my wife."

Lillian smiled. "Well now," she said as she whirled out of his arms. "That is quite an unusual proposal."

"Maybe. I'm guessing you think it would be better if we spend some time getting to know one another a little better before we make a life-long commitment. After all, we only spent a couple of wonderful days together in Philadelphia."

"Well, yes. That did cross my mind."

"I was perfectly prepared for you to turn me down on that basis."

"But I did not turn you down. I am just slowing you down a little, and I think that you know it is the right thing to do. Am I right?"

Two long strides and he was standing in front of her again. She looked up at him with adoring eyes. "I do agree."

"Besides, I can't wait for you to meet the rest of my family and experience this wonderfully, quaint little town of ours. Who knows? Maybe you might decide to practice right here."

"Maybe," he said softly before he pulled her to him and kissed her full on and passionately.

&

It was the second Sunday in July and Alexis was anxious about her first family dinner. Even though Lillian and Rebecca helped with the cooking, she still missed Cat's presence in the kitchen.

The sideboard in the main dinning room was against the wall with all the family's favorite foods. Alexis took everyone's favorites into consideration. As far as anyone knew, it was just a family dinner with no particular celebration in mind.

Lillian and Louis were the first to arrive and from the moment Joseph saw Louis, he knew something was amiss. Louis seemed a little different in his demeanor. Usually a very jovial personality, today Louis was happier than Joe had ever seen him. Joe extended his hand for the customary male bonding handshake. Louis shook his hand briefly and then pulled him into a bear hug, patting him on the back.

"Are you alright, brother?" Joe asked.

"Never better but I do have a surprise for everyone." Louis whispered. Then he pressed a finger to his lips indicating that he didn't want to speak of it anymore and he didn't want Joe to speak of it either.

Miss Ida and Jesse came followed by the Evans, who were always invited to family dinners. Samantha with Kira and David came next. Their happiness at being together as a family was written in the radiant smiles on their faces. David carried Kira, tickling, nuzzling, and kissing her every few minutes. No sooner than he entered the dinning room than great-grandma came and took Kira out of his arms. It was Lillian's first chance to hold and cuddle with her great-grandchild.

Rebecca and Benjamin arrived with Lilly and everyone thought that the party was complete until one of the boarding house guest appeared at the dinning room door. Lilly had invited Dr. Hamilton. He stood in the doorway and all eyes turned in his direction. 'Who was this beautiful, black, Naval Officer,' they all thought. Alexis thought he must have mistakenly gone to the wrong dinning room and she stood, intent on redirecting him to the smaller room near the front of the house. However, Lilly quickly moved to his side. "Hello, everyone. I would like to introduce you to Dr. Theodore Hamilton."

Ooo's and ah's went through the party before Lillian stepped forward and extended a hand to the young man. "Welcome," she said. "I am Lilly's grandmother." Then he got welcomes from everyone in the room and Lilly breathed a sigh of relief.

To everyone's surprise, two more guests came into the dinning room. Isaac and Catherine joined their families to much congratulations and happy smiles.

Everyone was allowed to serve themselves from the sideboard. Joseph had ordered expensive champagne and instructed Nan to fill the flutes around the table. Once everyone was seated and happily eating,

Joe stood to make the announcement. He tapped a glass with his fork to get everyone's attention before he began to speak. "I know that you are all wondering why Alexis and I decided to have this dinner. It is no secret that David and I have been working really hard. Our business has expanded so fast, it is more than we could have imagined. Alexis and Nan have also been working hard because the boarding house has more guests than it has ever had at one time. Besides all of that, we invited you here to tell you that Alexis and I are expecting again. This winter we expect to have an addition to the Bissett family." Congratulations were voiced among the party. "You each have a glass of champagne and I would like to drink to the child that my wife now carries and to our town's continued success and happiness now that the war has ended and we are all here."

"I couldn't agree more," Louis said as he stood. "I have something to add to Joe's good news. I have finally found a buyer for the boarding house." All the faces looked on in surprise and expectation. "The new owners will take possession one week from tomorrow."

"Who are the new owners?" Benjamin wanted to know.

"Mr. and Mrs. Isaac Simms are the new owners and the name has been officially changed to The Simms Timbuctoo House."

Catherine and Isaac stood to receive the congratulations and good wishes of their family and friends.

"Wow, this seems like a really nice little town." Theodore whispered to Lilly. "I could see myself settling down in a town like this. Is there a town doctor here?"

"Yes, we do have a town doctor but he isn't a surgeon and he isn't black and I'm not in love with him." Lillian said. No sooner had the words left her mouth than she regretted them.

'Too forward,' she though, until Theodore leaned over and kissed her cheek. "I love you too Lillian Bowman and I'm thinking that we can build a life here in this little town."

⁂

On a lazy hot day in August 1866, Lillian and Louis sat in rocking chairs on their front porch sipping fresh lemonade. "Why do you seem a little sad?" Louis asked Lillian.

"I am not exactly sad, really. Maybe a little bored. The kids are all grown up and married with their own lives. It just gets a little lonely with just the two of us."

"I know what you mean. I've been trying to get Joseph to take off a day so that we could go fishing like we use to do. He's just too busy. As soon as he and David complete one project, there is another waiting for his attention."

"Maybe he should expand the business a little. You know, hire more carpenters so he and David don't have to do everything."

"That sounds like a good idea. I'll mention it to him when I get a chance."

"Or, maybe you ought to teach me to fish." Lillian smiled.

"That's an idea," he said with a roll of his eyes and a smile.

They were both quiet for a time. Lillian fanned herself with the lace fan Lilly had brought her from Philadelphia. "It sure is hot today."

"Yeah," Louis said. "Its too hot to work but I'm guessing a strong thunder storm will wash all this heat and humidity away."

"Soon, I hope. This heat is miserable." Lillian squinted her eyes and put her hand over her eyes to shield them from the sun glare as she looked out down the road.

A very fancy buggy came slowly rolling down the road. "Who would be traveling on an afternoon like this? It is much too hot to be traveling."

"Whoever it is, it looks like they're moving. Look at the bags piled on the top and back of such a small buggy."

They both leaned forward trying to make out the emblem on the side of the buggy. When the buggy turned and began to come up their drive, Lillian stood. As the buggy turned the emblem became clear. "EM" was embossed on the door in gold lettering. "Oh my God," Lillian whispered as she stepped passed her husband. "I think its Beth."

The buggy stopped and a neatly dressed white woman with all white hair stepped down. She waved a gloved hand and Lillian screamed. "Elizabeth?" Lillian ran to meet her old friend.

She knew that Elizabeth was older than her but she almost couldn't believe that this old woman was Elizabeth Vance Martin. She looked very old and fragile.

Elizabeth stood with her arms opened wide and Lillian gently put her arms around her shoulders, as if she were afraid that Elizabeth would break under the weight of her embrace. "What brings you here? Why didn't you tell me you were coming?"

"Well, there are a lot of answers to those questions," she said as she leaned heavily on Lillian's arm. Louis came to take the buggy and horse around back. He took her bags inside the house while Lillian helped Beth to the porch.

"All of my friends have passed on and I have no family. I am old and all alone," Beth said. "I don't know how much longer I've got but I do know that I don't want to spend my final years alone. I want to be with people that I love and that love me. Some of my most precious memories were of the times we spent together in Philadelphia. As I've said to you before, we have come a long way, you and I. We have come from bitter enemies, rivals in love, slave and mistress, to great friends as close as family. I love you Lillian. You are the only family I have left and so I have come to you."

THE END